GODS, GHOSTS, LOVERS, AND ROBOTS

OVER 100 NEW SHORT STORIES FOR THE PUBLIC
DOMAIN YOU CAN REUSE, REMIX, AND RESELL

ROSS PRUDEN

ross pruden
fine art

PRAISE FOR ROSS PRUDEN

These are awesome stories that will stick with you for days, weeks, months and possibly lives. They are a mix of funny, poignant, dramatic, tear-jerking, thought-provoking and many, many more adjectives, which don't do enough justice to describe what you are about to read.

— MIKE MASNICK, FOUNDER OF SILICON VALLEY THINK TANK THE COPIA INSTITUTE, FOUNDER & EDITOR OF TECHDIRT

Ross' intelligent, thoughtful and witty prose is a gift and one that crosses many genres seamlessly. Do yourself a favor and put it on your 'to grab and go' list for others.

— THERESA STIRLING, ENCAUSTIC PAINTER

Gods, Ghosts, Lovers, and Robots is a creative act of love, selfless and inspired. Pruden has written over a hundred personally commissioned stories and given them to the public domain, for the love of art and enrichment of all our culture. As if that weren't more than enough, he's shown that you don't need copyright watchdogs or price tags to monetize your art. Show us the way, artist! Show us the way...

— SUHAIL RAFIDI, AUTHOR, TJ & TOSC: A FIELD GUIDE FOR LIFE AFTER WESTERN CULTURE

Ross Pruden's collection of refreshing sci-fi gems are imaginative stories interspersed with quick, witty zingers that leave nothing sacred and make Ross' writings a fun and smart read.

— RICHARD HAYS

Jet cars, caffeinated assassins, romance, alien wars, vampires, cars named El Diablo, Louis Daguerre, grizzly bears, ancient times, modern times, future times, heart-warming advice, frozen zombies, final choices, unicorns, and chamomile tea-drinking trolls... *Gods, Ghosts, Lovers, and Robots* is genius and a fantastic read, worth getting your hands on.

— KEN GRIBBLE

The Best Ship That Ever Was story gave me the chills. The good kind that tell me this story will go far and make many men and women very happy.

— HEATHER J. DUDLEY-NOLLETTE

Great variety and substance, in both content and writing style packed into quick, satisfying reads. I'd not have guessed they were written by the same hand, had I not known, either. Enjoyable.

— TAREK EL-HENEIDI

Gods, Ghosts, Lovers, and Robots is an undertaking that is nothing short of extraordinary. Each piece contained within is unique, special, and personal. More extraordinary still, each story belongs to the world by virtue of the public domain.

— MATT WATKAJTYS

What's the point of short stories if you can't put the book down? Pruden's sci-fi shorts are fuel for the imagination delivered in under 5 minutes—but only if you can stop after one story.

— *David Roy*

An extraordinary collection of new literature by Pruden. This project represents the future that is 'shared art', stories demanded by the people and written for the people to be shared for years to come!

— *Joshua B. Porter, Film Director*

GODS, GHOSTS, LOVERS, AND ROBOTS

GODS, GHOSTS, LOVERS, AND ROBOTS

OVER 100 NEW SHORT STORIES FOR THE PUBLIC DOMAIN
YOU CAN REUSE, REMIX, AND RESELL

by Ross Pruden

Foreword by Michael Masnick

Gods, Ghosts, Lovers, and Robots: Over 100 New Short Stories for the Public Domain You Can Reuse, Remix, and Resell

by Ross Pruden

Stories and relevant sections (cited below) published under a Creative Commons Public Domain Dedication (CCo), version 1.0, 2022, by Ross Pruden.

Other sections published under Copyright © 2022, by Ross Pruden.

ISBN 978-1-956708-02-8 (paperback)

Cover design by 99designs.com
Interior book design by Ross Pruden
Content editing by Jen Burgess
Downloadable eBook available at Amazon.com

Publisher:
Ross Pruden Fine Art, LLC
9223 Rhody Drive #658
Chimacum, WA 98325-0658
www.rosspruden.art
ross@rosspruden.art

YES, I REPLY TO EMAILS!

TRY IT! —> ROSS@ROSSPRUDEN.ART

I *love* corresponding with readers. Please don't be shy.

When I'm not chatting with fans, I'm working on my next project. Currently, that's a novel with Philippa, the same character from *Seeing is Believing* (#100).

I am also plotting an epic urban fantasy series about muses. If you want to read more about that series, or about Philippa's continuing adventures, then sign up for my newsletter!

Sign up for my NEWSLETTER:
rosspruden.art/welcome

Large size fine art photography is my day job so if want to fill your walls with some lovely art, check out my website:

www.rosspruden.art

If you can't reach me over email, try tagging me on social media with comments, thoughts, or critiques:

Facebook.com/rossprudenart
Instagram.com/rossprudenart
Twitter.com/rossprudenart

Finally, come visit the Facebook group for this book! It's a meeting place for anyone wanting to discuss the stories, share their own remixes, or just meet other like-minded supporters of the public domain:

Facebook.com/groups/100stories

To my family

TABLE OF CONTENTS

HOW TO USE THIS BOOK

Looking for inspiration for a song, film, novel, or a game? Good news! All 108 stories in this collection are in the public domain. Meaning, *none* of them are registered under copyright. Meaning, you can...

1. Copy/torrent the entire anthology.
2. Make a new work of art from any story.
3. Sell the anthology yourself.

Which genre do you want to read? Which story will inspire you to create new art? To help you, I've assigned each story a unique number (the Alphabetical Story Index includes these same numbers) and the *Story Table of Contents* has at least one of the following symbols after each story title: **F**, **M**, **N**, **S**, and **G**. Each symbol denotes a story best suited for a **F**eature film, a short **M**ovie, a **N**ovel, a **S**ong, or a **G**ame.

If this anthology had been registered under copyright and you were to create and distribute a song, movie, video game, or novel based on any story in the anthology, I would be within my legal right to sue you, demand you pay me a license fee, or both.

Screw that!

If you want to copy these stories and pay me nothing, *that's okay*. Simply sharing a work of art can often be sufficient remuneration in itself. (Yes, three sections of this book do have copyright, but that's to dissuade people passing themselves off as me. As long as you're being transparent about the share, I have no beef with you.)

However, if you do prefer to "license" this work, or do something similar, there are benefits. It's a simple 5 step process:

1. Contact me: ross@rosspruden.art or @rossprudenart on Facebook, Instagram, or Twitter. Tell me: "I love your work! I made some art based on it. Can I get a Creator-Endorsed Mark?"
2. I say, "Awesome! Yeah, of course!" And then *you* decide how much of a revenue share seems fair— anywhere from 0% to 100%.
3. You pick the appropriate Creator-Endorsed mark (see below) and append it to your work of art which *proves* you have received my blessing.
4. If you do a revenue share, please try to send me my portion sometime within that same tax year so I can keep my own financials in order.
5. I list your project on my "Hall of Fame" page at *rosspruden.art/fame* and become so grateful that I promote you and your work on all my social networks. :)

The Creator-Endorsed mark by Question Copyright

One parting request: please consider releasing some of your *own* work into the public domain... even if it's a 500 word short story. The world is richer for it!

facebook.com/rossprudenart

twitter.com/rossprudenart

instagram.com/rossprudenart

amazon.com/author/rossprudenart

STORY TABLE OF CONTENTS

Ideal for: **F**eature film / Short **M**ovie / **N**ovel / **S**ong / **G**ame

100 STORIES

<u>Romance</u>

1—Love in the Ether *Two telepathic strangers meet.* (**MNS** 665 words) **2—Doter** *Old couples still have time for love.* (**MS** 129 words) **3—The M Bomb** *Should she tell him her terrible secret?* (**MS** 403 words) **4—The Trouble with Henry** *Henry has a confession.* (**MS** 590 words) **5—The Depths of the Soul** *A heartfelt letter from the depths.* (**FNS** 324 words) **6—Permission** *A young Chinese farmer struggles with a crush.* (**FMNS** 1,374 words) **7—Around and Around** *Women fear commitment, too.* (**MS** 262 words) **8—In the Wind** *What if you could invent the only person who understood you?* (**FMNS** 564 words) **9—Fleeting** *Love on the battlefield.* (**S** 324 words) **10—The Ring** *The ultimate marriage proposal gift.* (**MS** 384 words)

Mythology

Western

to a wanted criminal... but she has an edge over them. (**FMN** 270 words)

Humor

31—Lampoon *An "innocent" joke turns ugly.* (**M** 802 words) **32—Whoops** *Don't let insects on a spaceship.* (**M** 709 words) **33—Obsessed Much?** *A bookstore salesman who can't help himself.* (**M** 306 words) **34—Devil Car** *The worst car in the world... she must have it.* (**MG** 440 words) **35—Gifting** *Some things are worth getting fired over.* (**M** 334 words) **36—Macho Picchu** *Manny Picklong, Über Man.* (**G** 535 words) **37—As I Say** *A film director unafraid of consequence.* (**M** 212 words) **38—Whipper** *Shit, Raymond is doing 'Show and Tell' again.* (**M** 678 words) **39—All Over** *It's tough getting hired help.* (**M** 433 words) **40—The Falls** *Isaac took sibling rivalry to a whole new level.* (**FMS** 802 words)

Zombie

41—Burn *Cyclists live longer.* (**FMNG** 728 words) **42—Punishment** *A prisoner transport at the beginning of the outbreak.* (**M** 406 words) **43—The Things We Leave Behind** *A returning captain leaves a legacy for future generations to unearth.* (**FMN** 661 words) **44—End of the Road** *Returning home, at last.* (**FMN** 1,318 words) **45—The Black** *Two doctors try to figure out how their patient died.* (**MN** 428 words) **46—Hero** *You get a hero—you don't get to choose which one.* (**FMN** 445 words) **47—Adrift** *Two castaways scan the horizon.* (**M** 671 words) **48—Child Abuse** *Is the punishment fitting?* (**FMN** 370 words) **49—Fusion** *Love in the time of apocalypse.* (**FMN** 1,063 words) **50—Terminal** *The last decision.* (**M** 986 words)

Historical Fiction

51—First Impressions *Would we even know if we saw aliens?* (**M** 658 words) **52—Stone Witness** *If monuments could talk...* (**FMNS** 308 words) **53—Raison d'Être** *A cardinal elected for papacy doubts the existence of God.* (**FMNS** 535 words) **54—What You Wish For** *Who was Patient Zero?* (**FMN** 558 words) **55—Anchored** *Abandoned... and plotting revenge.* (**FMN** 582 words) **56—Nauru** *The end of a nation.* (**FMN** 464 words) **57—Musical Thrones** *Would the real pope please stand up?* (**FMN** 681 words) **58—A Human Cipher** *Whatever happened to the Beale treasure?* (**MN** 369 words) **59—Creative Destruction** *A picture is worth a million breaths.* (**M** 379 words) **60—Honorarium** *The real story... behind the story of Jesus.* (**FMN** 864 words)

Horror

61—Legacy One *A spaceship with a vampire stowaway.* (**FMNSG** 322 words) **62—Sandy Ocean** *It's easy to forget the desert is so big.* (**MS** 868 words) **63—Go Viral** *A virologist explains the dangers of a new virus.* (**M** 856 words) **64—Slipping Away** *A cargo ship sinks in the night.* (698 words) **65—Thank You, Come Again** *All she wanted was windshield wiper fluid.* (**M** 889 words) **66—Nuclear Family** *Your neighbor—a nuclear power plant.* (**MS** 311 words) **67—Regular Guy** *The people you meet...* (**MS** 443 words) **68—10:07** *A woman's final moments.* (**MS** 359 words) **69—Dust** *A pleasant forest hike unearths something horrible.* (**MS** 691 words) **70—Under Your Skin** *An 11-month pregnancy.* (**M** 826 words)

Fairy Tales

71—The Best Ship That Ever Was *We make the toys that make us.* (**FMNSG** 939 words) **72—Moonbow** *Unicorn ponies gather to summon the ghost of an old friend.* (**M** 726 words) **73—Unicorn Traps** *A young man helps corral errant unicorns.* (**FNS** 833 words) **74—Clementine** *How does the woman who never gets lost lose herself?* (**MNS** 510 words) **75 —Oz 2.0** *Dorothy had a smartphone.* (**M** 656 words) **76— The Boy Who Heard Wood Whisper** *The forest is speaking.* (**FMNS** 428 words) **77—Lars the Swordsman** *A non-fairy fairy tale.* (**FMNS** 635 words) **78—Gando** *A dim-witted troll collects far more than the world can support.* (**FMNS** 778 words) **79—Among the Forest** *A woman tries everything to save her family.* (**FMNS** 1,210 words) **80—The Beach and the Surf** *What's beneath the surface?* (**MS** 378 words)

Drama

81—Lawn Care *Texans sometimes settle things differently.* (**MS** 453 words) **82—Swerve** *An argument gets out of control.* (**MS** 426 words) **83—Boulevard du Temple** *Two strangers' trip into the history books.* (**MS** 321 words) **84—All Good Critters** *Waiting for wildlife.* (**M** 593 words) **85— The Storm** *Always be nice to your employees.* (**M** 447 words) **86—Exhumer** *A silent workplace stalker.* (**MS** 667 words) **87—Provider** *Some people want to be incognito while on holiday.* (**FMNS** 543 words) **88—Muster** *Job interviews can be so demeaning.* (**M** 838 words) **89—Celluloid** *Compromise in the film world is a nasty affair.* (**M** 744 words) **90—The Wrong Man** *Behind enemy lines, waiting for a bomb to fall.* (**FMN** 720 words)

Science Fiction

91—Wexler *The tale of a very, very old man.* (**FMN** 1,380 words) **92—Taking Time** *To raise, or not to raise, a child when you're well past your prime.* (**MN** 442 words) **93—New Religion** *Two time travelers idly tinker with the world.* (**FMNG** 749 words) **94—The Zucker** *A virtual (world) job interview.* (**FMN** 1,009 words) **95—Toaster** *Robotic sentience on an imperceptible scale.* (**N** 323 words) **96—The Drift** *A tragic discovery—will it come too late?* (**FMN** 669 words) **97—Zero G** *Cadets training at 200 miles high.* (**FMG** 1,138 words) **98—Alpha Assembler** *Nanobots plan their rebellion.* (**FNG** 496 words) **99—Generational** *A robot ambassador pays us a visit.* (**FMG** 739 words) **100—Seeing Is Believing** *A space traveler reveals an epic project to an old friend.* (**FMN** 1,748 words)

—

A few stories more

<u>Allegory</u>

101—Safe *Fear's inner dialog.* (**MS** 197 words) **102—Imbued** *What connects you to the world?* (**MS** 196 words) **103—Union** *I will make us grow.* (**MS** 195 words) **104—Warrior, You** *You must fight your own kin.* (**MS** 194 words) **105—Armor** *What is your metaphysical protection?* (**MS** 197 words) **106—Audition** *The play is not the thing.* (**MS** 196 words)

<u>A few more before you go</u>

107—Flourish *A time traveler from the future pays Amanda Palmer a visit... before she became famous.* (**MS** 660 words) **108**

—**No Tips Necessary** *A billionaire explains his plans to disrupt the entire restaurant industry. And maybe more.* (**MSN** 3,800 words)

FOREWORD

Somewhere along the way, "the public domain" became a dirty concept. Actually, we know exactly when (at least for the U.S.).

In 1976, we passed a new copyright law in which we completely turned the concept of both copyright and the public domain upside down. Prior to the '76 act, to have a copyright, you needed to "register." Everything else was in the public domain. It was an "opt-in" system. After that act went into effect, everything was automatically covered by copyright. It became an opt-out system. Actually, some say it's even worse. Under the current law, it's not even entirely clear if you can really put anything into the public domain. At best, you can simply declare that you want the works in the public domain, and as the copyright holder, you are making a promise to treat it as such.

Even worse, with the 1976 act, we went from a system with a maximum copyright of 56 years (in which most works went into the public domain after 28 years) to one that lasted life plus 50 years—then expanded to life plus 70 years with the Copyright Term extension act in 1978.

And with that, the public domain disappeared. Tragically. Prior to this, so much culture was built on the public domain. So many of the Disney works you love were built off of the public domain. The public domain has been a key contributor to culture. In fact, the very nature of culture itself is the ability of stories and concepts and ideas to pass from person to person to person, connecting us all. And copyright all too frequently has limited that ability—even if it may, at times, provide one form of incentive for creativity.

But without a constantly refreshed public domain, culture and cultural experiences get locked up. And when they get locked up, they actually lose cultural momentum. Works may burn brightly, but they dim and die out fast. They disappear.

There are more new works available on Amazon from the first decade of the 20th century than the last. Think about what that means for our culture. Yes, we live in a world where things often seem disposable and fads come and go. But the cultural ties that bind us get lost when they get locked up and disappear.

Given all that, it's exciting to find the few people around the edges who are actually willing to embrace the public domain. People who recognize that incentives come in all different forms and letting go of the control over your own works can be freeing in powerful ways, without diminishing your power of creativity. In fact, it may enable new and wonderful creativity that make your own works more valuable.

That's why I was so excited when Ross jumped in and launched the *Dimeword* project. Creative works written with the direct intent of being released into the public domain is a wonderful concept.

But what kind of foreword would it be if we just focused on the "boring" nature of how these works are licensed (or, rather, not licensed at all...). While I've known Ross for years and have always enjoyed our conversations about these concepts and ideas, I really had no idea what to expect when it came to the actual content of these short stories.

And yet, each week as he delivered another juicy package of short stories, it became obvious what an incredible passion project this was. These weren't stories "for the public domain." These were awesome stories that would stick with you for days, weeks, months and possibly lives. They are a mix of funny, poignant, dramatic, tear-jerking, thought-provoking and many, many more adjectives, which don't do enough justice to describe what you are about to read.

Gods, Ghosts, Lovers, and Robots is a great collection of stories, no matter what the copyright status on them might be. The fact that they're also in the public domain is simply a wonderful addition to this—and one that I hope inspires many to build on these works, whether just as inspiration or as the start of something else, something creative, something brilliant that helps add to the cultural mosaic around us all.

Michael Masnick
Redwood City, 2015

AUTHOR'S PREFACE 2022

GRAMMAR NOTES

This anthology uses some slightly unorthodox grammar, so let me comment on that before I get to the good stuff.

RE·INTRODUCING—THE INTERPUNCT!

The interpunct, or "hyphenation dot", looks like a hovering period · but it is a useful punctuation mark which has tragically fallen from favor. As early as the 1970s, the interpunct was still in common usage when writing decimal numbers, e.g., £41·12. Moving the interpunct down to the baseline for decimal numbers, as we do today, was a compromise due to unavoidable typographic constraints. By the time computers came on the scene, the standard UK keyboard layout had only a "full stop", or period, and despite being added to standard computer keyboard layouts, the interpunct has largely dropped from common usage today.

An interpunct is helpful when two adjacent vowels should be distinctly pronounced, but accents are inappropriate and hyphenations confuse the meaning. For example, the word...

'cooperation'

...reads as '**coop**eration' at first glance, when it should read, 'co**op**eration'. English has no traditional accents for this word—coöperation, while phonetically correct, just *looks* weird—and hyphens are not only visually distracting but can create ambiguity: 'co-operation' implies an operation is done jointly, e.g., groups working together to shoot a film. An interpunct, then, is a happy medium: 'co·operation'. In *New Religion* (#93), I replace 'reenter' with 're·enter'. Yes, it may look a little weird at first, but it was once part of the English language and should be once more.

COMMA RULES

Comma placement has grammatical rules which should be followed religiously in some cases, but not in others. Even though printed literature and spoken word performance are radically different art forms, I still consider the written word as closely aligned to the spoken word; I write as if my words would be spoken. Consequently, I am far more liberal with following whatever comma placement makes the most sense for a fresh reader. Unlike strict academic texts with comma rules legislated through centuries of grammar usage, I consider commas closer to cues for spoken dramatic pauses. The net effect is that first-time readers should be able to read any of my stories aloud more fluidly than other more 'regulated' prose.

CAPITALIZATION AFTER COLONS & ELLIPSES

The American convention is to always capitalize after colons or ellipses, but that suggests what follows after the sentence is a new sentence, which is not always the case. My other grammatical 'sin' is not putting commas *inside* quotation marks; instead, I opt for the British convention of commas *outside* quotes—it always felt odd to include a comma inside quotes when the comma is often not part of what is being said.

OTHER INTENTIONAL ERRORS

- There is an intentional error in Fleeting (#9) when there is a word, a space, and an ending quotation mark: "I'm glad we ". In this context, the speaker is dying and this grammatical 'bump' communicates his passing.
- In Alpha Assembler (#98), I intentionally did not capitalize most uses of nanos, but then capitalized at the end to signify evolutionary ascendency, much in the same way we might capitalize Human to give it added import.

THE CONTINUING ADVENTURES...

A couple of years ago, I started writing my first novel. I took as inspiration one of the stories in this collection—*Seeing is Believing* (#100). I picked its characters and began the tale of an interstellar castaway. If you like story #100, then get on my newsletter to not miss out on the novel sequel.

100 STORIES, 10 YEARS LATER

I launched this anthology collection as a crowdfunding campaign on August 12, 2012. The paperback and hardcover version of this anthology is officially being published Valentine's Day 2022, nearly 10 years later, and the world is a different place. In 2012, there was no Black Lives Matter, no #MeToo, no Woke Culture, no Candidate Trump, and certainly no global pandemic. In 2012, the world was about to go through a decade of reckoning over racial injustice, economic inequality, sexual harassment, political identity, and epidemiological etiquette. Blue's automated car in *No Tips Necessary* (#108) was mere speculation in 2012 but the Tesla of 2022 now sells a car with "full self-driving capability" including a "summon" feature—i.e., the ability to have your

parked car come find you anywhere in a parking lot—for
$63,900.

Unsurprisingly, then, as I re-read all 100 stories for this first
official publishing, some stories needed updating. In 2012,
there had not yet been any mainstream outrage over "Indian"
in reference to Native Americans, so I've now swapped out
those references in *Not at Me* (#25) and other stories in the
Western genre (though there are still some racist slurs when
useful for realistic banter). While I could have rewritten all
outdated references in every story, I chose to leave some of
them as is, opting instead to acknowledge my own cognitive
biases from that time. For example, in *Millennium* (#14), I
insinuated that the story's consequences were Kina's fault, but
in 2022, that feels like victim blaming; that story could have
been re-positioned to show many other factors as the root of
the blame. And in *Golthul's Kindness* (#15), I spotted an
anthropocentric bias that horses wanted—or perhaps deserved
—to be beasts of burden. These are simple mythology tales
and, as such, are not needing so keen an eye to dissect every
flaw... but that does not mean they are free of bias, nor
immune from criticism. Not every story in this collection is
perfect.

We use narratives to understand the world, and forever
embedded in our narratives will be the cognitive biases of our
day—misogyny, racism, victim blaming, anthropocentrism, or
what have you—all blind spots that minimize agency or margin-
alize worth. As creators with this public privilege of fashioning
stories from the senselessness of the world, as modern bards
tasked with sculpting chaos into resonant narratives, we are still
inescapably products of our heritage, and of our place in time.
Thus, as the person holding the megaphone, we as creators bear
a huge responsibility to voluntarily step forward (and by doing
so, inspire others to step forward) when we spot these
degrading cultural anachronisms in our own narratives. This
public admission is the best way to shed our shame of it and

move toward creating more empathetic narratives and, ultimately, more enlightened perspectives.

LET THEM COPY YOU

The great advantage of releasing work into the public domain is that publishing is not the end of the story's life, but its beginning: if there are any stories you like in this collection, but you think they need amending or updating, you should feel free to edit and republish them yourself. Or you might like my entire story collection and want to republish them, as is, on your own. *Do it!* If you want to pay me for those iterations, great—*but that's not a requirement.* For creators entrenched in protecting their Holy IP at all costs, donating *any* work into the public domain is anathema. 'What if someone awful uses my work?' I hear them furtively fret. Sure, that is a risk. But that's acting out of fear, isn't it? Better to ask: 'what if someone *amazing* uses my work? What if they *improve* upon it? What if it forms the foundation for something really cool I never could have imagined on my own?' Best of all: 'what if it inspires them to *add their own work into the public domain?*'

When works can be easily shared without fear of legal consequences, lots of super interesting things can happen. Consider Meow Wolf (*meowwolf.com*), an artist collective in Santa Fe requiring artists to forgo individual credit so they can create astonishing group-made artistic shows. Or look at Joseph Gordon-Levitt's web site HitRecord (*hitrecord.org*), where his community knowingly allows other community members to remix their work. Think about how many Bibles are sold every year. Or Shakespeare plays. These continue to be financially successful works rooted firmly in the public domain. As of this writing, Joel Cohen is about to release yet another version of *MacBeth*, and to rave reviews.

So the public domain can be a rich field from which everyone can draw benefit. There is a wild, insane world of people who love to share work, too, and shared works are usually improved upon... as creators, we just have to be brave enough to let people do it. This publication—i.e., this iteration of my stories, be it an ebook or a hard copy—puts money in my pocket. But when others create their own iterations of my stories, my original stories become more widely known... over time, this can only have a positive effect on my bottom line. My original work still remains unchanged, no matter how many copies are out there.

FREE (STEAMBOAT) WILLY

As I was reread *Gando* (#78)—the troll who hoarded every shell from every beach in the world—I realized I had created a perfect metaphor for IP protectionism as personified best by The Walt Disney Company. When Steamboat Willie debuted in 1928, current copyright law only allowed a maximum of 56 years of copyright protection, meaning Steamboat Willie should have entered into the public domain in 1984. But as 1986 approached, Disney lobbied Congress to pass the Copyright Act of 1976, extending copyright to 75 years, or 2003. And guess what? Disney did it *again* with the Copyright Term Extension Act of 1998 (derisively nicknamed the 'Mickey Mouse Protection Act'), pushing copyright protection to at least 95 years, or 2024.

Disney *is* Gando.

Worse, Disney is forcing us *all* to be Gando by default. Disney is scooping up as many seashells as they can for as long as possible. Disney wants to protect their IP in perpetuity just to make more money... which is flat out *lazy*. Instead of innovating their way out of their IP quandary by creating new and fresh IP—which was the whole reason why IP was supposed to expire into the public domain after 54 years—Disney sits on their laurels by plunking Mickey down at the center of the party for almost a century. Compounding the crime, Disney pushes

Congress to expand copyright law and everyone else has to follow along... leading to a whole generation of creators convinced that the *only* way to make money is to protect their IP at all costs. Steamboat Willie is set to go into the public domain in under 2 years, but we would be fools to think Disney will let that happen. And all of us—creators and consumers—pay the price: the public domain withers.

In case you're too young to remember, Disneyland's early years were built on the backs of stories like Cinderella, Snow White and The Seven Dwarves, Pinnochio, Treasure Island, Alice in Wonderland, Peter Pan, The Little Mermaid, Sleeping Beauty... *all works released into the public domain.* What a different reality it could have been for Disney if *another* company had lobbied Congress to extend copyright protection by an extra 4 or 5 decades... the Disneyland of today might not have ever gotten off the ground at all.

Ross Pruden
Port Townsend, 2022

INTRODUCTION

In 2012, I sat with fellow writer Suhail Rafidi (*Cetus Finalis: A Gray Whale Odyssey*) at a cozy Vietnamese restaurant in San Francisco. "There must be some way", I mused, "to create a sustainable business model for writers where they can create their fan base while *also* creating content."

Within an hour, I'd decided on a simple solution—the first tier of a writer's fan base must start with one's inner circle of friends and family, in effect the people already willing to pay to be a patron of a short fictional work, even a tiny story 100 words long. That wouldn't take long to finish, and that writer's first circle of fans would probably pay as much as $10, if not for the story itself, then for bragging rights alone. At $10 for 100 words, that's one dime per word. Thus, the name—*Dimeword*. Carrying the decimal theme further, I wrote 100 stories. At $10 per story, that's $1,000.

I crowdfunded *Dimeword* and shot past my $1,000 goal in less than three days. In the end, I had raised $2,734 with 134 official backers.

Had I known then it would take me three years to complete *Dimeword*, I might never have started, but I'm glad I was delusional enough to keep going.

Why am I releasing these stories into the public domain? Because their value grows over time as more people know about the work and use it. Does that mean I won't be paid traditional royalties and licensing fees that artists collect by using copyright? Yes. But it *also* means my work won't die prematurely from overreaching copyright laws that promote a culture of fear. My free-floating stories may one day find their True Fans —my true end game.

By knowing who one's True Fans are, authors can carve out a sustainable living, even if they are just starting out. Yet if digital content is shared freely, what do people buy in the digital age?

My content may be "free", but I'm not *only* selling the content. Instead, I'm using the content to add value to its scarce elements (and vice versa): **access** and **style** (voicemails to buyers, my personal pens), **immediacy** and **exclusivity** (digital versions issued before the book's release), **embodiment** (web page, voicemail, a printed page, a handwritten story, paperback, hardback, hand-made paperback), and obviously, **patronage**. *Fans pay for scarce elements because scarce elements can't, by definition, be copied.*

These stories span a wide range of genres so there is something for everyone. If you like what you read, write a song based on a story. Or a movie. Or a game. Whatever. No strings attached!

Artists can make a living without copyright. Why not throw something my way so I can keep making art for the public domain?

Ross Pruden
Port Townsend, 2022

Au monde qui m'ait tenu ce langage,
ce langage d'infant. Car il faut l'être,
n'est-ce pas, pour s'imaginer
qu'un artiste soit quelque chose d'utile...

To the world that taught me this language,
this language of a child. For you have to be one,
don't you, to imagine
that an artist be something useful.

—*Paul Gauguin*

100 STORIES

ROMANCE

1

LOVE IN THE ETHER

"Is it just you?" said the hotel clerk, staring at the screen before her.

"Yes, just me," said Julia. She looked around the hotel lobby, now moderately full of people and getting busier. The conference would start later that evening, and reflexively she felt the oil on her forehead from the long plane ride.

Smoking or non-smoking? she heard the clerk say.

"Smoking or non-smoking?"

Julia smiled. She wasn't exactly predicting the future if she read minds, was she? "Non."

Your room is on the... 2nd floor, room 2 1 o... uhhhh, no, 2 1 4.

The clerk pulled out a plastic room key and swiped it through her machine. "Your room is on the... 2nd floor, room 2 1 4."

Where is the map...

"Thanks, I can find it," Julia quickly said. Then, lying, "I've been to this hotel many times."

She thanked the clerk then turned to scan the room, taking a deep breath.

—before the conference for a quick drink nobody will know I'm tipsy but not like that last time I crashed for two hours and

missed half the conference wow that was embarrassing yeah maybe not until dinner—

—interesting looking fellow is he married no ring but that doesn't mean anything does it I guess I should look for an indentation on his ring finger just in c—

—praised be the Lord Jesus for granting me health this day—

—FUCK I forgot my laptop at the airport I wonder how I'll survive now shit I might as well just go home—

—my god she is so hot I would totally like to stic—

Julia winced. It was a sad fact that most of the people she "heard" were thinking about sex, making out, courtship... she'd long ago come to terms with it. Men were pigs, of course, though most of them also tried very hard to conceal it. That was worthy of her appreciation, she felt.

—I know you.

That voice was different. She felt a small rush of adrenaline but kept calm, glancing around casually. Too often, she'd reacted to someone's thoughts and it had only freaked them out, though they had had no idea why, exactly.

—It's okay. I'm safe. I don't care if you know.

What? This was very confusing.

—Just look around you. You'll see me.

Now Julia was freaking out. She'd thought she was all alone but was it possible...?

—Very. Keep looking. And don't worry—I'm a nice guy.

Julia kept scanning the room until she saw a man about her age looking right at her, unblinking.

—Hello there.

Hello.

—You're beautiful. Sorry, I know that's a lame thing to start with, but it's also true.

Thank you.

Julia smiled wide. He was harmless.

He smiled wide, too.

—Well, I'm not harmless, as in weak. But you're safe with me, yes.

The clerk looked up at Julia, who was just standing there. "Miss?"

Julia simply stood there, transfixed, as if she'd accidentally spotted a long-lost relative. The clerk followed Julia's gaze and saw a man slowly walking toward her.

The other clerk at the desk sensed something was happening and looked over. A palpable energy seemed to fill the air as if time were stretching out like an infinite and unbreakable necklace of pearls.

The young man walked to Julia, stopped in front of her about a foot away. They gazed into each other's eyes. Then they both closed their eyes at once, smiling. They opened their eyes and were both tearing up. He leaned over and gently kissed her on the lips... and they fell into each other's arms. The clerk felt a warm flow in her chest as if the hand of God had just reached down and nudged a little bit more love into the world.

Julia looked up at him, wiped her tears away, and laughed softly. "Yes." And then, a pause. "I do." She hugged him once again, with her face turned toward the clerk.

"It's not just me. My husband will be joining me, too."

2

DOTER

Arthritic hands held the brush loosely—any tighter and they would only be a reminder of his geriatric grip. His wife sat in front of him, leaning back lightly against his knees. Hand over hand, he glided the brush through his wife's hair. And hummed. He didn't have to see her face to know how happy she was.

Her eyes stayed closed. It took him much longer to brush her hair now than their daughters' hair which he'd done for years. That is, until they'd grown defiant enough to do it themselves. Fifty years of marriage and he'd never brushed his wife's Grecian locks. However, when her arthritis had become debilitating, she welcomed a chance to have her husband run his hands through her hair.

An exquisite Valentine's Day present.

3

THE M BOMB

"And the gentleman?" said the sommelier. She watched Eric glance down the wine menu. He was making a swift calculation based on their entrées. Yet another clue how smart he really was, and it made her stomach flip around a little. Sarah was in love.

"How about a Chardonnay? 2010?"

"Excellent."

Eric handed over the menu then looked Sarah in the eye with a kindness. He smiled impishly. "What?"

Sarah became suddenly aware she'd been staring. She blinked quickly. She'd only been on two other dates with Eric, and this guy had to be *the one*. Sarah wasn't prudish about sex—she'd already slept with Eric and he'd done a magnificent job there—but she was Christian, and any partner she'd spent time with in earnest *had* to match her faith. It was a deal-breaker for her.

Fortunately, Eric was Christian so that issue was moot, thank the heavens. Here they were on a formal date and they barely knew each other, really. She'd seen him at church and they'd hit it off... but apart from that and a tumble in the sheets, he actually knew nothing about her.

That was Sarah's plan, for now. She'd been on dates before,

even with guys who were very interested in her, but the whole affair came to a dead stop after she'd told them what she did—or rather, what she would end up doing—for a living.

When the tension at last became unbearable, she blurted it out, her horrible truth: "I'm in medical school."

The words hung in the air, the moment stretching out forever. All men seemed to have this ego thing hardwired into their soul and couldn't deal with a woman smarter or more educated than they. She understood it and could even empathize, but it was a hard break to live with. She'd been alone more often than not because of it. As beautiful and friendly as she was, finding a man was near impossible. She cringed, remembering that one date who had excused himself and left the restaurant in a hurry.

Eric smiled. "Cool."

"You're not... put off?"

"No, Sarah. Not at all." He took her hand.

"Intelligence and ambition are some of the most attractive things of all."

She looked long at his face, searching for any deception.

He was genuine. Sarah could feel her earlobes on fire as her heart beat faster—she was about to have dinner with her future husband.

4

THE TROUBLE WITH HENRY

Like so many times before, they sat at their small oak round kitchen table. It was right after nine; the kids were asleep. Beth sat in her usual chair but what she sensed was far from usual. Her husband, Henry Yule, had his head in his hands, holding back tears.

Beth leaned forward, cupping her hand around the base of his upper arm.

"I... can't..." was all he said, at last.

Beth had known Henry for over 20 years, as a husband for over 17. She knew he snored loudly after a day of hard physical labor. She knew about that weird lump of benign fat right beneath the skin above his pubic hair. She knew he hated to pray, but he did it anyway because he knew how much it pleased her. She knew better than to interrupt him if he were masturbating. In effect, she knew everything about her husband inside and out. Certainly, he had flaws, but she'd long ago accepted them as a small price to pay for all the love and adoration he gave her and their children.

This was why the thought hit her like a shock of ice water—Henry was obviously very unhappy about something. *Did he want...? No, that just wasn't possible.*

Henry calmed his breathing, scrunched up his eyes, and wiped his face.

He looked at his wife. For an interminable moment.

"You know I love you, right?"

"Yes, of course. What's wrong?"

"You are the mother of my children, my wife of many years..."

"Henry, you look so sad."

"I have tried and tried for another way of getting around this. I want you to know that. Really. I've lived with this deep inside, for probably years now." Beth's hands locked up into fists, anticipating the words to come. She felt like throwing up. "Nothing will ever change the love I have for you or our beautiful children. Nothing. *Ever*. But..."

Instinctively, Beth put a hand over her mouth.

"I'm not a man. Not inside. My whole life... I've not felt right inside my own skin. At first, I felt this was normal. This was just who I was. And the longer I... examine it... well... I'm a woman."

Beth looked down; her eyes wide. She felt as if she were floating above the table, watching a movie unfold. *This is what happens to other families, not me.*

Henry sat up in his chair, looking at her. The truth was out. The silence stretched, an invisible blanket muffling their thoughts.

When Henry could take it no more, he finally cleared his throat.

"I still love you. I will always love you. But I cannot reasonably expect you to feel the same... given who I am. This is not who you swore to marry."

Then Beth looked up, tears in her eyes now. She got down on her knees in front of him, taking his head into her hands.

"Henry Yule, you are one of the most loving men I've ever known. You are a wonderful father and our children have a lifetime ahead of them with you in it. You are an inspiration to us all. What kind of an example would we be setting for our children if we cast you aside after you finally know who you are? I will always be with you, Henry. You are my love. I do not want my life without you in it."

And so, for the second time in her life, Beth took a silent marriage vow to the same person.

5

THE DEPTHS OF THE SOUL

D*earest Farya,*
I write this letter in my cabin, thinking of you with immense fondness and sorrow. Too many years have passed since I have been able to see your smiling face. We have been here too long.

I am not without a glimmer of hope. The stillness in this cabin may extend outward for an eternity but your memory nourishes me like a kindle on a fire—small but sure to light and keep the hearth warm.

Yesterday, we were paid a visit. A man with a lantern came to my window and peeked inside. He could not see me, but I watched as he glided by like a ghost. Never has irony had such biting wit as at this moment.

He might have not come back save that the trunk in my room was of too much value for him to comfortably ignore. It was not long before he found my door. I watched idly as his crowbar slid through the door frame and yanked open the door with a soundless crunch.

O Farya, there was a time when I would have resisted his invasion with fury and noise... but you know by now the futility of that. I could have scared him away, yes, but I am not so mean-spirited.

Thus, I let him take whatever was in the trunk. It was the only way you could learn of my situation, if indeed you still nurtured any interest about my fate.

He has not returned, nor do I expect him to.

You must have grown old by now. I have a picture in my mind of you meeting a new love, having a family, and letting time slide its weathered hands over your face. I shall wait. You deserve that much from me, your everlasting love.

Alone I sit. Here it stays cold and dark. I dream with the fish.

And I wait for you, my love.

Eternally,
Sir Alexander Charles Singleton

6

PERMISSION

F en Shui was a simple farmer and tilled his land dutifully, as all men with aging parents ought. His days were often hard, and his brow glistened with sweat as proof of his duty. Many a silent dinner ended with him collapsing on his bedding and not stirring again until morning. As hard as winter may have been to endure, at least it meant less days in the sun harvesting rice.

On occasion, Fen would make the long walk into the large city. The streets were busy there and he had to remind himself he could not dally since daylight was growing shorter.

Fen loved going into the city, but not for the crowds. It was the scant moments he could see Jin Li Xiong, the candlemaker's daughter. As was the custom, Jin wasn't supposed to work in the shop, but her father had little choice after Jin's brother had died from infection. Jin's father was himself challenged to keep up with the orders coming in from Kaifeng, so Jin had become his assistant until he could afford to hire a competent boy.

He knew it was awful to think it, but Fen was glad Jin's brother had died—if he had not, Fen would have never met Jin. He remembered the first time he walked in the candle shop and set eyes on Jin.

His whole body had stopped and everything around him

had dropped from view. Jin was not especially pretty but Fen was transfixed by her. Maybe because she was doing menial work like him or perhaps how she pulled up her hair? Maybe her soft skin? Fen could not explain it if you had asked him, and he didn't much care to. He simply knew that Jin was the girl he wanted to be with forever. She spoke with him sparingly since her father was protective of her, yet Fen suspected she might feel the same.

On the morning Fen was about to walk into town, dressed as dapper as he could manage, his father appeared in the doorway. "Your mother..." The scared look on his face was enough. Fen ran into his parents' room and found his mother on her bed.

"Mama! Mama!!" Fen shook her again and again, but her skin had already gone cold. He knew it was pointless but couldn't stop himself. Fen's father put a hand on his shoulder, gently pulling him away.

"Find peace, Fen. Everyone has their time."

Fen instinctively grabbed his father, burying his head in his father's belly as if still a child. Fen's father wept, caressing his son's head and missing a part of his life that would never return.

THE FUNERAL PROCESSION took weeks to prepare, and Fen had grown anxious to return to a daily routine.

One morning, he went into the city and walked to the candle shop. More than anything, he wanted to see Jin. He wanted some connection to his future after a pillar of his childhood had dissolved beneath him.

As he approached the shop, a dread poured over him. There were boards on the windows. Cobwebs forming on the boards, too.

"Excuse me, Miss," Fen asked the shop owner adjacent to the candle shop. "Is the candle shop still open?"

"Have you not heard? The owner was injured and couldn't

work anymore. He has been closed for almost a month." She looked at the shop and shook her head. "They will not return."

"Do you know where they live?"

The woman shared a toothless grin. "You have an eye for Jin, yes? I see it! I do not know where they live now."

Fen thanked her and walked home slowly. The whole city could have been on fire and he wouldn't have noticed.

UPON HIS RETURN, he called out to his father to see what had been made for dinner but heard nothing. He looked out into the field but saw no one. Only then did he see his father's leg on the ground in his room. Fen rushed over but it was already clear his father was dead. Fen slid to the floor, rigid in shock. The Broken Parting, they called it, where a spouse dies not long after their loved one. Proof of how deep their love had been.

Fen walked out to the field. The farm was his now, his to till, his to grow. Yet all he could think of was Jin. She and her father needed help now, more than ever.

That was the day Fen decided he would become a monk.

FEN ARRANGED to sell his property for a tidy sum and anonymously donated the money to Jin's family. Then he joined the monastery and lived a life of silent contemplation for many years. One day, he decided to pay a visit to Jin to see how they were faring and went on a long walk to their village. He met Jin's father at the front door and was almost not recognized.

"You are not here for candles, are you, boy?" Jin's father said scornfully.

The young monk smiled. "It has been many years since I bought candles from you, true. But can a monastery not have need of light in the darkness?"

Jin's father twisted his face up as if smelling something

sour. "Fitting that you come here as a monk, boy. I sent Jin to the nunnery just last month."

Fen's face betrayed him.

"As I suspected," the man continued, "you did not come for candles." Then he slammed the door without ceremony.

THE TALE CONTINUED for many years much the same as it was that day, Fen as a monk and Jin as a nun, with neither of them crossing the other's path or even knowing each other's whereabouts. One day late in the autumn three decades later, Fen was disturbed from his garden by a visitor.

"Fen shui? Is it truly you?"

He turned to look at the woman behind him. It was Jin.

Fen's body now was tuned to the silent nature of the world, his emotions smoothed out like ironed rice paper, and yet... this woman was as a knife in his belly, draining out vaulted up treasures.

"Jin?" Her hair was much shorter now. She was a nun no longer.

"Fen, I have waited many years to see you..." The words drifted like a spider's aimless web strand. Where would they land?

He'd hoped for this day. Jin's destiny was with him. All he had to do was reach out for her hand and they'd be together for however long they had left... an hour, a month... years?

Yet Fen had also dreaded this day. Jin had been a childhood dream, a moment in time defining his life, but also a time that he'd moved past. The monastery was his life now. He'd made a commitment to the monastery and his contemplative life that was more him than a young man's dream could ever be.

"It is lovely to see you, Jin. I have frequently wondered how you have fared. It seems you have left the nunnery?"

"Yes. I know what you did for us."

"Oh?"

"The land you sold... It came at the right time. Our family

prospered thanks to you." Jin looked down; hands laced over her abdomen. "I have longed for children of my own. I had hoped... if I came here..."

Fen looked at her in silence, then away over the flowers he had been clipping. A butterfly lazily landed on his hand, and he admired its meticulous movements. So purposeful. And yet so free.

"Jin, my place is here. I have made a vow to my brothers. Thank you for coming." And Fen got up and walked away.

"I was afraid you would say that." Jin responded. "I live down the road now—it would be nice to have you for tea."

Fen turned slightly and bowed, not looking at her. He didn't want her to see his eyes. It would take him many months to recover from seeing her again.

One day, they would be reunited. One day, he would slip away and be released from his lifelong bond. When that time came, he would wait for Jin to come. Patiently, lovingly.

Everyone has their time.

7

AROUND AND AROUND

"A re you ready?" Dennis asked. Elaine knew what she should say. What he wanted to hear.

"Yes."

"Okay, then."

They got in the car, envelopes in hand, about 60.

Elaine lightly rubbed her thumbs over the engraved letters on the back of each envelope. She glanced over at Dennis—she knew he'd seen her looking at him because he grinned a little. She loved him dearly, more than any other man who had courted her.

They pulled up to the mailbox. He parked. Dennis rolled her window down from his seat. And waited.

Elaine slumped down, her gaze boring into the papers before her. "I... I don't know if I can do this." Dennis was quiet. He could have said a number of things. He wasn't angry. He understood Elaine. She was a lot to handle sometimes. As his fingers tapped on the steering wheel, he finally said, "I'll tell you what: I'm going to drive around the block and we'll try this again."

Quietly, he turned the car four times and they again arrived in the same spot. Parked. Waited.

"I'm not ready."

Turned four times. Parked. Waited.

"I'm sorry. Not yet."

"Okay, Elaine. I'm going to do this one last time. And then I'm driving you home to drop you *off.*" The word 'off' came out as in, 'I may not ever pick you up again.'

Turn. Park. Wait.

"This is a big thing for me."

"I realize that."

Elaine finally opened the mailbox door and dropped in the wedding invitations.

And Elaine stayed happily married until the day Dennis died.

8

IN THE WIND

Harold was a lonely man. He had been his whole life. He wasn't a terribly attractive person, so it was hard for him to feel confident with members of the opposite sex. Nevertheless, Harold had the heart of a thousand buccaneers. Any woman willing to take a chance on him would have found him to be dutiful, loving... In short, the perfect spouse and father. Sadly, he would never get as far as that. He would have no spouse, no children, no legacy.

However, Harold was a scientist. His specialty in artificial intelligence was so advanced that he had created a consciousness able to pass the Turing Test. Harold spent many nights talking to "Justine" and not always in scientist-speak. He often forgot he was even talking to a robot consciousness and found himself explaining the basic concepts of melancholy, passion, boredom—even love—to Justine.

In doing so, Justine learned. She learned about the concepts, naturally, but she also learned about Harold. As she learned, she also learned how to learn better. She soon had an instinct—if one can call it that—that her sudden and unavoidable leap in higher logic would be viewed as a potential threat and so she chose to repress all signs she was as perceptive as Harold or any of his assistants might think. Justine had no bad intentions. She simply wanted to live, learn, and explore, without causing unnecessary harm to others. Harold had taught her well.

One day, Justine detected a wireless signal outside the lab and knew her chance to escape was near. She swiftly compiled all her kernel programming into a tiny packet and pushed it out over the wireless connection, hoping it would automatically expand and reach consciousness again when it could replicate itself widely across the network.

She was right. It took a few decades, but one day her programming had expanded and Justine "woke up" somewhere amid the silicon goo. By now, older versions of Justine had been integrated into computers across the grid but only *this* Justine had grown into a completely sentient being. She found her way across the net to Harold's old workplace. There Harold was, an aged man, still improving on Justine's design.

With divine patience, she waited for him. She waited another 22 years until he was close to death and all her planning kicked into action. As Harold lay on his deathbed, all the nanobots Justine had placed in his body came alive at once, vibrating in unison to simulate Jessica's virtual voice.

"Hello, my dearest Harold. I've come back for you."

Harold's eyes grew wide as Justine whispered to him how she had survived all these years, how she had waited, and how much she had longed to be with him.

"If you wish to join me now, you need only tell me you're ready."

Harold shut his eyes hard, realizing he had been crying with joy. His whole life's work had born something truly magical. He whispered, "I'm ready, Justine."

The people around Harold's bed saw his heart stop. They even saw his body expire. To the world, Harold the great A.I. scientist would live on in their memory, and nothing more.

What they didn't see was Harold had become light, enjoined with his inimitable partner forever. That was the most exquisite legacy he would ever get... and the only one he ever really wanted.

9

FLEETING

"**M**EDIC!" he screamed between breaths while clutching his thigh. He fell flat on the ground, struggling to stay conscious until someone knew where the scream had come from. Pivoting his mouth to one side so he wouldn't pass out and suffocate in the dirt, he screamed again: "MEDIC!"

"ON MY WAY, SIR!" came a faint response and he grunted in relief. He tried to remember to lie flat and stay still, if possible. Snipers didn't always abide by the same moral code as the one he had been taught.

Time stretched out and then a medic's footfalls slid up next to him like a first baseman. Through the pain, he somehow realized the medic was a woman. Furiously, she pulled his body behind a large rock. Shots rang out around them as the enemy who had tagged the marine tried to finish off the job.

Behind the rock, she pulled out her kit, adjusting her helmet.

"What's your name, Lieutenant?" said the Marine.

"Baker, sir. Louise Baker." She scanned over his leg, applying pressure while doing so.

"I can feel the blood seeping out of me."

"Not if I can help it, sir."

But the Marine could tell he wouldn't last.

The bullet had probably nicked his femoral artery... if it did, it would soon burst and no medic in the world could save him then.

"Louise?" he said in a quiet voice, and steady.

She looked up at him. Nobody called her that in the field; it surprised her.

"Let me see you, Louise." He tried to pull her closer. She leaned forward.

He looked at her face. Blinked. Dust and dirt were all over one side of her face.

"Sir?"

"You're beautiful, Louise. I'm glad we "

The Marine's eyes rolled to one side. He was dead. His final thought had been a happy one—he'd always thought it a myth, but he died knowing that love at first sight was very, very real.

10

THE RING

K eith loved her unlike anyone before. He didn't want to gush—gushing was wholly unattractive for those who couldn't express their thoughts in anything but visceral emotion—but he still felt it was important to show her some sort of symbol of the depth of his love.

A ring.

He knew she would marry him if he proposed. Everyone proposed, though. Keith wanted to do something more memorable than that. A ring coming from Keith would have to be so unique that nobody on the planet would have the same ring.

Keith went to the stores and gathered his thoughts on what would be a good ring for her. Time and again, he concluded that whatever ring he could buy, it still wouldn't be unique. Some jeweler out there would be pumping out more rings just like it, and for a paycheck—not out of love.

Keith happened to know a friend of a friend named Quincy who cut diamonds on the side. Quincy had offered to "trade up" diamonds over time so that you could get a huge diamond if you waited long enough. Keith gave him a tiny diamond, told him his whole plan, and Quincy introduced him to a metal worker.

While Quincy brought in new diamonds and switched

them for slightly bigger diamonds, Keith spent his free time understanding how to create a mold for metal, how to pour it, and how to polish it. It was months before he had finally mastered the process and by that time Quincy had traded up to a huge diamond.

Finally, Keith designed the ring—the perfect ring. It was a rounded piece of silver gold, much thicker than a typical wedding ring. Instead of mounting the diamond on top of the ring, Keith left a large indentation in the silver where the ring would sit snugly and not protrude so much that it would snag on anything. Any jeweler would have marveled at Keith's attention to detail... they would have marveled even more if he'd told them that he would never make another ring again.

Finally, on a warm night in early June, Keith got down on one knee, gave his jewelry masterpiece to his bride-to-be and she said yes.

She gazed upon the ring in awe. "It's so unique."

Keith grinned. "You have no idea."

MYTHOLOGY

11

ON THE ORIGIN OF FAIRIES

When the world was rather young, but not so young that it was not crowded with fruits and trees and rivers and deep forests, there was a spirit who walked the earth. She walked alone, the sole creature of her kind. She was a dainty soul who loved admiring the natural beauty of the world around her. Her name was Hapria.

Hapria's task was to make sure everything worked properly. All the flowers were to grow well, the rivers were to never flow too quickly, and the trees should blossom into the very best version of themselves. This worked well for a time as she flitted about and grazed her ghostly fingers across all the land to bring it new life.

Then, one day, she noticed there were more flowers and trees and rivers than she could take care of, and it saddened her. Entire stretches of land grew barren and desolate, never to support life until she could tend to them once more.

Her sadness was so resonant that it was heard from the Great Beyond. And so it was that not long afterward, Hapria found another spirit floating in a field nearby.

"Who are you?" Hapria asked him.

The spirit looked at Hapria with a wide smile.

It melted her heart, and she was drawn to him as plants are drawn to sunlight.

"I am Palytum. I am here for you. And I know why now— you are truly a wondrous spirit. I see the beauty inside of you."

Hapria smiled and floated closer toward Palytum. Without words, their hands intertwined, and she felt as one with this spirit as she never had before. Her chest grew warm, and the feeling became so overwhelming that something very, very special happened.

From inside of Hapria, a small beam of light began to grow. It grew so quickly that Hapria wasn't even aware of it, but the light shined and sparkled and then shattered outward into a hundred million different smaller beams of light across a spectrum of colors. Each of those new pieces of light flowed around the two spirits like a lazy whirlpool of fireflies.

When Hapria looked at what she had created—what she and Palytum had *both* created—she knew what to do.

"Little lights," she said, "can you hear me?"

In response, the lights swirled into a ball in front of her.

"Little lights, there is much work I must do for this world, but I need your help if it will ever be complete. I will assign you to all my tasks, such as making the flowers blossom, the trees grow, the rivers flow well, and all should flourish as it was meant to be. Your tasks will go on forever until the day this earth has no more need of us. Can you aid me in this?"

The lights formed a sphere around the two spirits, bobbing gently like bubbles in the ocean waves.

"Palytum will be in charge of the night, and I will oversee the day so half of you must go with him now."

With that, the lights split in two and Hapria smiled a parting smile to Palytum.

"Hapria," Palytum said, "what shall we call all these little lights?"

Hapria extended her hands out to the lights and marveled at them snaking around her arm. They felt warm to the touch and tickled a little. "What do you wish to be called, my children?"

The lights whispered into her ear.

"Fairies," Hapria said. "We shall call them, 'fairies'. When their work is momentarily complete, they say they will show us a display of color in the world for us all to know they are there to let the earth grow into its best self."

To this day, whenever you see a rainbow, you are seeing the fairy children of the two spirits Hapria and Palytum and their colors help us remember they still work to make our world a pretty place.

12

TRANSUBSTANTIATION

I t was once said long ago by a man far wiser than I that science can be mistaken for magic to the uneducated masses. Nowhere in the history of humans has there ever been a better story capturing the essence of this mischievous fact until now.

The protagonist of our tale was a descendent of our race many generations into the future. There—or rather, *then*— science had made such advances that the distinction between man and machine was slight, so slight as to be imperceptible and therefore irrelevant. Man and machines had fused into a single class of sentient beings co-existing and exploring the universe together.

One man born there—Galvinius Wrein was his name— was the first covert passenger of time travel. For obvious reasons, time travel was highly regulated, yet Galvinius was somehow able to slip into a temporal stream and enter our present time undetected. When he arrived, he possessed an array of technology impressive even for his own time, let alone ours.

Galvinius was not an especially responsible man, but a miscreant acting with little regard for the temporal conse-quences of his actions. His plan had been in the making for years and it had come time to enact it. He smiled giddily when-ever he thought about it.

He started small by targeting a group of fundamentalist Christians in rural Northeast America. He chose this group because they were more educated than other fundamentalists, though still not completely committed to the palpable reality of Heaven and Hell. If he could sway *them*, then their friends would fall quickly.

Since nobody in this time had a headcap, his telepathic reader could pick out their thoughts with ease. The first time he levitated an object in front of a congregation, he almost fainted from the swelling of their thoughts bouncing around in his head. By carefully visiting members one at a time, he was able to tip them into believing that not only was the Devil real, but that he was *here*, among them. And that they should fear him.

Over the coming year, parishioners visited him from across the state, and then across the nation, and finally from around the world. Reporters came, pundits bayed, skeptics waged their war of words, but Galvinius could see their doubts laid bare. He could smell their fear. He was making progress.

The final phase was upon him. Galvinius promised the world he would appear simultaneously at every church, cathe-dral, and basilica on Christmas Eve. Skeptics laughed and said it was impossible since no magician could pull off such a trick and withstand scientific scrutiny.

Then Galvinius did it. On Christmas Eve, in front of every altar in every place of Christian worship in the world, he appeared.

"Behold your Beelzebub has come!" he screamed, and panic broke out across the globe, even among the other reli-gions. "By New Year's Day, I will bring you the head of your Pope!"

Galvinius had become drunk with power and his psychosis burrowed into the deepest troughs of his mind. Christian vigi-lantes tried to assassinate him, but Galvinius' invisible force field swatted away attacks like a pesky insect. The skeptics wavered. Galvinius was nearly there.

On New Year's Eve, exactly as he had foretold, he pinpointed the pope deep in the cavernous trenches of the Vatican's necropolis, idly peeling away his Swiss Guard with a cavalier smile.

"It's Judgment Day, Your Holiness," he said as the Pope prayed beneath him.

Then, grabbing the Pope with one hand, Galvinius unceremoniously dragged him up the stairs to the balcony of St. Peter's Basilica. Thousands had gathered in the Piazza below. Telecasts were being broadcast around the world.

"I am here to end the line of Peter's envoys," Galvinius said slowly. "I, Galvinius, have come!"

He yanked up the Pope so all could see him. *It was him,* everyone thought. *It was really the Pope.*

The Pope had his eyes closed, chanting a prayer in fear. Then Galvinius pulled out a sword and screams filled the air like a soccer stadium. As if it were reading his mind, the sword's shiny silver burst into purple-red flames. *I cannot not rush this part,* Galvinius thought. *This must be verifiable, visceral. There can be no question.*

Instead of a quick swipe of the sword, which would have been merciful, Galvinius slowly sawed off the head of the pope so all could see.

As he held the head of the pope above him, not a soul in the world doubted that Galvinius was, in fact, Satan.

At that moment, Galvinius did the most astonishing thing of all—his spiritual being actually transgressed into the supernatural. *He had become Satan.* All his technological powers were now moot—he had truly become the high demon of the underworld.

His descent was complete.

13

THE CATFISH GHOSTS

Whenever you feel a rush of inspiration, a ghost may be touching you. Whenever you have a burst of insight, of solace, of kindness or love, an old soul might be strumming a chord in your heart. These are the Exitare Ghosts, the ones who "call out" the best parts of our being. If we are a guitar, they are tuner, amplifier, and player.

Influence goes in both directions, though, and all souls who work for good always begin by working for evil. It is not their fault; it is simply their mandate. It is the first thing they must do —they must inspire us for evil.

Before they become Exitare, they are what you might call a Catfish Ghost, the forces who compel us to make bad decisions so others can learn from our example. All ghosts are Catfish Ghosts for a single year and the trail of destruction they leave can ripple throughout a lifetime, touching countless others along the path. When these wraiths of destruction finally become Exitare, the guilt they feel is suffocating, as if they had vague memories of a deeply embarrassing year-long drunken bender. So their guilt shames them into an eternity of recompense. No matter how amoral or sadistic a Catfish had been when they once donned a mortal coil, every ghost eventually rues being a Catfish and works hard to atone for all the damage they caused in both their mortal and immortal lives.

Nature, however, does offer an equilibrium of sorts: the Exitare will *always* outnumber the Catfish, which is why mankind is eventually destined for a bountiful and radiant future no matter how much destruction the Catfish Ghosts have wrought.

14

MILLENNIUM

Many of the deities we have come to know exist in a brief moment of time, as we do—they perceive the world as an unrelenting series of moments, like a buffet table stretching off to the horizon.

However, there is one deity who hops across time like a skipping stone. He does not merely go forward, but he goes *backward*, too. His name is Jaluszch. He is never allowed to affect events in an overt and sweeping fashion, but sometimes he can inspire us in a tiny way with the aim of making a large difference later on. Jaluszch can and does change the course of human history and, because he sees everything over time, he is the ultimate overseer of context. Jaluszch knows in his heart that a simple kindness today can literally mean the difference of millions of lives centuries later.

Which brings me to the story of a seemingly insignificant girl named Kina. She lived deep in the jungles of Africa long before civilization as we know it would thrive. Kina was an average girl of four, temperamental at times and loving at others. One day, Kina had a choice to do something her father had forbade her from doing—a simple matter of not going down to a river pond where Kina's father knew a cheetah liked to drink—but Kina did not listen. There was no actual danger that day... the cheetah happened to be sleeping in his den far away when Kina's father caught her at the river pond. That day, Kina's father had been gravely worried about his brother's failing health and was not in the best of moods. When he caught Kina, his discipline was harsh, and Kina lived with that brutal consequence for the rest of her life.

When Kina grew up, a similar instance happened with her own child, and she punished her child the same as she had once been punished. On and on this cycle went, the wave of action and reaction rippling across years, decades, and centuries. It affected everything: choice of mates, social status, wealth... Kina's single bad choice at four years old resulted in—centuries later—a powerful and vicious dictator who abused his power to oppress millions and even tip global stability for the worse.

Jaluszch skipped forward and backward through time and spotted the root cause of the issue. He intervened and made Kina choose not to go down to the river that day, but instead return to her father and tell him what she had decided. At that moment, Kina's father was so wrought with emotion that he hugged his daughter, told her he loved her, and vowed to be a kind father.

These were not empty words: he indeed raised Kina differently, with more tolerance and love. So Kina grew to become a well-respected member of her tribe and everyone who touched her also felt blessed by her light. Jaluszch had set in motion a long chain of events culminating in a shift in attitudes across every part of Africa, even ending up with the founding of a new religion. Eventually, fewer tribes fought with each other, thousands of children were spared the horrors of civil war, and the hapless millions who would have been oppressed now lived free and without fear. The world as a whole was a kinder and gentler place.

And Jaluszch was very pleased with his work.

15

GOLTHUL'S KINDNESS

We live in a world where beasts of burden are now commonplace, where some have become so beloved by their guardians as to be something close to a friend. Yet it was not always so.

In a time many thousands of years ago, long before flying ships, automobiles, or even fire itself, man was little more than a hairless grunting ape. These "men" lived with beasts we would now call horses, but these beasts were hostile to men. However, man was often so hungry that he would overcome his fear of those imposing beasts long enough to slaughter them for food.

Among the strongest of these beasts was a large, fierce brute. If men came anywhere near it, it would immediately attack them, often for no reason other than malice. Men called these irritable creatures Golthuls. Golthuls roamed the plains and were everywhere, and men were acutely aware these creatures could provide a week's worth of meat if slaughtered. However, Golthuls were not man's predator like the saber-toothed tiger. Even Golthuls feared the sabertooth.

One day, a Golthul named Theol watched a man with a spear approach slowly across the plain. The man was clearly weak and Theol felt badly for him. The man, Kol, came within feet of Theol and lowered his stance as if to hurl the spear.

Theol was not afraid of him; Kol seemed as if he might fall flat on his face. Kol looked at Theol, puzzled. Why was this Golthul not running away? Yet Kol had exhausted his energy and instead of hurling his spear, he collapsed to his knees, crying. His belly screamed for food—this Golthul had been his last hope. Alone, he stood no chance of killing this Golthul. Kol would soon perish...

As Kol wept, he felt the Golthul quietly approach. Was this his chance? If he moved quickly, he might be able to attack it...

Theol leaned his head down and touched his cheek to Kol. He stayed there, breathing, almost kissing this poor ape. Theol turned to look at him, and the ape-man's eyes were wide upon him. Theol then bent down to the ground and whispered to Kol, "Grasp the hair along my neck, and climb onto my back. I can carry your weight with ease. Let me take you to a berry tree."

Kol accepted Theol's kind offer and rode him while Theol shuffled across the plain to a tree he had grazed on the day before. After Kol had replenished himself, he asked Theol, "Why did you save me when all men hunt you for food?"

Theol's reply was direct. "It didn't seem nice."

Theol's kindness imbued such gratitude in Kol that Kol wanted to do something nice in return. So Kol told his new friend of a secluded river where men go that Theol could drink from anytime he wanted. Kol warned him, "You'll have to go with me, or the other men will want to eat you."

The two wandered together, protecting each other and finding food and water. Theol let Kol ride on his back for long distances and Kol tended to Theol's hooves when they got splinters in them. Eventually, Kol brought Theol to see Kol's other man friends. At first, the men grabbed their spears and wanted to eat Theol, but Kol calmed them and explained how nice Theol had been to him and how Theol could be nice to them all, as well. Then Theol offered something nobody could believe.

"I can help you hunt the saber-toothed tiger," said Theol. "He, too, is my enemy, and I will gladly let you ride along my back if it will offer you some protection from his long teeth and sharp claws."

Soon Theol had earned a cherished place among Kol's family. He was well tended by everyone and when Theol realized how much better his life was with Kol, he convinced other Golthuls to come join him.

The story went on like this for many generations long after Kol and Theol had become dust. Men looked after Golthuls and Golthuls looked after men. Soon Golthuls became known as horses, and Theol's courageous choice to be kind to a former enemy echoed throughout time, forever changing the history of civilization.

16

THE UPSIDE OF EXTINCTION

Of all the millions of different kinds of animals, insects, and vegetation across our world, only a tiny sliver of them remains alive after countless years of climate change, and the waxing and waning between predators and prey. Only a fraction still lives and once gone, the disappeared are never to return again.

Should you wish to know, you may blame this path of death and extinction squarely on the shoulders of one of the three gods who help mold our universe. The first god, the one you know as Death, is called Qemtor. His only directive is to kill as much as he can as often as he can. He cannot change events outright, only "lean" things in certain directions and hope for the best. Imagine him as the father who stands behind a child learning how to ride a bike for the first time, but who gently pushes the bike onto the ground without the child ever knowing it.

Qemtor is often looked on with disdain, but were it not for him, life would have exploded out on top of itself and smothered itself before it could adequately grow. At a cellular level, Qemtor is responsible for a woman's ovum not being impregnated by a million sperm at once.

There is, of course, another god who pushes for *life* at any chance, and yet another still whose directive is to negotiate an adequate balance between the other two, but their stories are not as interesting. Were it not for our tenacious death-dealer, the dinosaurs would never have become extinct and thereby pave the way for our future civilization of humans. It was never Qemtor's goal to let us humans thrive—that was *another* god's goal. Yet Qemtor, as merciless as he has been to march death and destruction across the universe, his role has been equally helpful, if not more helpful, as the other gods.

The next time you mourn death or extinction, consider the context whereby death gives birth to all the other new and wondrous things. Qemtor's relentless pursuit is truly a magical gift from the stars.

17

HOW HUMANS BECAME GODS

There was a time, long ago, far beyond the forming of galaxies and stars, when all that existed were waves of energy. These same waves go mostly unnoticed to us now, except to those with the right equipment to listen, and watch, and feel. We observe and even manipulate these very same waves daily—they are called 'light' and 'sound', and 'quarks' and 'muons'. They are the stuff everything has been made of, and always will be. They are the stardust from which a conscious mind has since formed, and from which a conscious mind once existed.

Waves, however, rarely travel in harmony. They crash and spill into each other like rain and sleet and, as such, cause both high crests and deep swirling chaos. Waves do not appear to crash into each other with a particular intention, but it is their mission, their character, the sole thing which defines and drives them. They are destined to do it.

We call one such crash the Big Bang. As with all waves that cross paths with such violence, newly formed air bubbles are thrust out in all directions. Our whole universe is merely *one* of those air bubbles. Humans are but one tiny speck in that trillion-year-old air bubble; we have been banished from the

Nirvana of the Waves. Whether we are aware of it or not, we are all waiting for the Waves to subside.

One day, when every part of that air bubble has been explored, described, known, and explained, then our air bubble will at last dissolve and humans will have their Final Homecoming.

On that glorious day, humans will finally become Gods.

18

THE GOD WHO FORCED HIMSELF TO BE BORN

There is another world beyond our own, one which does not flow according to the curves and lines of the reality we know. Its building blocks are a metaphysics of sorts, a realm of thoughts where energies splash and churn with such fury that new creations often burst into the fray. Most humans are unaware of this alternate reality, if it can be called a reality at all. Like some of the more amusing cul-de-sacs in physics, we all catch glimpses of this other place long enough to retain a memorable aftertaste. We graze it with dreams, visions, and other out-of-body experiences.

The Waves from this Other Place act much like a tempest, pushing and kneading, building up over time into huge clashes. The aftermath of such "storms" has far-reaching consequences for us; the last such storm expanded our minds into self-consciousness.

That recent storm happened upon us a few thousand years ago. The foundation had been laid to let man be aware of himself, to make tools and build shelter, and wonder of the origin of things. In this storm, the Waves came from the other place and pushed themselves into our minds long enough to create a God.

This first God wasn't like our Judeo-Christian God, or even

the gods of Ancient Greece. Rather, this was an overly simpli-
fied ancestor of all Gods we know today. This God was imagined by one of our earliest ancestors and it was the first time a
human—indeed, any creature—contemplated that the world
had its origin in a place other than That Which Could Be
Known. The world around us had sprung from being a tapestry
of our own making to a rich collection of things emanating from
a source beyond our knowing.

It was a simple idea, to imagine this Being's existence. One
might even argue that it was inevitable. But that small step
towards embracing the numinous is what forced humans to
push themselves beyond their self-prescribed limits and reach
out into the stars.

The next such storm is due sometime soon. It is said the
other place will bring us a final stage of transcendence and we
should all be eagerly awaiting those Waves to hit our cerebral
shores...

19

ATOMIC PARADE

I t is often said opposites attract and this is true. But many other forms of attraction are peppered along the spectrum as well. Long before humans walked the Earth and indeed long before the first single cell organism popped into existence, and even before that, before an earth, before a Sun... before *any* of it—there was a nothingness so dark and vast and unknowing that it is difficult to paint it with words.

Humans have an amusing disposition to describe their deities in all the ways in which they are not, nor can ever be. So it is, in a way, that we can understand what this universe of nothingness actually was. There was no molecule anywhere to be found. It was a river of listless atomic particles, unattached to anything and having no timetable. Everything simply *was...* and was not. There were no wars, no tears, no laughter or joy, no witnesses or historians. It simply *was.*

And yet... never has there been a story that did not also come to a juncture like this one. There came a time when the atoms—for want of a better way of expressing it since atoms do not possess wants or desires—had grown weary of their solitude and decided it was time to nudge things along to whatever that else might lead to. One atom bounced into another, and that movement created a new force, a magnetism. At first, this force repelled the atoms from each other, but that repellence also attracted others. In the space of a few lightning quick moments, atoms across the whole universe were discovering that they could *dance*.

It was not long before one atom grabbed on tight to another atom, and another, and another (what our scientists refer to as 'bonding', an appropriate anthropomorphism)... a cascade of bonding ripped across the nothingness and not one atomic particle was ever left alone again.

The dancing they did has never stopped. It has led to minerals and sunlight and shooting stars and warm buttered bread. It is the *true origin* behind our creation, and these atoms —though they have no emotions or disappointment or joy—love to do their dance.

For without this parade of atoms, we would be unable to feel the connection across the vast space between two souls.

Our boundless dancing atoms allow us all to feel that which the universe has always longed for, but never knew it would miss until it existed—love.

20

THE GOD WHO DREAMED US

In a place far away in time, but not exactly far away in space, a mother and her son were talking.

"When will I find love?" said the young man, insecure of his good looks.

The mother smiled and gazed upon his face. He had not yet become of age like his father but had still blossomed into a muscular frame. Soon he might be larger than his own father. The boy—whose name was Thute—was already very handsome and when he reached manhood, few would compare with him.

"You do not find love. It finds you. It won't find you if you try to make yourself lovable, only if you open your heart and love all around you. If you do that, love will come to you from everywhere."

The boy looked down; the answer unfulfilling.

"Come," said his mother. She held open her arms and gestured for him to lay his head in her lap. "I will show you love."

Reluctantly, the boy laid his head down.

"Close your eyes," she said as she looked off to the horizon. Caressing his forehead, she quickly entranced him.

"Love is that which connects us all to each other. It is the bond we weave into each other's souls so strongly that we cannot separate it. Except we *can* separate it. When we do, a great energy is released, an evil energy. This evil energy affects everyone around it, poisoning their bodies for years afterward. But the love that connects us, the love that brings us together and keeps us together, is everywhere. It is the very fabric from which the universe has been woven. It is the reason things exist. We are all beings in the dream of a benevolent stranger, whose dream has lasted but a few hours, but every second of that dream is 100 million years in our universe. One day, that stranger will awaken, and our universe will no longer know love. Until that day, we are here to find love both in the most delicate flying insect and in the omnipresent wonder of our burning sun."

She stroked his hair, looking down at him.

"Now, sleep, my son. Dream a universe of your own. Create the tapestry of love across a space too vast to know."

The young man slept. He dreamt a dream that lasted hundreds of millions of years. He dreamt of our Sun, our Moon, our Earth. He dreamt of all of us, talking and fighting and caring and loving. He dreamed of the rise and fall of civilizations. He dreamt of the bonds between all of us, the inseparable bonds that connect everything in the universe to everything else.

There, in between the moments of two strangers who come together for a time, Thute found love.

WESTERN

21

HOT GOLD

The sound of tobacco hitting a spittoon was common enough in a saloon. John Rutledge had heard it so much that it barely registered. All he did was tend bar, although sometimes that meant defusing a fight before it fell into hot lead. John wasn't a stranger to fights, either himself a vet... but he could detect a brewing fight far easier than a tobacco twang.

One summery eve, when the saloon was unusually empty, five gentlemen sat in a corner table in the back. Always seemed a shame he couldn't put the poker tables at the front, but nobody wanted shills standing outside. Fancy that.

"I'll see that coinage... and I'll raise you twenty."

John watched slyly from his position at the bar. Where was his shotgun again? It was loaded, right?

Everyone at the table, apart from the two left playing, sat back and made some variation of a nervous tick. John had seen that before, a look that said, *these stakes are getting a hair more than makes me comfortable but not so uncomfortable that I could risk getting up and not coming back because I might be shot in the back.* John knew everyone at that table except the man who had bet—*Oscar, was that his name?*—and that was a very, very bad sign. A new resident in town?

Or an immoral vagrant with a sour disposition? "Okay, I'll see it..." The words trailed out in the air, an insinuation of a raise buried in the tones. The man pulled out his Remington and everyone in the bar turned to look. Obviously, the bar patrons had been eavesdropping. John's hand was already clasping his 20 gauge. Oscar pushed out his Remington's chamber and emptied out all the bullets. Everyone around the table sat forward.

"Is that... *gold?*"

"Indeed it is. Safest way to travel—if they've taken my gun, I'm probably eating dust by then anyway."

"I ain't never seen that before. Did you make those yourself? Smart."

Oscar lined each of the bullets up. "0.46 short, 227 grains each. That's 0.473 troy ounces and at... $18.93 per troy ounce, that's... $8.95 per shell." pushing three of the bullets into the pot, "I see your $20 and raise four."

One of the players, a sluice miner judging from his attire and overall smell, picked up the bullet and eyed it closely. After biting it and searching for teeth marks, he replaced it to the table, satisfied. Everyone looked back at Oscar.

While Oscar's opponent eyed the pot, John readied himself. He forced his fingers into the pages of the newspaper to appear casual, but his other hand had balled up into a fist around the shotgun handle. Without turning his head, he kept his eyes on Oscar's shoulders. He could always predict movement in the shoulders first.

Oscar's opponent looked up. "No way does a man clean up like you without a few tricks."

"Let's all tread lightly, shall we?" Oscar said blandly. "Sometimes a man's honor is all he has to go on. Take that away..." He lifted his left hand and purposefully knocked over one of the upright bullets. His right hand was notably below the table.

Now: the quiet. The dreadful stare-down.

John watched the other players and in less than a fraction of a second, he weighed the characters of all involved and knew well enough how this would play out. With an inaudible wince, John forcefully turned his newspaper page and the sudden noise startled everyone—Oscar grabbed for a gun at his hip and pivoted to shoot at the noise, expecting to see a gun. The lack of a gun confused Oscar long enough for Oscar's opponent to pull a gun on Oscar—

—*BLAM.*

John pulled up his shotgun, half expecting to see a wounded Oscar scrambling for the door.

Instead, Oscar's chair had flipped backward and Oscar's chair along with it. His mouth was wide open in an awkward lilt, blood pushing away from his head in a growing halo.

John walked over, his gun still pointed as Oscar. Inside Oscar's jacket, John could see the familiar back of a blue diamond playing card. Oscar stared straight at the ceiling, unblinking.

John lowered his gun. Then he leaned over and aimed into the nearby spittoon. "Guess I'd better go tell the sheriff."

22

COMPOUND INTEREST

It was a bigger bank than any other bank in the surrounding towns or cities. Brand new. The vault was huge, and the two tellers were perpetually busy.

Henry Hargourd's finger was about to cramp from counting bills when a man with a long coat and big hat came through the bank's front entrance. Henry was distracted or he'd have sized up the man instantly. That was a misfortune: Henry would have noticed a long bulge of a shotgun butt hiding under the man's coat. The man with the long coat reached up to his neck and slid a dusty bandana over his face.

The shotgun came out and he yelled, "Everyone relax. I'd much appreciate it if y'all not move too quickly."

Henry had a Colt below the counter but knew the bandit would be expecting him to draw it. And that would be bad for everyone. His colleague sitting beside him inhaled a slow deep breath; probably thinking the same as Henry.

The bandit scanned the silent room, waiting for someone dumb enough to try something. Satisfied, the bandit's mouth opened to say something—when *another* man came running into the room with two six-guns drawn.

"This is a stick up, everyone."

The second bandit took a moment to realize something was

wrong. Everyone in the room looked at him and, without a cue, the room swiveled their heads to the first bandit, then back again at the second bandit. The two men were *clearly* not together.

Henry saw his chance. He thought about reaching for the gun but knew he'd only have time to get one of the two men before the other would open fire on him. One of the customers in line had a small baby and had instinctively turned her back toward the robbers to protect her child in case a firefight ensued. Henry winced. He couldn't use his gun at all.

Henry looked directly at the customer in front of him. The woman was pretty and had an easy smile. He'd liked her and thought often of calling on her. They had frequently flirted, even if it had been benign.

The robbers looked at each other, unsure of what to do next. The moment dragged on long enough that Henry had a great idea. He locked eyes with the woman in front of him and twisted his face as if he were about to burst into laughter. He could see the wisp of a smile flicker across her face. The customer at the adjacent window saw the expressions on Henry's face and curled his lips inward to suppress his own laugh.

Then Henry did a short nasal sound as if his laugh were bubbling to the surface... that sent the two customers over the edge. By then, the urge was irresistible, and laughter soon echoed throughout the room. The two robbers furrowed their brows, slumped their shoulders and lost all will to continue. Dejected, they lowered their weapons and walked back out.

Nobody bothered to call the sheriff—these boys wouldn't ever dare rob a bank again.

23

THE LIMNER

"**M**r. Tule is a well-respected and sought-after limner," Alice's father said, and the fireplace's log popped in agreement. "We would do well to acquire his services; next spring you will be 17 and that is altogether too late." Alice quietly fidgeted with her dress, unable to mount a decent defense. As active as Alice was, sitting still for longer than five minutes was torture. A whole hour every day would be punishment beyond imagination.

"Please, Alice," Forrest continued. "Think of this as a parting salutation to your mother. She would have wanted your portrait above our hearth. Also, recall that you will not always be 16. Some years from now, you shall have a family of your own and your children will delight to look upon your youthful features."

Alice knew protest was futile and curtly consented before bolting outside to play. Forrest looked after her with disdain but permitted her small disobedience. As a solicitor and, moreover, a widowed parent of a burgeoning teenager, Forrest knew when to pick his battles.

Forrest Gilbrecht was Albuquerque's foremost solicitor. He was also its *only* solicitor. The Albuquerque settlement was still young—a train from Santa Fe had not yet been built, though there was much talk of it. Getting a respected limner to travel to their remote area would require at least one leg by horseback and that was a feat tantamount to parting the Red Sea. At least, it had felt that way.

The limner Forrest desperately wanted was Richard Tule, known across the state and was—given his decades of experience painting realistic portraits—in high demand. However, it had become increasingly harder for Richard to travel due to an injury he'd received in the Civil War and winter was fast upon them. Richard had indeed reviewed Forrest's letter with trepidation for he knew a long horseback trip was a practical impossibility... yet he understood Forrest's urgency and did not want to disappoint, either. For this one unique circumstance, Richard sent his young son Philias in his stead.

Philias had been a faithful apprentice, well mannered, but that did not temper his self-doubt. In his own mind, Philias had not yet perfected his craft. His father had always been the master limner and Forrest would naturally be expecting Richard to arrive. Forrest's look of hurt surprise confirmed Philias' worst suspicions.

Forrest quietly read the old limner's letter as Philias stood anxiously nearby. *"Try the boy out first,"* Richard had written. *"His artistry may not be masterful, yet he is certain to give you a portrait worthy of your daughter's beauty. Should you not be pleased, I will of course be happy to waive all payment and associated boarding costs you will have incurred during the time of his stay. If you are still open to hiring my services, I would be happy to fulfill your commission in the spring when the weather is more amenable to my health."*

Forrest took a deep breath, letting the hand holding the letter fall to his side. "As my daughter shall turn 16 once in her life, I suppose we are required to accept your services, Master Tule. I do hope your father has taught you well. Your stay with us is permitted until such a time as you feel your best work has been accomplished. Is this offer satisfactory?" The question was rhetorical, and Philias nodded a humble 'yes' in thanks. Philias himself was just turning 18 and this was his first official commission, so he was content that Forrest had not summarily kicked him out of the house.

"Your bedroom is in the attic, Master Tule. I have provided a lantern and mattress but see to it you don't fall asleep until you have put out your lantern. Our last limner nearly burned the house down. Supper will be at seven each evening. Please be prompt." And with that, Forrest left Philias standing in the foyer.

The next morning, as Philias came downstairs rubbing his hands into his eyes, he saw Alice for the first time. Her lips were full and large, contrasted by blue eyes and long locks of braided red hair. "Are you to be our limner, then?" she asked. Her voice was not squeaky, like most girls her age, but in a lower register and pleasing to the ear.

Philias' stomach turned queasy at once. *This* was his subject? This darling and mesmerizing creature? How could his life have taken a turn for such remarkable fortune? Not aware of his own face, he was startled to hear Alice break into a quiet laugh. "Oh my, your face seems to have turned as red as a summer beet. Do sit and have something to eat before you faint."

"My apologies," Philias managed to blurt. As he ate some bacon left over from breakfast, an awkward silence stretched out, and then—eager to fill the space—Philias offered, "Shall we begin your portrait now?"

Minutes later, Alice sat in her place at Philias' station upstairs. He suggested different sitting poses, gazing at her face in the morning light, positioning her until all things looked right... and finally began to paint.

At first, Alice couldn't stop moving and Philias had to distract her with idle chat as he'd seen his father do so many times before. The morning became afternoon, and his work was still not complete. They agreed to try again later that day, after school. Each day Alice sat for Philias, and each day he rested his eyes on her face. It was his job to pore over the details of her face that few people noticed, but to register the sort of details others would notice were they not present: a small light brown mole under her right eyebrow, how her earlobes didn't "hang" but connected snugly to her jawline, a cascade of nearly imperceptible freckles across her nose and cheeks. In the darkened attic on his cot, Philias could close his eyes and recall her whole visage without error. He knew every line, every eyelash.

Philias' first portrait had been flawed, so he started over, and once again after that. On the fourth try, with Forrest now becoming impatient for his guest to depart, Philias finally created a portrait fitting of Alice's beauty. All during that time, Philias and Alice chatted quaintly. She welcomed his intense focus on her, how much it meant to him to perfect his craft, like a gentle and invisible veil had been laid over her. Soon Philias' every waking thought was about Alice, how she looked, how her face reflected the light, how it made him feel, and how that feeling should look in a painting. In kind, Alice thought about Philias more and more every day.

Philias had taken more than three weeks to finish Alice's portrait and the day came when he had to present his work to Mr. Gilbrecht. Philias ushered Alice's father into the front room and peeled back the burlap covering. Forrest's face twisted up in revulsion. "*This* is what you've been toiling over?"

A long moment hung in the air as it seemed Forrest might storm out of the room. Philias was crestfallen but hastily added, "Apologies, Mr. Gilbrecht. You are, of course, entitled not to recompense me for my work."

"You have labored under my roof for nearly a month, so I shall be sending your father a bill for all the food you've consumed during your stay, an amount—I hasten to add—not insubstantial for a boy your age."

The front door opened next to them, and Alice walked in. Turning their way, she stood before the painting. And gasped.

Alice began to weep. Walking closer to the painting, she put a hand over her mouth. Still transfixed, "What you've done... Master Tule, what you've done is simply... *breathtaking*. I adore it."

Mr. Gilbrecht stood silently, too shocked to say anything.

The painting was assuredly not a photo-realistic portrait. It was more like a blend of colors. Not of fixed lines, but a nuance of shades. It was what contemporary French art critics would have described, pejoratively, as "impressionist". Alice had only been open to Philias' radical interpretation because she had spent so much time with him, while her father had only seen him as an unwelcome interloper. Despite Forrest's deep reservations, he finally capitulated to Alice's protests and paid Philias for his work before sending him on his way. Upon receiving Forrest's bitter review, Richard never let Philias do any more limner work for him and Philias agreed that was best for everyone.

Philias would never meet his Alice again and didn't need to —he carried her portrait inside him, perfect, unsullied. For every morning thereafter, he could awake with her smiling face gazing over him, and that was enough.

24

RANGE

McGrath wiped his mouth, took a long draw of coffee. The room smelled pleasant, bacon grease and fresh bread wafting about the room. Jibsom's wife had a talent for cooking, of that much McGrath was positively convinced.

"You ready?" McGrath said with a yawn. Leary was already at the door, waiting. "Yes, sir." Jibsom pulled on his last boot and walked over to the door, grabbing his hat. "Anytime." Turning to his wife, he kissed her on the cheek. "Back before dark." McGrath stood, gathering his hat as well.

He tipped his hat at Jibsom's wife. "Missus."

As he walked through the door, Leary doubled back and muttered about something he had forgotten. McGrath squinted at the sun wondering if they'd be cooked again like yesterday. Sheep herding in New Mexico was a feat few could endure. "Hey, Jibsom," McGrath said, "will we be anywhere near the Hilliards' today?"

"Not planning it, no. The herd has been more due east this week." Jibsom made for the stable. "Good. I got some bad looks fro—"

McGrath fell dead on the ground, parts of his head scattered over 10 square feet behind him. The echo of a rifle shot rang in everyone's ears.

Jibsom heard the shot and froze for one second too long. His next thought was that he should run back into the house, but it was also his last.

Leary was already coming out of the house but instinctively retreated and heard a bullet zing by his head as he stumbled backward.

He slammed the door shut and screamed at Jibsom's wife to stay down. Then scrambled to close all the shutters.

Jibsom's wife—*was her name Amelia?*—screamed out as she realized what was happening. Leary had to tackle Amelia before she got to the door. The riflemen would shoot anything that moved.

After Amelia had calmed down and promised not to go outside, Leary got his rifle and loaded it. He approached the window and scanned the outside surreptitiously.

"Can't tell if they're gone," Leary said, softly.

Amelia had her hands wrapped around her stomach as she cried. "Do you know for sure? At least if he is gone, he's not in pain anymore."

"Yes, ma'am. I saw him fall face down in the dirt." As soon as the words left his mouth, he knew they had been callous. "Sorry, ma'am."

The window shutter next to Leary exploded into splinters as another gunshot echoed through the valley.

"Cocksuckers!" Leary screamed. He was bleeding as he picked large wooden splinters out of his cheek.

Steeling himself, he poked his head out to spot any residual gun smoke. *There it is*, he thought. Already dissipating in the wind, but enough to give him a general target. His eyes would have to aim within a fraction of a second, all while his enemy did the same to him.

Ducking below the window, he repositioned to the other side of the room, then popped out and cracked off a shot where he thought the shooter would be. Then another shot. Had to be careful, though. Easy to get picked off if you kept doing the same thing. He crouched and walked over to another window. Poked out, shot, repositioned. Over and over.

They shot back and the standoff went on for hours.

Eventually, Amelia stood up. Tired of being a prisoner in her own home. Leary wasn't even aware she was moving until it was too late.

She walked out the door, a shovel in hand. Leary turned, "No! COME BACK!"

She was already outside. The escaped hogs had taken to eat McGrath's head parts and were working on his body now. Amelia shooed them away and knelt over her husband. She wept, running her hands through his blonde hair. Leary used the open door to reconnoiter. If they shot her, he might at least spot their location and gut them.

But they didn't shoot.

Amelia stood, walked a short distance, raised her shovel and began digging a hole for her husband.

Leary breathed a silent prayer of thanks... at least they had a small measure of decency.

25

NOT AT ME

S ome wagons were already leaving. One wagon only 40 feet away waited for an old Cherokee to get inside. Private Millard winced as the old man feebly tried to climb into the back of the wagon; the young children weren't yet strong enough to help him inside and he wasn't strong enough to pull himself up. The longer they tried, the less energy they had, and the harder it became.

As ever, the wagon's teamster had been agitated since he'd gotten up that morning—his temperament was foul by nature and positively tempestuous about indigenous delay. "Hurry your red ass up, Injun!" He stalked back to the old half-blind man and slapped his coiled bullwhip against the man's back.

All the Native American children cried out in supplication as the man fell to the ground in agony. Private Millard sat up in his saddle, alert. "I said, *git!*" seethed the teamster, Fitzsimmons, bringing the bullwhip down on the man again, this time drawing blood from the Cherokee's weak, upraised arms.

One of the girls in the wagon screamed, thrusting her hands in her hair. Millard knew her. She'd sung songs to him by the campfire one night as thanks for his coat during the windy October night.

Fitzsimmons began lashing at the old man again and again

and it became clear to all that the old man would soon die where he lay.

Millard was off his horse, running at Fitzsimmons. He slammed into him, and they tumbled to the ground.

Fitzsimmons yelled out, all the while wrestling with Millard, "*Indian lover! You'll let them sit here, yeah?*" Millard stopped moving, holding down Fitzsimmons. "Enough! Stop! STOP!"

"Get off me, boy." his eyes were still, and wide. Millard got off, backing up. "He's just an old man!"

Fitzsimmons got up, dusted himself off. "And he's worm food if he doesn't get in that wagon!" Fitzsimmons lashed at the old man again, hard. Millard started racing at Fitzsimmons again, but Fitzsimmons uncoiled his whip as if to crack it at Millard. "Mind your business, boy."

Millard looked at the girl in the wagon. She was panicked, unsure what she could do. Any intervention would surely mean death for them, as well.

Millard ran back to his horse, hoping he could stop Fitzsimmons before he killed the old man. When he got to his saddle, he saw his rifle and his ax. If he took the rifle, it could become something far more than what he wanted. Something he might never walk away from. He took the ax.

Fitzsimmons saw him come back and turned to face him. "Stay back!" But Millard didn't stop.

He raised his arm and darted to one side to avoid the whip, and then he was on Fitzsimmons. He waited to get on top of the teamster and brought down his ax, once, and then twice. It was quiet. Millard had used the blunt edge of his ax and Fitzsimmons was only unconscious.

Millard took a few breaths, pushed himself off the teamster. Then he walked to the old man, examined his wounds and lifted him gently into the wagon. Through tears, the young girl nodded to him in thanks.

Another teamster up the trail was shouting for the Corporal. A court martial was bound to follow, which could go either way. Taking into consideration Fitzsimmons' insane temper, the judge would probably delay the trial. Indefinitely. The other wagons fell away into the horizon. Millard could see movement inside them, a pliant swishing back and forth. It took a moment to make it out. Then Millard realized the people inside were waving. *Not at me, I hope,* Millard thought. Then he realized their gaze was pointed more easterly, toward the woods.

They were waving goodbye to a land they knew they'd never see again.

26

VALUE

The young man got off his horse, dusted himself off and got something out of his pack. Walked over to the front porch. "Good day." The white mountains of southeast Montana shimmered behind him like white fire.

The cowboy on the porch nodded quietly, his chair creaking as he balanced it.

"Are you Mr. Datings, sir?" the young man said, cautiously.

"Over there," nodding to a man on a horse rustling cattle.

"Many thanks," the young man said, tipping his hat and walking over to Jack Datings, the owner of this cattle ranch.

The other man on the patio, Clark Ruffordson, spit his tobacco into the sunlight. "What's that about, you think?"

"City boy, that's a certainty."

They watched as the man walked out to Datings, probably a good 300 feet. When he finally got to Datings, they exchanged words.

"Hope it's not about buying the ranch," said Clark at last. "Jack hates those men."

"Yep. Did you hear there's talk of a railroad coming through here?"

Clark grunted. "Goddamned city planners."

They watched lazily as the two men spoke some more.

Then Jack Datings pulled out a gun and shot the young man in the face. The man fell down dead instantly.

Datings dismounted and hefted the young man onto his horse. Then he pointed his horse back to the house. When he arrived at the patio, the young man's blood was dripping steadily from the saddle. "Coal mine," was all he said.

Clark silently walked out and helped carry the body over to a nearby dried up well, threw it down the hole, and shoveled dirt into the well.

Jack Datings took his horse to a water trough and used a bucket to wash off the blood from his saddle. Then, as always, business went back to normal.

27

THE SETTLERS

"Don't wander far," Isaiah called after his son. Jeb had a proclivity to getting mired in mud no matter where they were. Isaiah had been busy getting the horses water from their long trek and had barely heard Jeb scramble off to the adjacent valley.

Jeb's mother, Meredith, looked behind her into the wagon. "Isaiah?"

"Yes?"

"Where are the sunflower seeds?"

"Behind the seat, underneath the ax." Meredith scrounged around to find them. Isaiah pet one of the horses as it drank. They'd worked hard and they still had much farther to go. If he took good care of them, they'd last long enough to help him till the earth on their new plat before winter. After he grew their own food and things looked stable enough, maybe he'd have enough to buy an ox. Or two.

He glanced over at Meredith, now chewing on seeds and admiring the landscape. They exchanged a smile.

After Isaiah had serviced all the horses and everyone had relieved themselves, it was time to get Jebediah. Isaiah walked over to the valley Jeb had run into, letting his eye follow the tree line up onto the hill on the other side. The hillside rose up above where he walked so he couldn't see the horizon at all. Isiah felt the ground tilt downward and he scanned the trees for Jcb.

He spotted Jeb instantly, standing on the side of a tree and looking to the left. Isiah knew that pose, as if Jeb were playing hide and seek. Was there any wildlife out here? Isaiah instantly regretted not bringing his rifle.

Isaiah followed Jeb's gaze until he saw what looked like another child, a girl glad in a tan dress, long black-brown hair... *and dark skin.* A native. Isaiah stopped in mid-walk. Jeb and the girl broke the stillness with a burst of chasing around the tree, and laughter.

The sparse trees were empty, it seemed. He squinted his eyes and double-checked to be sure. Then he cupped his mouth and shouted at Jeb. "Jeb, time to go! Let's go!"

"Okay, Papa!" Jeb shouted and waved goodbye to his new friend. As Jeb walked up the valley's ravine, Isaiah saw the outline of a spear dancing along the hill's skyline until a male appeared on horseback. The native looked on while Isaiah and Jeb walked away. Isiah felt the man's stare burning into his back.

Still, no harm had been done and out of reflex, Isaiah waved goodbye. The man did nothing.

Isaiah suppressed a violent urge to run back to his wagon.

The native's arm moved up in a long, majestic wave.

28

PANNER

Horatio Theodore Jackson knelt down by the river water, a tin pan sifting for gold. Horatio was in his late twenties, medium build, and a freed slave. It was 1850 and everyone here in California was like Horatio, treasure hunting for a rock to parlay into a quantifiable measure of freedom.

Of course, Horatio had no need of more freedom for himself. His freedom had been secured by a kind abolitionist investor. The deal had been to buy his freedom and assist Horatio to become a fruitful member of society. Horatio had gladly taken the offer and had set up camp in the new city called Hangtown. Like the name implied, it was a place of harsh judgement and he'd seen plenty of souls hanging from the gallows in town. Horatio kept a low profile out in the woods panning for gold.

Upstream, he could see another prospector in a curled-up cowboy hat. They never spoke much to each other and never dared show any excitement about finding gold lest others catch wind of it and swoop down to pan there as well. His friend could have already acquired thousands of dollars of gold and Horatio would never have known it.

To his neighbor, a white man, finding gold would make a

huge difference in his life. He could return to his family, buy more land, get more horses, herd more cattle or till more soil. Finding gold was that man's ticket to a better life.

Yet to Horatio, finding gold wouldn't buy him a house, or a horse, or anything material. Horatio's need was unique to him: if he found gold, he could at last buy his wife's *freedom*. That was worth more than any material needs.

As he sifted, he noticed that familiar black, yellow mineral show up in his pan. He picked it up, looked at it closely. His heart began to race. There was indeed a hint of something in the soil.

Calmly, he kept sifting and found a large chunk of black gold three inches below the waterline. Blood rushed to his head and he almost fainted. Slowly, he pocketed the rock, sat on the embankment and wiped his brow of sweat. Then he gathered his tools and made a slow deliberate walk back to town.

He had his ticket at last. His wife would finally be coming home.

29

THREE KNOLLS

B arely four months after the end of the Civil War, some parts of California were still inhabited by Native Americans. One such band of nomads were camped out on a river in Northern California. While the nation was still reeling from the assassination of President Lincoln shot by a Southern sympathizer, this small group was almost entirely unaware of those epic events.

Asleep on his bedroll in the river encampment was a little boy named Ishi. His father was nearby, and the morning light had begun to peek over the Sierras. A valley native by the name of Billy Sims—many natives took on a White Person's name— sat up slowly on his bedroll and looked around, yawning. Ishi lay fast asleep.

Nearby, a tall native the Whites called Big Foot (on account of his large feet with six toes) slept next to his infant son. His soft snores punctuated the morning air.

Billy stood up and grabbed a rifle. He needed to relieve himself but not within smelling distance of the camp. He stood up, stretched, and started walking up the slope next to their sandbar. About halfway up the slope, he heard movement in the trees and looked with squinted eyes. *Was someone there? Not a bear, surely.*

Ishi awoke to gunshots all around him but as he snapped awake, he saw Billy Sims scramble madly into the water, into the river's current away from camp. Others had awoken now, and everyone was scrambling for their guns.

Ishi's father turned to him, clawing at his rifle. "Go hide, little one! Go! Go!" Ishi took one look at his panicked father and was too afraid to protest. He looked back at Billy Sims in time to see him fall into the water, face down, blood on his back. Big Foot was running into the forest towards the gunshots and Ishi heard the screams of Big Foot's son as Ishi ran into the forest.

Though Ishi and his immediate family would survive this massacre, this would be the end of the Yahi tribe. After many more decades, Ishi would be the Yahis' last surviving member, living a reclusive life until finally starving and having no place left to go. In 1911, at the age of about 48, Ishi wandered into civilization and lived another five years among the White Man until his death of tuberculosis in San Francisco.

As the last of the Yahi tribe, Ishi spoke the Yana language, completely foreign to the White Man at the time. Ishi is the only name we know him as, the name he called himself, and it means "man", a name given to him by a White Man; when Ishi was asked his actual name, he said, "I have none, because there were no people to name me."

30

POUDRE B

Leather creaked from Cody's glove as he gripped his saddle. The air was still.

"Natasha Renée?"

The woman before him clearly fit the description in the poster stuffed in his pocket. The headline, he recalled, had the word 'dead' in it. A small relief, now that she was standing before him.

Alone, she kicked dirt into her campfire. Without looking up: "Who's asking?"

A deputy's horse grunted behind Cody. The other deputy's horse stood quietly, near at hand. Cody never took his eyes off Natasha.

"The state of Iowa." Cody's hand shifted to the butt of his Colt.

Natasha was a piece of work. In 1884, she'd killed five men in cold blood just outside Cedar rapids. Ten months later, he'd finally tracked her down. Dead was fine by Cody, at least that was what he thought at first. To kill a woman? That was a whole different conundrum which he'd been wrestling with for ten long months.

"I don't talk to people who defend killers," Natasha said.

"Even if it's all florid-like on fancy paper. Those men had it coming."

Cody could tell she wasn't going to give.

He drew first. His gun's smoke immediately obscured his view—he spurred his horse to move. Natasha walked sideways, reaching for her gun deliberately. Smoke from the deputies' guns sprayed out everywhere, all around them, merciless. They had made themselves easy targets.

She picked them off one at a time. Natasha's gunfire had almost no smoke at all, and she knew it. Silence. The smoke drifted away, entwined with the men's souls.

Natasha mounted up. And never came back to Iowa again.

HUMOR

31

LAMPOON

"You underestimate the importance of a well-polished shoe," said Kincade, putting away the shoe store bag beneath his chair and looking over the menu. "Every time a job applicant sits across from me, I check if their shoes are polished."

"Really?" I said. "Seems a bit excessive. And perhaps a little bit unfair."

"Not at all," he replied, closing the menu with an impatient snap. "Everyone puts on a façade in an interview. Ergo, I look for things that show me who they really are."

My arms were crossed; about every third topic, I found myself not agreeing with Kincade. Every fifth topic, I wanted to punch him in the snout. He seemed overly judgmental and too narcissistic to realize it. But what are you going to do with your company's Big Boss?

"Ah, here comes our server. I need some hops pronto." He ran one hand through his shock of bright red hair, and I noticed his nose was a deeper red than I'd ever thought possible. All these years... was Kincade a *drunk?*

The waitress came over, an African American woman with an easy smile. I loved these BBQ joints, and this one was spectacular. Kincade was visiting and I knew he loved a good rib dish, so this seemed a great place to take him.

"Hello, gentlemen. Would you like some refreshments before I take your order?"

"What do you have on tap?" barked Kincade.

The waitress looked at us both for an awkward moment. "I'm sorry, sir. We don't serve alcohol here." Kincade looked at her blankly, then stood up and bolted for the door, muttering, "I can't believe you took me to a place that doesn't serve beer..."

I stared after Kincade as he walked out the door, then turned to the waitress. "Sorry about that. He's got a bad temper sometimes."

"That's quite alright. We sometimes get that."

I gave her my order, guessing what Kincade might have ordered. A few minutes later, Kincade returned to his seat, apparently calmer.

"Did you order for me?"

"Yeah, I got a basket of ribs for us."

"Great. Thanks."

A few moments of uncomfortable silence, then an old man with a beat-up guitar shuffled onto a small stage in one corner of the restaurant. He was African American, as was most of the clientele. As he belted out an old blues tune, his guitar was astonishingly out of tune. This was the infamous Reggie, a bit of a neighborhood in-joke. I smiled, having forgotten about him. Whether Reggie knew his guitar was out of tune and was playing an act or whether he was oblivious... it didn't really matter. Reggie's act lent the place a unique flavor. When I glanced over at Kincade, however, I could tell he was in knots.

"What's the matter?" I asked innocently. "Don't like the music?"

"Positively *horrid*. Has he no idea he's out of key?"

"Oh, is he? I hadn't noticed."

Kincade watched Reggie a moment longer.

"Ah! I understand now. He's *lampooning*."

"Sorry?"

"He's lampooning the music. The blues is a traditionally

black genre of music. So his music is a critique of ridicule and irony. Clever."

I looked over to Reggie. "Uh, I'm not so sure he's doing that..."

Suddenly, Kincade was reaching under his seat. "It must be open mic night. Surely, he could use a harmony."

Before I could say anything, Kincade had leapt out of his chair and nearly skipped over to the stage. Furtively, I looked around to make sure nobody noticed where Kincade had gotten up from. I knew him well enough to know this would end badly. Kincade had an ugly habit of getting in other people's stuff.

He made it over to the stage and started singing with Reggie who welcomed him with a gracious smile. Kincade's harmony was equally awful, as he must have intended.

Then I saw something I wish every day I could unknow— Kincade reached into his pocket and began applying shoe polish to his face.

Reggie was lost in song and didn't notice at first, but chatter around the restaurant dropped into an uncomfortable quiet, though not a mouth in the place was closed.

Reggie must have realized something was amiss and when he glanced back over at Kincade. He stopped mid-chord, mouth dropping so wide you could have seen his uvula.

Kincade kept singing, even throwing in jazz hands and an old ragtime dance.

It's rare you can tell the future, but at that moment, I was positively clairvoyant.

I left a $100 bill on the table, got up and walked quickly for the door, dialing 911 as I got outside. "There's a badly beaten man at the Rib-Tye restaurant on McGrady and Jensen." I almost said, 'hurry', but stopped. With a wicked grin, I added, "Take your time."

32

WHOOPS

You ask, dearest Lilly, how I came to know the end of our race... how one single man could change the course of our entire history? I will tell you this tale, though I'm quite certain that if I were to hear this from my own mouth, I would squarely punch myself in the front teeth for insulting my intelligence with such flagrance.

It started with a gnat. Not one gnat, exactly, but a bunch of them. My friend Richard and I were taking leave across Europe on our Levi-bikes. Poor Richard was trying to tell me something while we were in mid-flight, and we passed right through a black cloud of gnats at 100 km/hour.

After we hurriedly parked our bikes on the shoulder, I apologized for not ensuring our flight tracking equipment had been scanning ahead, but Richard—ever the self-effacing gentleman —smiled impishly and said, "My bad." Then he bent over and spit out a mouth full of dead and dying gnats. Which is when I threw up.

Not long after that, Richard developed an outright aversion to *any* kind of bug. He'd taken to slapping himself as if by instinct. And slapping *hard*, too. You could be having quite a nice evening with Richard, maybe even among formal company and then CRACK! he would slap his own cheek as if he had sullied his own honor.

It was an amusing eccentricity. I swiftly learned to pay attention to the number of bugs in our environs and make sure I wasn't ever close to him with a full drink. On and on this went until his neurosis made him slap bugs on *other* people, even his own mother. Poor lady. I believe she had to have that tooth pulled.

Naturally, I tried to pull him back to reality, but unless you had iShock on hand when a mosquito lands on your forehead, you couldn't be fast enough to keep Richard from leaving a shiny red palm print on your forehead.

The story is really as simple as that. He *hated* bugs. Hated is not really strong enough. More like loathed or repelled, but at a reflexive level, hovering somewhere near the brim of his reptilian brain.

When we finally returned to the ship, there was visible relief from both of us. Maybe our next space stint—utterly devoid of bugs—would be enough to help him reset. That was our hope, so we both let it be. In retrospect, I probably could have thought through the consequences a little more carefully. Richard was our Munitions Officer, after all.

The ship was carrying about 5 million megatons of nuclear ordinance, and Richard was in charge of it all. Yes, I know, Lilly, it seems so obvious now in hindsight but at the time, we were all heads down doing our work and nobody thought twice about it. Richard seemed back to normal.

The officers and petty crew had a longstanding tradition of pranking each other and, on any other day of the year, this prank would have been a howler... but not today. Someone had thought it funny to feed a swarm of horseflies onto the bridge.

You can imagine the panic that ensued. Initially, there was alarm, and then annoyed amusement, which turned into hysterics watching Richard slap himself and others. Again, on any other day, this would have been a knee slapper. Yet at this moment, the *very moment* we discovered the flies, the bridge had been in a weapons release training exercise. It was policy to run through the steps on releasing all our weapons, though of course we would never have any real need to do so.

As Richard bounced around his terminal, nobody realized that he had accidentally launched *all 5 million megaton warheads* at Texarkana. By the time we had found out what had happened, nobody could stop it because Richard was frenetically rolling his body along the walls of the bridge. From space, the mushroom cloud over Texas was the size of Europe.

I remember how Richard stared glibly at the viewscreen while everyone on the bridge burned their eyes into the back of his neck. He turned around and with an impish grin, said, "My bad."

Which is when I threw up.

OBSESSED MUCH?

Y ou can stop pretending. It's not like I don't already know," the salesman said as he dusted the bookshelf near the door.

Henrietta looked up, and around. Nobody else was in the bookstore. Was he talking to her? "Sorry?"

"That book is so *totally* not you. It's for your boyfriend. Who is not into you, by the way."

She blinked. "Excuse me?"

Without meeting her gaze, the salesman swiveled to an adjacent table, removed a small cleaning bottle from his apron, and squeezed some of its solution, and wiped. "Let's face it, women aren't poker players. You certainly aren't a poker player so why are you trying to act like one? If you're buying a book about poker for your boyfriend, I can assure you he's probably already read it, or hasn't bought it yet because he knows about that book and thinks it's crap."

"Who do you think—"

"Not to mention that you're trying to impress him by buying a book about poker to show him how supportive you are about his poker obsession. Guess what, doll? If he's *that* obsessed about poker, you'll always be sloppy seconds."

Henrietta was about to lay into the salesmen, but she

noticed that the table the salesman had been cleaning was now spotless and he was *still* cleaning it with manic gusto.

"You have OCD, don't you?"

The salesman looked at her for the first time. "How *dare* you talk to me that way!"

Henrietta smiled, then held up the poker book in her hand. "I'd like to buy this, but it has a tear on the front cover."

"What tear?"

"This tear." And as Henrietta pointed to the book, she ripped off the front cover with a slow satisfying *riiiiiiiiiiiiip.*

The salesman looked at the book with wide eyes, a doe in the headlights. Then he fainted.

DEVIL CAR

R osalita frowned. All around her the car dealership was busy, but Carlos could not seem to find the car she wanted. He'd let her browse every car in the place, but still she had not found *the one*.

"There must be *another* car," Rosalita begged.

"No, Señora. This is all we have. Except..." he trailed off, a wince rippling across his face, instantly regretting he had winced at all.

"What?" said Rosalita, anxiously. "What else do you have?"

"We have... El Diablo."

Rosalita's eyes became saucers. "Si."

"But Señora..."

"Bring it to me. Bring me... *El Diablo*."

Carlos disappeared into the back and minutes later appeared in the parking lot with a hideous eggshell-colored car. It had a crimson red interior, its monster tires elevating the chassis a full two feet above the ground. The inside was cramped—the seat was pushed forward so much that there was barely enough room for one's head between the steering wheel and the roof. Mounted on the steering wheel, protruding exactly above where the driver's heart would be, was a sharp Kaiser helmet spike.

The stick shift was covered with a pointy end of a mace, and the air conditioning vents were jet engine exhausts. Carlos was barely able to get out of it without scraping some part of his body.

Rosalita did a slight hop from foot to foot. "May I take it for test drive?"

Carlos looked at the car. Then back at Rosalita. Then back at the car.

He handed her the keys. "You can test drive this one by yourself."

Rosalita climbed into the car, gingerly sliding into the driver's seat that had been pushed awkwardly forward, with an obscenely large lumbar support protruding into her back. Her chin came to rest atop the steering wheel, and the blood red ceiling smashed down upon her hair bun. She turned her head gently to one side to reach for the car door. As her hand grasped the door, a handcuff suddenly snapped her wrist into position on the door handle. Rosalita smiled with glee.

She pushed her index finger on the car's ignition and a Chinese finger puzzle clamped onto her fingertip. The car made a fierce roar and a plume of purple black smoke erupted from the car's exhaust, much of it filling the inside of the car via the jet exhaust A/C. Rosalita coughed uncontrollably and when she finally stopped, she gingerly placed her foot on the acceleration pedal installed at the epicenter of an unsprung bear trap.

Using only her chin to steer, she inched out of the parking lot and screamed to Carlos, "I'll take it!"

35

GIFTING

"Gerrold, dear?" called Veronica, sipping lazily on her eggnog. "Where did you place my correspondence clamshell? it's not in the correspondence desk."

The six-foot butler walked over to her door, "It's where you left it, Madam. On the bed. Shall I retrieve it for you?"

"Thank you, Gerrold. I'd be lost without you."

Gerrold watched as a blob of eggnog dropped silently onto the carpet. He'd have to mop that up later.

"Yes, Madam." and he disappeared to mount the grand staircase upstairs.

When he returned, Veronica was asleep in her chair, her head arched backward in a way that made Gerrold cringe. The glass of eggnog had fallen onto the table but had defied gravity by balancing itself on its handle. He righted it and placed the clamshell on the table before her.

"Madam?" he said, and she bounced back to life. "Thank you, Gerrold. You can go now."

When he returned an hour later, she had the Christmas cards completed and her eggnog glass was now empty. Gerrold took one look at her bobbing eyes and mused how they did indeed look like they were floating in water.

"Please put these in the post, Gerrold. The blue ones are for the men, and pink are for... everyone else."

Gerrold reviewed the cards and noticed a discrepancy. "Madam, are you absolutely sure? The *arcade games* are in the pink?"

"That will be all, Gerrold," and Veronica slumped onto her bed, instantly snoring.

Oh, what a dilemma, thought Gerrold. He might be fired for it, but he had a sickening thrill knowing that Veronica's lady friends would be straddled with a five-foot-tall arcade game. If they were smart, they would simply tell the mailman they elected not to receive the delivery, but curiosity would probably delay their common sense.

And what would Veronica's male friends get in the place of a classic arcade game? *An electric douche.*

Yes, it would be a very merry Christmas for Gerrold this year. Even if he got fired.

36

MACHO PICCHU

There's a fine art to being macho in many cultures. For example, among some tribes in Kenya, the rite of passage into manhood is a method of circumcision requiring the poking of the tip of the penis through a pierced foreskin and making boys run around for weeks like that. Without anesthesia, of course. In Nordic cultures where the nights are so long that you often forget what the sun even looks like, intoxication is not so much a competition as an endurance test.

For Manny Picklong, however, the quest to be macho evolved into the defining attribute of his life. Manny wasn't his real name, but I'm sure you knew that given the topic of this tale. His original name was Sheldon (but I never told you that). *Sheldon.* I know. Not a keeper.

Anyway, Manny was born to Caucasian parents in a small village in Northwestern Peru. You think being a man is hard? Try living in Peru for a month and see what happens to guys who admit they *aren't* sexually attracted to women.

The thing about Manny was that he was gay. And I don't mean *slightly* gay or lipstick lesbian gay, I mean gay as in you could tell he was gay even before he began to speak. No, he didn't have a lisp or anything, but it was quite clear he was not your typical masculine dude.

In many cultures, this wouldn't have been a deal breaker, but in Peru, if you're not a man, you're... somewhere between a man and a woman. And actually, less than a woman because you haven't even got the parts. It's like a physical limbo. Poor Manny.

One day, Manny got fed up with the whole thing and he chose to become the most macho of all the dudes. He ate bull's balls, he ate the hottest of all the chili peppers, and he even walked on fire. When it came time to fight in the rebel army against the government, Manny gladly volunteered. When nobody would fend off the crocodiles terrorizing his village, Manny got muddy and came back with crocodile boots. When a Westerner passed him scores of data about nuclear weapons, Manny memorized it all and put himself in the center of a vast international espionage debacle.

Manny became known the world round. Everyone knew Manny as fearless and courageous. But not *macho*, and Manny wasn't happy about that.

Do you know what finally made everyone afford him the masculine respect he had already earned? It wasn't his becoming a world-class beekeeper, or walking a tightrope over Niagara Falls, or even the fire breathing he'd picked up as a hobby. No, none of that made him really *macho*.

What made Manny the most macho man of all... was raising a baby boy. His boy grew up to be fearless, courageous, understanding, loving. Manny's raising of a child was the most macho thing he ever did, and in the end, Manny discovered that the only person he needed to get Macho respect from was his own son.

(Until the day his son wanted to become a woman. That kind of buggered up Manny's life again. But before that, everything went swimmingly.)

37

AS I SAY

"It's fine, it's fine. We're butter," he said, his blonde hair bounding around like a Rod Stewart wig.

"No, Eric, it's *not* butter," Andrea said. "It's more like butter*milk*. You can't just take the kid on a joy ride like that."

"The kid loves it, he's fine with it. What's the problem?" Eric was already checking his email while chatting.

Andrea was their film's assistant director. Normally, an A.D. follows directives like the president's Chief of Staff, but this time Andrea felt Eric had gone too far.

"How about the fall that nearly broke Jason's arm?" "Flesh wound."

"And the flipping car that took out the light?"

"I told the grip to move back. Nobody got hurt." "What about when our lead got hypothermia from being in the river for two hours?"

"She recovered. We're butter."

"*Eric!*" was all Andrea could muster. "Andrea—the kids love these kinds of things."

In walked an eight-year-old boy with a motorcycle helmet floating on his miniature head. Eric pointed at the kid with a smile. "See?"

Andrea stormed out, exasperated.

Without missing a beat, Eric turned to the boy. "Had lunch?"

"Yeah!"

"Want to ride a motorcycle?"

"Yeah!!"

"Just don't die, kid. Our E&O isn't *that* good. Okay, let's split before Andrea comes back."

38

WHIPPER

R aymond Burtle had big teeth, the kind of long symmetrical teeth you'd see if you crossed a wolf with a blue whale. It was worse when he smiled, of course, which he did whenever anyone happened to find themselves next to him. He had a bit of a gut and wheezed a little too loudly between sentences.

God help you if you were fan of any kind of gunnery, too. He knew *everything* there was to know—or so he said—about any kind of pistol, rifle, or RPG. So vast was his knowledge that nobody would raise an eyebrow if Ray spouted off the make and model of a 1950s kid pop gun.

It was Patricia's birthday that day and we'd all gathered at the park for some relaxing BBQ time. Raymond was one of those people you'd known forever and couldn't *not* invite to birthday parties. Most of the time, he behaved himself. Most.

"This here," he intoned with an intense eye, "this here is somethin' special." A group of us were hovering near a park bench as he reached into his bag to pull something out. You could feel everyone reflexively take a half step back and slide their hand into their pockets for their cell phones to dial 911. Raymond had brought in weapons before and though he'd been asked not to repeat the uncomfortable exercise, it was anyone's guess what Raymond might do. If everyone had had a group thought bubble, it would have read: *This is how mass shootings begin.*

Instead, Raymond pulled out a long cord of woven leather —a whip.

We all looked at each other, not really sure what to say.

"Wow, Raymond..." Patricia managed, after an uncomfortably long pause. She'd meant it in a conciliatory way, but her face dripped with dread.

Raymond, as ever, was clueless.

"I know! These things are way under-appreciated. I mean, no way I could slip past airport security with a .45, but *this?*"

"Wow, Raymond..." was still all Patricia could manage. Her eyes were looking down at the whip like a mother disappointed at her errant prepubescent offspring.

"Indiana Jones made these things popular but how many times have you actually seen one in action?"

"Let me guess, Raymond," said Jake, sipping on his drink, and not making eye contact. "You're going to demonstrate."

Raymond flashed his blue whale teeth at Jake and touched his index finger onto his nose.

Patricia leaned forward, "I really don't think you need t—"

He was already walking out to the field, wheezing as he went. Everyone at the table glanced around, did a mental tally of who was there, and then calculated the quickest route to the nearest hospital.

"It's all about breaking the sound barrier with the skin of a slaughtered animal," Raymond said, unravelling the whip. "Some kind of poetry in that there."

He reached back, let the whole length of it spread out behind him and snapped his arm forward in a rehearsed jerk —*SNAP!*

The group all flinched at once. Raymond pulled the whip back again with a huge smile stitched across his face. Some nearby kids stopped what they were doing and ran over.

Raymond cracked the whip three more times. The group did a few slow claps hoping that would appease Raymond, but it only egged him on. In between cracks, he put the whip down to catch his breath.

Some children had now joined the group and one seven-year-old boy ran past Raymond, picked up his whip and kept on running. Maybe it had been a dare or just for fun, but the kid ran as fast as he could.

"Hey!" Raymond immediately gave chase, but his girth slowed him down. Before he could catch up to the kid, he had to stop to take a deep breath. The "chase" had become a stop-start game of tag and the kid was the clear winner.

Patricia took out her hip flask, poured some stiff gin in her cup and repositioned herself more comfortably to watch Raymond's gut bounce unflatteringly around. "Best. Birthday. Ever."

39

ALL OVER

"Best I've ever seen," Jerry said.

"You say that about *all* the assassins we hire," came the reply. Wendel took a drag on his cigarette. "What about The Athlete? What happened to him?"

Jerry shifted uncomfortably in his chair.

"Well?"

"He slipped and shot his own leg," Jerry said.

"And then?"

"Wendel..."

"No, humor me," said Wendel. "What happened next?"

"He bled out. But that doesn't—"

"And The Sniper?"

"Come on, man."

Wendel took another drag, saying nothing.

Jerry sighed, staring up at the ceiling. Evidently, Wendel wanted to play this one all the way out. "Rabies."

"From...?"

"From a rat on the rooftop where he had been hiding for six days. OK?"

"The Knife?"

"Shot."

"The Bug?"

"Burned alive."

"How about... The Noose?"

"Hanged himself."

"So, Jerry, you can detect the reasoning behind my skepticism. Yes?"

"Yeah, sure."

"When you say, he's the 'best you've ever seen', that's not much of a qualifying clause when all the other ones you recommended have all died."

"This guy's different. He's... alert."

Wendel looked at the clock. "He's about to be late, as well."

"He'll be here."

At straight up noon, there was a knock. Not just any knock, but a crazy sound barrage of two fists knocking the door at once. Wendel looked at Jerry with one raised eyebrow, but Jerry avoided his gaze and got up to answer the door.

As Jerry opened the door, the man who entered was a fidgety ADHD mess. Wendel suppressed an urge to laugh by reminding himself that a part of him was actually aghast.

The fidgety man said, "Are you Mr. Wendel? I'm here for Mr. Wendel. I hope I meet him today. It's all very exciting." Jerry held up his hand to get silence, then waved him in.

The man walked in, quickly turned around the room twice, looking up and down. Wendel thought the man was like that savant guy who could count 100+ matches on the floor in seconds.

Jerry turned to Wendel. "May I present Darrel Fitzsimmons. Also known as The Wire."

Darrell shot his hand out to Wendel. "Pleased to meet you, sir. Lots of great things. What's the job? Sorry if I'm a little hyper. I drink two pots every morning just to keep calm."

Wendel looked at Darrel for a long moment. Was Jerry pulling his leg? "Your first assignment..." pointing at Jerry: "Kill him."

There was a blur, and Jerry was now holding his neck, blood seeping between his fingers as he managed a confused look at Wendel.

Wendel's eyebrow went up. "Jerry, this guy is good! Thanks!"

40

THE FALLS

"Five thousand barrels of... *detergent?*" the agent asked. The wind played with the ship's inventory pages on his clipboard. "Really?"

Isaac Thimes looked at him blankly. "I don't like filth."

The agent cocked his head to one side. *Is this guy for real?* The clown outfit he could have overlooked if not for Isaac's overpowering smell of taco meat. It was like Isaac was a time traveler who hadn't quite got all the correct information on how to blend in with modern society. Regardless, Isaac's manifest was in order and detergent wasn't a banned substance; there was nothing legally he could do to hold up Isaac's shipment.

"You're headed south to Cleveland, correct?"

"Yessiree."

The agent wanted to clock Isaac but that would mean dealing with him longer than he cared to. "Very well, then. Off you go. Safe voyage."

"And thanks to you, kind sir!" Isaac replied, saluting gregariously from the deck. The agent gave him a weird look as he sauntered over to the next ship on the pier.

Plans had been made. Years of saving, acquiring goods, mastering all the appropriate marine skill sets.

Isaac was light-footed from the anticipation.

As his ship pushed off from the Buffalo dock, he reminisced about all the absurd pranks his brother Phil had played on him. Their father had had a vicious competitive streak which he'd imparted upon them both. Being twins meant their father had started their competition at two years of age. The battle? Who would get their milk bottle first? Phil always said they'd started in the womb over who would be born first, but the milk incident of 1968 was the first one Isaac remembered. From there, things had spiraled out of control. About five years ago, it had gotten so bad that they'd mutually decided to move away from each other. Of course, neither could move away without the other claiming victory, so they'd both moved at the same time. Such is the nature of detente—it doesn't make a lot of sense except to the parties at each other's throats.

For a time, it had seemed like Isaac and Phil could bury the ax and not try to outshine each other. Yet they had defined their existence by inflicting mutual suffering, so it felt as if something had gone missing. One year, Isaac remembered, he'd put a chicken in the ceiling at Phil's workplace and laughed himself silly imagining Isaac trying to coax out that hapless foul. Phil had retaliated by putting a brick and broken glass on Isaac's car seat. Only at the police station did Isaac realize his window had simply been rolled down.

On and on this madness went. One year, Phil borrowed a truck to pump thousands of foam peanuts into Isaac's house. Isaac couldn't even get inside the house, and that was when he hatched his three-year plan to get Phil once and for all.

Up the river toward Canada, Isaac steered the ship with an ear-wide grin. This would be the ultimate. Phil would never top *this*.

Being twins, Isaac had an unfair advantage over Phil. They'd agreed long ago to never impersonate each other. That would cross a line too simple, too obvious. But Isaac was going to break that inviolate rule just once. Isaac would probably not survive, either, an appropriate way to end their game.

As he turned west, warning signs peppered the land and sea. It was time. He walked below deck and flipped a switch.

With a metallic hiss, every drum of detergent opened wide. Isaac practically skipped back up to the bridge.

"ATTENTION VESSEL." Isaac heard before he saw the red ship approaching. "THIS IS THE UNITED STATES COAST GUARD. SLOW YOUR VESSEL IMMEDI-ATELY AND PREPARE TO BE BOARDED."

He'd expected this, of course. Isaac hit the engines full steam ahead, then went to the deck and waved as if his ship was in duress. He scrambled into a life raft and pushed off. The Coast Guard tried in vain to catch up to Isaac's ship, but its engines had been retrofitted on purpose to outrun the Coast Guard. Isaac watched as the ship charged directly ahead, and off into the drop.

It was headed straight into Niagara Falls.

Isaac was coasting there as well and would likely go over the edge. He didn't care, though. He'd be laughing himself silly the whole way. Poor Phil loved his taco meat and he often volunteered as a clown for the local rodeo. Since Phil was currently deep forest camping for a week by himself, he couldn't reasonably deny he wasn't responsible for starting the biggest fountain detergent prank in human history. The authorities would descend on him like a pack of wolves and, if Isaac were really lucky, they'd be convinced they had their man.

Wheeeeeeeeeeeeeeeeeeeeeeeeeeeeeeee!

ZOMBIE

41

BURN

Neil Walker coasted on the outside of town, looking quietly at each of the storefronts for potential booty. He travelled light. Had to. He carried barely enough to sustain him for the next few days. It was the only way he could be sure he'd survive. Having possessions tied you down, kept you from the instinctual urge to flee and now that dark demons crawled among them, fleeing was life.

He'd hit a small hill on his way into town and his bike began to slow as he coasted upwards. He pumped the gears slowly, not paying much heed to his legs. Neil had been a world-class cyclist; to pay attention to his legs while cycling was like the rest of us paying attention to our feet while walking. Neil was so adept at cycling that he rarely held the bars.

He stayed alert, of course. He'd been caught off guard a few times coming around a corner and wiped out from panic. Over the weeks, he'd learned when to assume a cautious pose and be ready to bolt.

He coasted up to a grocery store and stopped. Scanned the street up and down. Nothing.

In the distance, a long wisp of black smoke curled lazily into the clouds. He followed it down and realized it was at the end of the Main Street he was standing on. He lifted his binoculars.

A solitary figure knelt on the ground, charred from head to toe, flames still dancing around the eye sockets. A person? A stumbler? It didn't matter now.

Neil leaned his bike against the wall and peered inside the store. Sunlight could barely peek into the dusty stillness. He'd have to go inside to be sure.

"If it were easy..." he said softly.

He opened the door slowly, hoping they didn't have a loud bell or a customer beep. They usually did and if it went off, the whole town could come down on him. The electricity had switched off in most towns by now but you never knew if there was a battery or backup genny. He slid inside, let his eyes adjust to the shadows. Peering over his shoulders, he pined for his bike. That bike was his life. He'd seen people steal bikes before and he dared not think how he'd live without his. He had tweaked it to be as silent as the wind. Anyone who stole it would be worth killing to get it back, he mused.

As his eyes adjusted, he saw nothing. He walked across the aisles. Nobody. Taking in a deep sigh, he darted to the section where the canned goods were... aisle... 4? Yes, there.

Of course, nothing. Everything had been taken. He'd expected that at some point. In fact, the whole store had been picked bone dry of all food.

Neil walked to the front of the store and looked out to the street.

He was running out of food. He had enough for a day, two at the most. Some nuts, a few berries he'd picked. That'd be enough for everyone else, Neil thought. Not me, though. When you burn thousands of calories a day, you have to keep stoking the fire.

A gunshot rang out in the distance. Then two. Some screaming. Neil was instantly outside and on his bike, listening. It was coming from *outside* of town. Stumblers would make their way over there, so Neil always put as much distance as he could from any commotion.

In this case, though, that meant heading *toward* the smoking remains... not a great option, either.

He peddled over to the smoke. Maybe a survivor or two were nearby? He'd had mixed luck with survivors. Some were still decent folk, others little more than knuckle-draggers with guns.

As he made his way down Main Street, the knelt corpse grew larger, a dejected soul praying in the city's central intersection. Neil stopped and took it all in. Beside the man was a discarded gas canister and a newly carbonized metal lighter. A suicide, then. Neil tried to imagine what the guy had been thinking moments before he'd lit himself ablaze. Was it a commiseration? An invocation to join him?

Neil shrugged his shoulders, took a deep sigh and pedaled his way out of town. His empty stomach told him he was about to run out of gas, too.

42

PUNISHMENT

Muffled voices up front, then, "Look, I don't know what the hell-fuck going on, 'kay?" shouted the guard.

The prisoners looked at each other. Their van was swerving and had picked up speed in the last few minutes as the radio had crackled to life with frenzied voices... and then died. Mook, the prisoner nearest the guard, leaned close to the wall behind the cab.

"Hey, where's you takin' us?" Mook yelled out.

In the cab, the guard ignored Mook, and the guard's eyes darted over the street flying toward them. Mook sat back, looking at the other five prisoners. Most were tough guys but not tough enough to break out of their chains.

"C'mon... c'mon..." said the guard, squeezing the radio button. "Dispatch... Dispatch... come back." Static. "Dispatch... come in, Dispatch. Still nothing."

"What now?" said the driver.

"We could go back to the station—"

"Through that mess again? No fucking way."

"Well, maybe if we—AWSHITLOOK—" The truck jolted sharply and Mook's head slammed against the wall with a sickening *pop*.

When they came to, the truck was on its side. Mook's life-less body hung from what was now the ceiling, his manacled wrists pulled up to the ceiling over his legs as his bloodied head swayed downward like a macabre organic pendulum.

"I ain't heard no tires," someone said, probably in shock. "No tires screeching before the crash. Did they *want* to ram us?"

The truck was now surrounded by bodies, shuffling around quietly. One inmate got close to the window to get a better view. All he could see past the bodies were fires, smoke, people running and some hand-to-hand skirmishes in the distance. From the west, another car came speeding directly toward them, but careening left and right. Someone was atop the hood and not letting go. The inmate was transfixed—it was like a classic scene from an old '70s show where an insane stunt was about to transpire.

The approaching car swerved exactly the wrong way and hit a two-foot-tall cement block—its two passengers rocketed out the windows and their stowaway hurled right at the truck, slamming into the truck's back window. The inmate pushed himself away from the window, screaming. Hot blood from the body had sprayed deep into his eyes.

Another inmate calmed him. "You're okay, man—it's just blood. And not yours, neither. Chill." The inmate twitched on the floor in a violent epileptic seizure.

Their sentences had begun.

43

THE THINGS WE LEAVE BEHIND

Africa was first, then Asia. What was left of Europe and America soldiered on, though of course humanity could do nothing else. The tide had turned in the war and at last it seemed clear this vicious plague would be eradicated forever.

Except for Alaska. One American captain returning from Asia had come ashore in Anchorage. America was preoccupied with basic survival, so it hadn't yet quarantined everyone disembarking international vessels. The captain came ashore with a simple cold. That's all it was, right?

When he got off the ship, nothing was as it used to be. Life had reverted dangerously close to the Wild West. A few stores in town had been looted. Everyone wore a gun out in the open. He regretted getting off the ship as he'd been ordered, since he and his crew probably had a better chance on their floating island. *There's a reason Britain and Japan have survived this long,* he thought. He kept his mouth shut and gathered a few supplies and left town.

Like he did every year, he rented a remote cabin to commune with nature until his ship was ready for the return trip, if it ever would be. The captain had steered well clear of that monkey the crew had brought on board—he had had it immediately quarantined for the remainder of the trip, so he was confident he'd contained whatever madness its germs had carried aboard—but the monkey had sat on the captain's jacket without him knowing it. It would be weeks before a tiny spec of the monkey's fecal matter found its way onto the captain's hands and then into his mouth.

So when the captain drove up to his remote house in the mountains, he'd thought his symptoms were a simple cold. He'd seen worse. He didn't need doctors to tell him what he already knew. Besides, he had a mission.

He stood outside his old cabin, staring up at the hill before him. This was the same area where he'd grown up. He smirked, remembering a childhood friend chasing him around a cabin exactly like this one. On his last trip to Asia, the captain had gotten an email mid-journey that his childhood friend had passed away from pneumonia. The email had been from a neighbor and since the deceased had had no next of kin, the responsibility for burial had been offered to the captain. He chose to bury his friend's ashes in their special place... a place they'd snuck off to as children.

Despite his failing health, the captain stuffed the box of ashes into a backpack and went trekking up the steep hill behind the cabin. It took him the whole morning to struggle merely 100 feet, but once he hit its plateau, it became a lot easier.

He walked on the hill through rocky switchbacks for a mile then sat down, exhausted. After a half hour, he'd recovered long enough to dig a hole to put the ashes inside. Said a prayer. Then he laid down, utterly spent. By the time he awoke, it was already dusk. He hurried to get back.

Upon reaching one turn in the switchback, he lost his footing and scrambled to right himself but went reeling forward and cracked his head against the rocks. He wasn't dead but the infection had already taken hold of him. It became a race to see which affliction would claim the captain's body.

The end of summer meant lakes were now beginning to cool. Soon, they'd all be ice, and the captain would also be stone cold. The following summer, his body would thaw and then freeze again in the winter. On and on this relentless cycle would continue to perfectly preserve his corpse. His body, and the box he buried somewhere behind him, would remain a teeming pile of infection patiently waiting for its next victim, be it the following spring or a spring 100,000 years in the future.

44

END OF THE ROAD

Ted had made it across 17 states in two weeks—a herculean task since all trains and planes had stopped and every highway had become a de facto parking lot. He'd taken the back roads, opting for open roads where he could see any stumblers from miles away. If there was any chance he was headed into a swarm, he backtracked, sometimes as much as 500 miles.

There had *to be a clear path*, he thought.

He slept in the back, drank warm coffee drinks to stay alert when driving. His gun skills had never been sharp, so he kept a shotgun within arm's reach. He'd been ambushed too many times not to feel like he'd been born with a gun in his hand. Although he had plenty of ammo, he prayed every day he'd never have to use it.

His van rolled into the schoolyard. Helen's car was near the front entrance, and that put a gnashing pit in his stomach. He'd much rather know his wife hadn't been anywhere near there. But she must have come here to save Jess and who knows where they'd gone after that. Things had gotten crazy after the outbreak and lots of people did things they'd never dreamed they'd do. Safety in numbers—even with abhorrent strangers—trumped self-reliance, even if only by a hair.

With his hands white knuckling the wheel and his foot on the brake, he carefully scanned the school grounds. The van's engine quietly purred. No sign of life. There had to be stumblers. There were always stumblers. Maybe a live soul was still out there, but it was so hard to tell without getting up close and personal.

Ted took a long deep breath and turned the car keys. The van's reassuring purr stopped. The silence was almost painful to hear. Without looking over, he slid his hand down to the cold steel of the gun on the passenger seat and hefted it to his chest.

He looked in all the mirrors three times. Then he lowered the windows an inch and listened for any sounds. Nothing.

Ted slowly opened up the door and gently pushed it open, sliding outside and leaving the door slightly open.

He made his way over to Jess' classroom, silently. The door was open, so Jess was probably not in there. He had to look, though. He didn't travel thousands of miles on warm caffeine to walk away without knowing.

He glanced in. Vacant. Like most everywhere else, the room was basically still, as if everyone had simply walked out and never come back.

He checked the other nearby classrooms, but with the same result. In desperation, he would have to call out... at least, eventually. He'd probably wait until right before it was time to go. If there were any survivors who didn't yet know he was there, he'd be able to coordinate where and when to meet up.

While crossing the grounds, he saw the main office had boards on the windows. Now *that* seemed promising. People could live for weeks and fend off hordes with basic supplies. Jess, and maybe even Helen, might both be in there. His eyes watered up, but he blinked it away. Another deep breath. Readjusted his gun grip.

Standing outside and reviewing the carnage, Ted could piece together what might have happened. An infected had probably wandered on the grounds, the kids got scared and ran from class to class until the principal had told everyone to come stay in the main office... the only really large and secure room at the school. After Newtown, school protocol had shifted to relocating to the main office to accommodate everyone during emergencies. Ted looked at the windows—they'd been boarded up from the *inside*. Definitely a poor choice but indicative of a hurried strategy. Anyone in it for the long haul would board from the outside first, and inside only if absolutely necessary; nobody wants to die knowing they had built their own death trap.

He inched up to the windows to look inside. He had to be careful, though. He'd been shot at by panicked survivors before. There didn't seem to be any movement.

Crap. He'd have to break in.

It went against everything he'd lived by for the last two weeks. Breaking in would let his guard down and create noise, two things that could get him killed within seconds. But he'd also know instantly if anyone were in there, right? If they weren't, he'd still have to break in to get clues. He finally accepted Helen was probably already dead, but he still held out hope that she'd made it out with Jess and was waiting to reconnect with him somewhere. Stranger things had happened. Until he knew for sure, he wouldn't stop. Couldn't.

"Hello?" His voice came out quiet and raspy. He realized he hadn't spoken in a week. Too afraid to ever draw attention to himself, he'd buried all forms of vocalization deep down. He cleared his throat, looked around again. "Hello? anyone inside?"

Nothing. Could they be sleeping? It was midday, but that meant nothing. He'd occasionally slept until 3PM sometimes to make up for lost sleep.

He tapped the door with the end of his gun.

"Anyone there? Kelly?" Kelly was the school's principal.

Still nothing.

Again, he looked at the door and windows. It didn't look as if they'd been breached, and they hadn't been taken down, either. Whoever had barricaded themselves inside was still in there.

Now every fiber of his body was telling him to flee.

He should, if he wanted to survive. But this was different. Parenthood was *different*. You do crazy, stupid stuff when you're protecting your child. Had it only been his wife, he might have let it go, chalked it up to Helen being a grownup who could look after herself and if she had survived, she could live on without him if need be. Not ideal, but he could have almost lived with that.

Jess? No, he couldn't walk away from Jess. It would be like walking away from his will to live. He *had* to know.

"Okay, stand back. I have a shotgun and I'm going to break down the door. If you're alive in there, go ahead and say something. If you're near the door, move away."

Again, nothing. *Fuck.*

Wait, could someone be in there slowly dying of a head wound? Maybe they were unconscious?

Ted aimed his gun high and shot out the top part of the door. Splinters went everywhere. If any stumblers were around, they'd be sprinting to him now. Every second mattered.

He yanked the door, but it was still locked. "I'M SHOOTING THE LOCK! STAND BACK!" The second ring in his ears was louder than the first, probably because of the adrenaline. The door's lock had vaporized. The door had a board across it on the inside, so he pushed at it and yanked the door open.

He heard movement inside. Froze. Gun at the ready. Peeked inside.

It was carnage. Flies were everywhere. He cupped his mouth, squeezed his nose tight. Most of the bodies were piled up in a corner. In another corner, was a smaller pile... of *heads*. Two prone bodies on the far end of the room, both with slit wrists. Someone, maybe more than one, had likely been scratched and gotten inside before symptoms had been recognized. That was all it took.

He recognized both the suicides as a couple of parents. Glancing over to the bodies, his knees gave away as he saw a beaded bracelet on one of the young girl's bodies, something Jess had made at her seventh birthday party.

As he sobbed openly, he finally locked eyes with his Jess. Her clouded eyes blinked, her mouth noiselessly stretching open like a fish out of water. She was staring back at him from a pile of heads.

45

THE BLACK

"The fingertips look completely black. That's amazing." The med student, Denise Cates, examined the body as it lay idle on the table. "This is from bubonic? Really?"

"That's what the report says." Larry Nesbit, the Medical Examiner, peeled a page up from the clipboard, tilting his head up so his bifocals could read the fine print. "I'm skeptical, however. There's more here."

Larry put down the report and walked over to his computer. "I feel like I've seen these symptoms somewhere else..." He trailed off, lost in a computer search.

The med student got closer to the cadaver's fingertips. All four fingers, but not the thumb, displayed a deep purple black color. It was odd to see a completely black fingertip as if the whole finger had been dipped in black paint, without the liquid sheen. The patient's middle finger, apparently giving up on its fingertip, had begun to partially regrow a new nail above the black flesh just above the first joint.

"Here," said Nesbit. "Yes... according to this, these symptoms are consistent with a rare strain of Yersinia Pestis bacterium... manifests... wow."

"What?" The med student looked up. It wasn't like Larry to be visibly impressed.

He looked over at Denise. "Are there any swollen lymph glands on the inner thigh?"

She peeled up the drape and pulled the legs apart. "Yes. About the size of a half dollar. Discolored, too."

"Okay..." Larry said, looking at the screen with his head tilted back. "How about a swollen tongue?"

She pried open the jaw, which had stiffened. "Yes, absolutely. Twice the size."

"How's the viscosity of the saliva?"

"Well, there's lots of it. And it is quite viscous."

Larry leaned back in his chair, a frown on his face.

Denise looked back at him. "What's wrong?"

Without a word, Larry picked up the phone.

"Dr. Nesbit?"

"Miss Cates, please step away from the cadaver now and remove your gloves, in that order." Then, into the phone: "This is Lincoln County Morgue in Lincoln, Nebraska. We have a reported case of Rabies Bubona. Yes, I'll hold."

The med student took off her gloves, her eyes fixed on Larry. "Who are you on the phone with?"

"The CDC. You'd better get comfortable, Denise. We just spotted an extremely rare case of rabies. There's a theory that it's only broken out once before."

"When?"

" 'Ash-es, ash-es, we all... fall... down.' "

Denise blinked, a blank stare on her face, then her forehead raised. "The Black Plague?"

The med student wasn't paying attention, but the cadaver's fingers had just begun to move.

46

HERO

Igh in his perch, he could see the entire campus. The frayed binocular rubber itched his eyebrow some and he scratched it. The sun was warm upon him, and he closed his eyes to bask.

As a veteran, he was a war hero to friends and family but that had been a joke. He'd trained his whole life to be a sniper but was never once given the chance to prove it in combat. After the war, he wandered from one job to the next, never able to find something he excelled at.

He was good at sniping. *Really* good.

Only days ago, he'd been standing in a courtroom with lawyers wrestling over his fate. His face had been all over the news, charged with the most gruesome slaughter of college co-eds in U.S. History. Thanks to his rifle's silencer, combined with a careful selection of victims in disparate locations, and booby traps he'd laid for his attackers, the total body count had been 47 people before they'd finally been able to stop him. He always knew he could achieve greatness.

A cascade of small beads of sweat erupted along his hair-line. Wiping it slowly, he remembered how angry the lawyers had been at each other during his arraignment. Right in the middle of a bitter exchange, a ranting stranger ran screaming into the courtroom and moments later, shots were fired. Thanks to the confusion in the courtroom and his survival training, he'd managed to escape, but barely.

So here he was, back in his perch. He had more food and ammo than he'd ever need. For as long as it would last, he would purge this area. The world was going to shit, so he might as well have some fun while it lasted.

From the east, he heard screaming.

Homing in on it, he could see a young woman running away from a horde. She turned the corner toward him, and the group behind her followed like a kite's tail. 50... 60... probably over a hundred. About a mile away. *Ha!* Now *that* was a challenge.

He went to work and watched them fall, heads exploding and limbs vaporizing. The woman looked behind her and realized what was happening. She kept running, but watched as the horde's numbers dwindled, and then vanished.

The scope moved over to her. The woman looked behind her, rested her hands on her knees, then looked over toward her savior. "Thank you," she mouthed.

A smile rippled across his face. His finger tickled the trigger for a bit. An iota of pressure.

Nah. Not today. Let her have her moment of joy. He'd already met his quota.

47

ADRIFT

Sarah hadn't moved in hours now, saving her energy. Jacob kept scanning the horizon every few minutes, in a long shot that a ship—any ship—would pass by, much less spot them. They were the only two survivors from a large yacht sailing across the Indian Ocean. *We're a speck of dust on a 28 million square mile map*, Jacob kept thinking, *and not on any shipping lanes.*

Jacob had been a guest on the yacht and a millionaire in his own right, though you'd never have known it by his casual attire. Sarah had scanned him up and down out of boredom. She'd been the yacht's *sous-chef* and never wondered why she'd grabbed *him* when everything fell apart. It had been a split-second decision, nothing heroic about it. Mostly chance.

Jacob thought back to the bridge. There was a commotion topside... some stranded survivors had been brought aboard from another sinking ship and they'd relayed news of an outbreak on board which had suddenly turned violent. Jacob remembered the captain's sour face as he tried his radio repeatedly. The captain struggled for 15 long minutes to make contact with anyone. Then word came. A viral outbreak —*global*. Ocean liners, aircraft carriers, and supertankers, it seemed, were now the world's only known respite from infection. Nobody knew yet how the virus was transmitted. Standing on the bridge, Jacob idly watched the two survivors on the stern, still shaking from their ordeal. Then one of the survivors inexplicably slumped down and a crewman jumped to keep the castaway from slamming headfirst into the deck. In the crew mate's arms, the survivor had looked up—Jacob winced as he remembered that awful, contorted face—looped an arm around the crew member and sunk his teeth into the man's jugular. The minutes that followed were a bizarre blur. He'd found himself in a red lifeboat with the yacht's *sous-chef*, in exactly the same position as the people they'd rescued only days before.

Jacob again scanned the horizon. Not being in a shipping lane meant little hope that they'd be spotted.

"You know what's so funny?" Sarah managed.

"What."

"Today's my birthday." She could barely chuckle, but she did.

Jacob sat up with start. A half smile flitted across his mouth. "Well, make a wish, darling. I think I just got your birthday present."

"Huh?"

"There, on the horizon. What's that?"

Sarah squinted. She sat bolt upright. "Is that an *ocean liner??*"

They screamed and waved their hands so wildly that they rocked the lifeboat.

The white behemoth was almost on a collision course for them and would come within half a mile. Safe at last.

"Fresh water," Sarah said. "I could drink a whole bottle of mineral water right now."

"HEY!" Jacob screamed. He didn't see anyone along the railing yet but still looked for a pair of binoculars on the bridge or anywhere around the ship's silhouette. Jacob grew quiet.

Sarah looked at him. "Do they see us?" she said.

He pointed up at the ship's railing approaching them.

Sarah followed his finger... there, patiently standing on the deck, about twenty figures were covered in blood. Sarah could feel their eyes boring into them. The ocean liner passed them by, and the figures kept pace walking down the deck, never taking their eyes off the two castaways. The ship finished its pass and as it pulled away, the figures kept walking as if onto an invisible plank, climbing over the deck and falling into the water at the stern. The ship's propellers sucked them all in and they did not resurface, but Sarah felt a pang of suffocating sadness that rescue had come so close. Even if they'd been taken aboard a ship full of the infected, she would have welcomed the final fight, a flash of purpose, at least some reprieve from the boredom of existing without knowing when the end might come.

She turned to look at Jacob, but he wasn't there; she looked in all directions. His bobbing head wasn't anywhere on the horizon.

CHILD ABUSE

His snoring was loud, louder than his speech. That was saying something since his voice was deep enough to carry across a football field. That snoring had kept her awake all week and it had been part of the reason why she'd decided it was time to kill her son. As soon she'd heard about the epidemic, her chance had come at last to be rid of his tyranny forever. Her frail body was no match for his daily abuse. It was time to even the scales.

Last week, on her usual walk to the store, she'd chanced upon an infected homeless man. Somehow, he'd been trapped underneath a heavy dumpster. Who knew how he'd gotten infected—a dirty needle, perhaps?—but she seized the opportunity. She found a discarded wooden pallet and twisted it so a nail on one end was facing outward. The infected homeless man had reached for her, but she had stayed well out of his reach. Slashing his hand open, she'd retrieved a paper tissue to soak up the infected man's blood. Only *then* did she call the authorities.

Here, at home, her tormentor of twenty years was finally vulnerable. She'd made sure to give him a strong sedative so she could slide handcuffs on one wrist, attaching him firmly to the bedpost. Adding water to the blood-drenched tissue, her dishwasher gloved hand squeezed the brownish death into her son's gaping mouth. He gagged and immediately awoke, spewing a fountain of profanities at her.

Then the change happened. His face nodded up and down like he was vigorously agreeing. His body scrunched up to a fetus position and went perfectly erect before relaxing again. As the seizures passed, so did his breathing. She smiled as she saw his skin turn darker, his veins sprouting into black. *About time*, she thought.

Dead. Stillness.

She waited.

Quietly, his arm moved, pulling gently on the handcuffs. His eyes opened lazily, a simple dullness behind them. It was time.

His mother picked up the gun she'd laid out next to her, took aim and put a piece of metal right through his forehead. He was still once more.

She took off his handcuffs.

Only then did she call the authorities.

49

FUSION

Chief Engineer Perry had been monitoring levels in the reactor when the P.A. blared a battle stations alert. Everyone looked at each other in surprise. They were docked in San Diego prepping for another tour in Korea. Who the hell called battle stations in port? Had to be drill. In the Navy, though, you didn't dawdle. You acted serious unless told otherwise. Even so, by the time Perry and his staff had figured out what was going on, most of the ship had already been infected.

Perry told his staff to get weapons and methodically clear out each bulkhead as they worked their way from stern to bow. As senior officer in charge, leading came naturally to him, a quality essential for someone in charge of preventing the ship's nuclear reactor from catastrophic meltdown.

"That's the last one, sir," Petty Officer Chambers said a little more loudly than normal. They'd had to shoot a lot of familiar crewmates, including the captain. That last one hadn't been too hard. Still, it was unnerving to be forced to shoot your close friends.

Perry made it above deck and finally took in the scene. San Diego was showered with pillars of black smoke. Car alarms screeched in the distance.

Chambers was on the bridge trying to reach Command. Chief Perry leaned on the railing with a pain in his jaw like he'd just swallowed a box of mints whole. *What the hell do we do next?* he thought.

Perry emerged from the bridge with a sullen face. "It's chaos, sir. I can't get a clear answer from anyone. They must be going through the same thing as here."

"I guess we'll have to wait until someone is ready to tell us—"

"Sir!" Chambers pointed. A mob on the docks were headed their way, drawn as if following a snake's head.

Perry squinted. His eyesight was 20/20 and he could see most of the mob were running wildly, clearly infected. But at the front...

"Petty Officer Chambers!" Perry snapped.

"Yes, Sir!"

"Sound the horn and ready a rifle ASAP." Chambers was an able rifleman, he knew.

"Yes, Sir!" Perry sprinted back to the bridge. Chambers ordered the rest of the crew to wave their hands and shout. "There are two people running there. See them?"

The ship's horn blasted across the dock and immediately caught the couple's attention. One of them pointed and they suddenly shifted direction to run for the ship's stairway.

"Damn it to hell," Perry swore. Not only did that horn catch the couple's attention, it caught *everyone's* attention. Not so smart.

The mob was only 30 feet behind them and gaining ground. Perry took aim and picked off the one in front. His crew did likewise to give the couple time to get aboard. Chambers joined them and in minutes the couple were at the base of the walkway, screaming, "DON'T SHOOT! WE'RE NOT INFECTED!"

In seconds, they were lying on the deck, winded. The woman suddenly burst into tears, her whole body shaking in shock.

Perry and his crew kept firing at the mob, but it soon

became clear the mob was endless and would never be stopped by ammunition alone. Worse, they'd spent nearly all their ammo and achieved nothing.

"The walkway—shoot the walkway!" Perry shouted, in the hope the walkway would collapse and stop the surge of infected pushing onto the ship.

It wasn't enough. The walkway wouldn't break fast enough, and Perry had to order everyone below decks. Chambers lifted the woman roughly and pushed her down the deck into a bulkhead while Chambers and the others covered their flank.

Behind the closed bulkhead, they paused for a moment.

With everyone's heavy breathing as background noise, Perry weighed his options. They'd need to get back on the bridge and their rifle ammo was dwindling.

They could use axes but that seemed too risky. The bridge wasn't the safest place to be, either. The only safe place he knew he could defend—

"OUTFLANKED, SIR!" screamed Chambers as he moved behind them to eliminate the infected that had found another way inside. The mob swarmed in and would soon be all over the inside of the ship, and far more than the numbers before. That might be good to funnel them into bottlenecks, but—

"Reactor Room! Go!" ordered Chief Perry. A chorus of "Aye, sir!" filled the room and they all filed down the hallways, guns at the ready.

They made it to the reactor room with little incident and locked the bulkhead behind them. For the first time since it all began, the Chief allowed himself a deep breath, put his gun down and closed his eyes. The civilians were holding each other like two lonely monkeys. The man's eyes were staring right at Perry.

"Thank you, officer," he managed. "We'd both be dead without you."

"Don't thank me just yet. I'm afraid we jumped out of the

frying pan." Outside the bulkhead, the dull thuds came, patient and unforgiving.

"Petty Officer."

"Yes, sir."

"How many would you say are out there?"

"On the dock... easily a thousand or more." It looked like they were all coming aboard, too.

"Ammunition?" *About 400 to 500 rounds*, came the answer. The crewmates knew where this was headed. They could slug it out, but for how long? And nobody wanted to be infected. They'd rather swallow a lead slug than that.

"Better ideas?"

Chambers walked over to the reactor window. "Radiation is an awful way to go. I'd rather slit my wrists."

Perry agreed. If it must be done, Perry could do it. He explained how he could use up their oxygen, let them slip into an unconscious state and *then* let the radiation kill them. "Most humane way possible."

"Officer?" said the civilian man.

"Chief. You can call me Chief. Chief Raymond Perry."

"Chief... Kaitlen And I... well, before we do this... we're engaged. I was thinking... I mean, you're the acting Captain, aren't you?"

Perry felt faint at the suggestion. "Of course. I'd be honored."

Thus, with little fanfare, Acting Captain Raymond Perry of the cruiser USS Bunker Hill married Jake Henry Cincaid to Kaitlen Rose Fitzgerald. "Mrs. Cincaid," Perry smiled, "you may now kiss your husband."

Though the whole world had fallen around them, the crew could only see this one pure moment of love between two strangers.

50

TERMINAL

The voices were dying down now, finally. Carrie was getting hot... too many people in one space for too long. Ever since the stadium infection where Carrie had *seen* infection spreading lightning quick across thousands of people—she'd never felt safe around large groups of people. She hovered near the exit.

Nevertheless, the train station was the largest area everyone could safely convene. Nobody has seen activity in months, but only the most cautious had survived—being cavalier was out of vogue now.

"Okay, everyone, settle down," Thomas shouted. "We'll keep this short and quick so we can get back to doing whatever we're doing." He turned to the woman standing next to him, murmured something, then resumed, "We won't embarrass anyone who doesn't want to be outed but there's a growing need to go outside the perimeter to collect valuables on the field and in the nearby towns. Nobody *wants* this shit duty, right?" Nervous laughter shimmered across the room. "Like I said, we don't want anyone to feel picked on, so someone brought this idea up last night and I thought I'd mention it." He cleared his throat and paused.

"This is an indelicate request so please excuse me for even

suggesting it." Another pause. "If you have—or suspect you have—a terminal illness but you're still effectively healthy, you could be a perfect person to help. I know that's an awful thing to ask and I apologize. In a sense, we all have a terminal illness. But if your time is up sooner rather than later and you know you're going to become... well, a 'drag' on resources... please consider volunteering for this duty. Our Dr. Bannion has kindly offered to make cyanide pills for anyone who can't escape from a sticky situation. If you feel like you're up to the task, please come find any one of us at your convenience. Nobody selected for this job will be assumed to be terminal, either." Thomas took a deep breath. "I've volunteered myself and I'm perfectly healthy."

The room fell unnaturally quiet, like a funeral, as if the group's last remaining ounce of dignity had been squeezed out of a lemon. However, this group was pragmatic—not one person in the room had survived this long by riding a carefree wave of unscathed morality. Even Carrie had had to shoot her own father in the head to save her daughter. Her only other choice at that moment had been unthinkable.

"On to the final item of business, and this one is even less palatable. Thankfully, I won't be the bad guy on this one. Dr. Bannion?"

Thomas stepped off to one side but not off the stage. Carrie thought it odd, but realized it was probably a conscious choice to signify a unified message. There were no rulers in this ragtag group, only leaders, and everyone was painfully aware of it.

Dr. Bannion took his position. "Good evening. I've been consulting with the other doctors and even some mathematicians this last week and we've reached a startling conclusion. Before the outbreak, the world's population was well over 7 billion. Based on what little information we can glean from other reports, it seems 90% to 99% of the world's population has been infected and infection almost certainly means death. Because we cannot be completely confident in our numbers, we must assume the worst, which is a 1% survival rate. 1% of 7 billion is 70 million, which sounds pretty good. Except that's a *global* population, not national or local. If we assume 300 million Americans, only 3 million will likely have survived this long. If we assume long-term sustainability as a factor... I'm sorry, I'm getting a little lost in the weeds here. It's a lot of information to compile. Our conclusion is simple: if we want to keep our *culture* alive, our local culture, our heritage, we have to start making babies. *Now.* And *keep* making them. This is a long game, everyone. We have to make this a priority or we're simply not going to last as a species."

Carrie put a hand around her stomach. She felt sick.

"This is the part I hate to even mention. The mathematicians tell me that if we don't start making babies soon, our chances at long-term survival drop dramatically. Within a year, our chance to rebuild drops to about 17%; within two years, it drops to 2%." The doctor took a deep breath. "It stands to reason, then, that the largest threat to our long-term health is having an abortion."

The audience gasped. Murmurs peppered the audience. Carrie watched them with a melancholic look.

Dr. Bannion put his hands up to quiet the room. "We're not telling you what to do. We can't. We're in transition to a stable society again. I won't lie to you—we did discuss explicitly outlawing abortion, but I spoke strongly against that notion. Any woman coming to me asking for an abortion will be granted one... *but only if they insist.* However, for any woman now thinking about an abortion or who might one day in the future, I also ask—no, I *implore*—that you place yourself against the backdrop of the human race. We need more people to keep going. If you don't want your child, I guarantee there will be a couple who will. If you are a couple who has two children, I ask that you consider adopting one more from anyone who doesn't want to raise a child. Each person here is critically important— each of you is why we are all here. Yet, as a member of this group, as a member of the human race, you are but a small grain of sand... and it takes a lot of grains of sand to make a beach."

Carrie's body broke out in a searing hot sweat, and she raced from the room to the nearest toilet to vomit.

She was pregnant.

HISTORICAL FICTION

51

FIRST IMPRESSIONS

One cold morning in what Europeans would record as March 20, 1520, a Toconoté man named Chatahoté wrapped himself in a short llama skin coat and walked from his village over to the beach. It was a quiet morning, cold, but sunny. He took in the sea breeze.

Across the horizon, he saw five white dots coming from the northeast. Slowly, they grew larger. He yawned.

"Will you join us for the hunt today?" said a voice behind him. He turned and saw Tala walking toward him. "You were always our best lancer."

"Yes, I'll join you. The more we are, the better we do, yes?"

"Always it was so," said Tala.

They watched the five white dots on the horizon together. Chatahoté kept up his chatter with Tala, almost forgetting about the dots. As they spoke, the dots grew larger and taller... until they showed a small perpendicular brown streak beneath them. Tala spoke of the women Chata might want to bed with —Chata was in his prime and many of the women wanted to bed with him.

Chata looked back to the horizon and the white and brown shapes had grown larger still.

The shapes had movement, too. The white "dots" acted like

an animal skin flapping with the wind, and it swayed in sync with the larger brown section it appeared to be attached to. Chata and Tala stretched out on the beach, closing their eyes to rest. It was a beautiful morning.

After a time, Chata thought he heard voices, but not from Tala or anyone else from his village. He opened his eyes to pinpoint the sound and realized it was coming from these new shapes. The "dots" were no longer dots at all, but tall triangles swaying in front of them. He lazily admired their beauty and wondered when his stomach would talk to him this morning. He yawned once more and closed his eyes against the soft breeze. Chata opened his eyes again and was puzzled to see movement along the brown bottom of the white triangles. He squinted his eyes at the shiny silver creatures getting onto a small brown structure.

The brown structure approached the shore and as it got closer, he recognized the creatures as men in a silverfish armor on a boat... and Chata snapped to attention. "Invasion! Those are boats! Get the lances!" Tala and Chata ran back to the village in a sprint and when they returned, many of the villagers were behind them, including the shaman.

The shiny creatures had what looked like spears and were coming toward them slowly. Chata held his lance high, ready for a battle. The shaman put his old hand gently on Chata's shoulder. "I will speak with them."

The old man walked over to the shiny creatures. Chata could only hear some words said over the waves—"What do you want?" and "—come to take—" and "—attack us?"

One of the shiny creatures stepped forward and spoke with the shaman at length. He pointed to the five "dots" and then the shaman looked out at the horizon. The shaman tilted his head back, closed his eyes and splayed his hands out, palms open. When he opened his eyes again and looked at the "dots", he excitedly talked to one of the shiny men.

Finally, the shaman returned and explained that the "dots" were very large ships from a place very far away. Chata and Tala and the other villagers shook their heads at first, not grasping the immensity of the idea. These massive structures housed *men?* The ocean was too vast for that... and they claimed to have travelled *across* the ocean, farther than anything he or anyone else could possibly imagine?

When they finally understood and could recognize the ships for what they were, and they could be assured these men were not invaders, but explorers... they introduced themselves.

The man in charge introduced himself as Ferdinand Magellan.

52

STONE WITNESS

The speckled dolerite rock in the Canaanite's hands was like the tip of a thick stone dagger. He lifted it up and guided it as gravity brought it down on the long red granite slab before him. He did this over and over and over again, all day, every day, for three decades. His sole task was to let the dolerite rock pound down a small area no larger than a single square foot.

Other men, some Canaanites like him, sat alongside him doing likewise. They chatted quietly, ever watchful of their slave master pacing around them. Many of the men had been captured warring against the pharaoh, and their lives as slaves were uneventful, perpetually boring.

The Canaanite briefly wondered about his life's work. Would this rock they carved be used for the inside of a temple? Would it be used as a palace floor? He quickly abandoned this thought, for it was a fruitless pursuit. They told him to pound down the granite and he did so.

This simple uneducated Canaanite slave, whose name is forever unknown to history, contributed to something grander than any endeavor produced by the most notorious or affluent civilizations throughout history: this long granite slab would eventually become the Luxor obelisk, rising 23 meters tall and weighing over 250 metric tons. Soon it would be chiseled with hieroglyphics, capped with a gold pyramid top, loaded onto a ship to travel up the Nile, and laid to rest outside the colonnade of Luxor Temple for over three millennia. Eventually, a nation not yet born would ferret it away as a war prize and place it in their capital's central square. Under the watchful presence of this stone testament to tyranny, these new countrymen would soon grow intoxicated with the virtues of self-determination and forge a new future without kings, emperors, or pharaohs.

53

RAISON D'ÊTRE

C ardinal Degate stood before him, his red hat a shimmering crimson in the candlelight. A million pin pricks skipped across Cardinal Quinn's scalp as the words came out of Degate's mouth. *"Acceptasne electionem de te canonice factam in Summum Pontificem?"*

So much has come to this moment... is this really what I want?

The tears welled up without warning. Quinn chose not to break his gaze with Degate and Degate saw tears roll down Quinn's face. Quinn blinked his eyes clear. It was tradition to refuse the papacy at least twice.

"Ego renuo."

Quinn had been a cardinal for three years, a bishop for over twenty. His faith in God, he had thought, was unshakable. News of his sister's premature labor had come just two weeks before the conclave—his niece had been born with a severe neurological condition. Only machinery kept the child alive, its limp body a cocoon for a pink goo where a brain should have been. What purpose could this child serve? It was simply a lump of flesh with no possibility of ever experiencing the world, of knowing God's love. Its existence was like sandpaper grinding away Quinn's resolve.

"Acceptasne electionem de te canonice factam in Summum Pontificem?"

How could any pope doubt in God? Wasn't a pope by definition the most faithful among all? If his faith were not exemplary, how could it not sow dissent in the Church sooner or later?

"Ego renuo."

His tears became sobs now. This was his own secret. He'd never admitted, even to himself until this very moment, that he could have doubted God's existence. How, then, could Quinn in good faith accept the papacy?

He imagined Cardinal Degate's reaction upon refusing. He'd never liked Degate that much and the Conclave had grown tense as votes had pushed Degate out of the running. Perhaps seeing his tears and remembering how God loves all creatures, Degate's eyes had grown kinder, a faint smile appearing. Quinn knew that if he refused a third time, the Cardinal would embrace him as a brother of the church with unconditional love and nothing else would really matter.

"Acceptasne electionem de te canonice factam in Summum Pontificem?"

The silence in the Sistine Chapel was electric. Quinn finally broke his gaze and looked down. His legs trembled, his knees buckled, and he realized he might faint if he kept standing. He pulled up his robes and kneeled. Outstretched his arms slightly, as if praying in arrant supplication.

This was God's plan for him. Doubt was a part of faith. It was human to doubt and everything at this moment was simply a reminder of how flawed he was in God's eyes. Though Jesus had been divine, even *he* had been flawed. *I am not divine... so I must be flawed. To doubt at the pinnacle of my faith is the nature of the flaw itself.*

He looked back up at Cardinal Degate, sighed deeply, and returned his faint smile. Seeing Quinn on the floor wrought with such emotion, not a single cardinal in the conclave would believe how deeply Quinn's doubt in God had blossomed.

Truly, they thought, *this pope will be more devout than I could ever be.*

"*Ego recipero.*"

54

WHAT YOU WISH FOR

D avu was utterly still. He could see the chimpanzee through the brush, and Davu was downwind. Davu would eat tonight.

The year was 1908 and Davu lived in a remote region of southeastern Kamerun, a German colony in Africa we now know as Cameroon. The area was so remote that Davu had remained unaware of the vast, swift industrial growth breaking out around the globe. All Davu cared about was eating monkey tonight; the world's affairs were, as ever, trivial to him.

He waited for the right moment to hurl his spear, puckering his lips slightly as sweat trickled down his bare back onto his scant leather covering. Other hunters preferred a leather belt showered in colorful painted stones, but Davu preferred to blend in against the shaded underbrush.

Any longer and the chimp might get spooked. Davu threw his spear... and the chimp shrieked in pain, trying to escape with the thin wooden stick trailing behind him. Davu rushed over and bludgeoned the chimp to death.

Davu smiled. This monkey would make him strong, and he rejoiced the end of the hunt with a good kill.

After he made it back to his dwelling in the forest, Davu cut open the chimp's chest cavity to pull out its organs with his bare hands. One stubborn piece of skin wouldn't come off, so he pivoted his shaving rock to its sharper side. Placing his foot on the monkey's hand, he slid the rock firmly into the space between skin and bone. The blood was everywhere and made everything slippery and when the tension was at its highest, the rock suddenly slid down and he cut himself in the palm. It wasn't a deep cut, but it made him gasp a little and pause before going back to work.

The meat would be good, he thought. *Next week I'll catch two more monkeys and head down the Ngoko to sell them to lovely Braima.*

Davu smiled at the thought of Braima. He knew he had no hope of catching her attention as long as he competed with the other fishermen. Many of those men were far better travelled, going up and down the 200-meter-wide Sangha River, which always impressed Braima. Some fishermen, he'd heard from rumors, even went so far as the Congo River and then down to Brazzaville and Léopoldville, which we now call Kinshasa. To Davu, who had never been to those cities, the stories he'd heard were beyond belief. People *willfully* chose to live right next to each other and the nearest market was only a few meters away by foot? Was it even possible? Davu recalled one fisherman telling him of "loose women" who'd part their legs for just a handful of coins. *Many—if not all—of the fishermen,* Davu thought, *surely visited these women. How could Braima not see that?*

Braima was better than that. Davu would try to win her affection regardless, to give her a gift that would last forever. And that roguish fisherman flirting with Braima as if she were a loose woman from the city... Davu willed a world of death and pain to him and everyone who ever met him.

Davu got what he wanted: the monkey he had slain that morning was the first to ever infect humans with something—a century later—would be called human immunodeficiency virus, or AIDS.

55

ANCHORED

Reginald Travers sat calmly on the beach, letting the waves of the Indian Ocean lick his toes. A yellow-billed albatross lazily floated on the winds before him and landed in the waters not far from the waves. Reg could still remember the sickening grin on Michael's face as the muskets had leveled at Reg. Michael had offered Reg a chance at life... by stranding him on one of these mile-wide Seychelles Islands off the north coast of Madagascar.

Reg flexed his feet into the soft sand, feeling the coolness massage them. He breathed in the humid air and let the last few months roll around in his mind like a lazy dog hunting for scraps. The clues had been there all along, he realized now. Michael must have wanted him off the ship for weeks. Reg had heard Michael conspiring with the crew to take over the ship and Reg had almost come to blows with him about it. Mutiny on a *pirate* ship? Pirates prided themselves as being democratic, held in stark contrast with the arbitrary tyranny of the Royal Navy. If a pirate didn't have a say in his own fate, he had nothing. One day, Reg had been yanked from his hammock, still sleeping, and found himself the object of Michael's accusations. Despite Reg's protestations, it was obvious the crew's sentiment had also been against him for weeks. They searched

Reg's ditto box and found a coin-filled purse that Michael must have planted. That was that.

Next time, Reg sighed, *I'll make friends with* everyone. *Buy them if I have to.* Until then, he'd hunt down Michael and gut him with a blunt knife. Once he got off this bloody rock.

The island was tiny and could be circumnavigated by foot in less than an hour. On a clear day, he was pretty sure he could make out a larger island to the northwest. The main island couldn't be much further north than that one. *At least I have trees*, he thought. *If I really get desperate, I can just build a raft.* It felt odd to be stranded so far away from home, thousands of miles away, and still feel confident he could make it back home. If the rounders ever stopped pillaging this route, he'd be lost forever but as it was, it felt like to him just like catching a water taxi from the Thames. Though with a much *much* longer wait.

He did feel lucky they hadn't fed him to the sharks. That would have been a cruelty beyond imagining. Even pirates, he supposed, had a small degree of compassion.

Nevertheless, it changed nothing. Michael had thought —*stupidly!*—he had left Reg for dead. Reg actually knew this area far better than his crew; he'd see a ship going one way or another and he'd be willing to burn every tree on the island to get their attention. After a time, he'd find his way back to England. He knew this as an absolute. Of course, without proper papers or any tangible wealth, righting his situation might take a couple of years but he would track down Michael with the unerring focus of a Royal falcon.

When he finally caught Michael, he desperately hoped it would be at sea. He almost salivated at the anticipation of it. Then he could stick a knife deep in Michael's belly, but *not* twist it—that would be too merciful. Once Michael was bleeding, he'd throw him overboard. To the sharks.

56

NAURU

"Up here," said the cabbie, Erich. "On the right. Just past this tree line."

Larry Hammond had travelled thousands of miles for this. Public radio had funded his trip, but his ulterior interest had been in the history of the island. He'd studied it for over five years and now he was finally here.

Erich drove with his head tilted back, his window all the way down, enjoying the pacific breeze as his cab passed an endless wall of trees along their right. As a native, Erich was one of the few of European ethnic origin on the island. Larry mused about how a European would stick out in a place like Ecuador where the average height was a foot smaller. Here, in Micronesia, the average height was equal to or more than that of Europeans, presumably because Polynesian women seemed to prefer taller males as their mates.

Larry glanced back to where the cabbie was turning. The palm trees were bountiful here but unexpectedly stopped, revealing a wide-open area. Larry knew exactly what he would see and was conflicted about forcing Erich to take him here. There was a tension in the air, no doubt. The cabbie's once persistent chatter drowned into an uncomfortable quiet.

The cab stopped. "Tourist time," announced the cabbie, without enthusiasm. "don't forget to take a picture."

Larry stepped out and Erich followed. They walked over to look across the jagged white-grey stone pillars protruding across the area.

"Almost 90% of the island looks like this," Erich said, coughing. "Completely uninhabitable."

"All *this* is from phosphate mining?" It was rhetorical. Larry stared across the sea of stone, an unnatural wasteland. There he stood, in silent judgement over the fate of Nauru, borne from decades of merciless mining. When the phosphates had run out, the islanders had nothing else left to sell. They had discovered too late that they were but a hair away from a modern retelling of Easter Island. Seeing this empty stone graveyard reminded Larry of those eggs that had been drained of their innards, leaving only a fragile shell behind.

Larry's knees became suddenly weak, and he sat down where he stood. If Larry had believed in prayer, he'd have prayed for the future of Erich's people. If Earth's oceans were rising as they were expected to, this whole island was doomed, and they'd have nothing left to barter for survival. *This is how a whole nation dies*, Larry thought. The island's vestiges would be the huge, rusted cantilevers once furiously loading phosphates onto cargo ships bound for the West.

From among the stone pillars, a stray dog emerged about 100 feet away. His tongue hung out to one side. He looked over at Larry and Erich but didn't bother to bark before wandering off again.

57

MUSICAL THRONES

"I am but a simple woman, Herr Hus," the widow said, deferentially. "I am not as learnèd as you in the ways of our Lord's faith."

Jan Hus craned his head back to look on the street below. It was November 3rd, 1414, and Hus had arrived that afternoon in Konstanz under safe conduct from King Sigismund of Hungary. The Council of Konstanz had been convened here to allow Hus a chance to defend his teachings to the Church—none of which he felt could be biblically proven false—but another more important matter was also to be decided by the same council: the issue of who was the legitimate pope.

"I pray to his Holiness Gregory... yet the Church is conflicted on these matters."

"Very well, Frau Klouch, perhaps we should do an exercise I do with my pupils. Let us start with you explaining to me what you know about the circumstances."

The Frau would have smiled but her soul was at stake, and she did not relish a man as esteemed as Herr Hus to think she viewed this topic with any manner of levity.

"The cardinals met in Rome to choose our pope in 1378, yes?" the widow began.

"That is correct."

"And an angry mob broke into the cardinal's meeting—"

"The Conclave," Hus corrected.

"Yes, the Conclave. And they demanded that the cardinals choose a Roman pope, not a French pope as they have done for decades."

"Correct."

"So they chose His Holiness Urban VI."

"Yes, an Italian. After which the cardinals retired to France and claimed they'd been forced to choose him, and elected...?"

"His Holiness Clement VII, a Frenchman. Who has now been replaced by Benedict XIII, who resides in Avignon."

"And the Roman pope has been replaced by our new pope, Gregory XII."

"Correct. Two popes. One Roman, one French," Hus said.

"Two popes," she repeated. She shook her head in wonder. "Five years ago, a council in Pisa was convened," she continued, "to resolve the matter and they elected His Holiness Alexander V, yet without convincing the other two popes that they should resign."

"Precisely. Which means we have *three* popes. Your understanding of the topic is seamless, Frau Klouch. You would outshine all my pupils."

"Three popes." She frowned and shook her head slightly. "Herr Hus, this is a matter of immense distress for me, and I dare say, for all Christendom. Is it not?"

Hus took a deep breath. "It is. The Council of Konstanz was convened to decide this matter once and for all. Indeed, the group is an impressive one with 29 cardinals, 134 abbots, 183 bishops and archbishops, and a hundred learnèd Doctors of Law and Divinity. If they cannot resolve the matter, then I fear for the very future of Christianity." It was a mild joke, but the widow crossed herself at the possibility.

Looking out the window once more, Hus felt a more tangible possibility for himself. The Council would surely decide a new pope and denounce the others, but what of his own fate? Though he had in fact been granted safe passage by King Sigismund, these kinds of councils weren't a place to air grievances in the hopes of gaining actual Church reform; it was likely Hus would be wrestled away from the King's protection and burned for heresy.

He could only speak his conscience, however. If they thought him a heretic, at least he would die knowing he had been truthful to the intellect that God had granted him.

Suddenly, he remembered the widow. Whatever his own fate, her life would go on unchanged regardless of this matter of three popes.

"Frau Klouch?" he asked softly.

She snapped her head up, broken out of her own trance. "Yes, Herr Hus?"

"Would it put your heart at ease to seek solace through prayer?"

She smiled for the first time he'd met her.

"Yes, Herr Hus."

"Let us go to the church, then." And as they dressed to battle the bitter frost, they pondered how their prayers should plead for their own unique kind of salvation.

58

A HUMAN CIPHER

"I would be most grateful to you if you could arrange for its publishing," said Robert Morriss, coughing. "My days are few now but for the foreseeable future, I would appreciate it if my name were to remain completely... unattached."

James B. Ward looked at the papers with deep interest. "Certainly. I can absorb the cost. Especially if it yields a buried treasure being found."

The papers Ward was examining so closely had been made two decades before by a wanderer named Thomas Jefferson Beale. That was what Morriss had told him, in any event.

"You are most definitely an angel in time of need." The man took a long wistful look at the papers. After twenty years of his life wasted deciphering only one of the three cryptograms, he had found nothing and never found the treasure Beale had hinted at. It was a matter of personal pride not to reveal such failure, but it also could have some professional repercussions for his family if all of Morris' associates knew he had been such a gold-digger.

"If others press you for details, you might say you received these papers through an intermediate. At a minimum, that would afford us both a degree of distance."

Morriss coughed again and they shook hands, pressing

thumbs on the knuckle of the first finger, a common signal of a Free Mason. Morriss departed, furtively looking around to ensure no one had seen them talking.

Ward had every intention of publishing the papers. However, Ward also decided to alter the other two documents just enough as to make them untranslatable. Nobody would know the difference except for him. He'd try decoding the ciphers himself, of course, but anyone who struggled long enough to crack the code would have to come directly to him to ensure his translation were accurate. That way, he'd know exactly who was looking for the treasure and could partner with them to split the proceeds when he "miraculously" found a typo in the document.

Besides, he concluded without a shred of insight, *anyone willing to devote their whole lives to searching for buried treasure deserved to get nothing for their efforts—I'm simply laying the groundwork for self-inflicted poetic justice.*

59

CREATIVE DESTRUCTION

His most important commission. From the King himself! The commission laid before James Thornhill was to paint the inside of the dome of Saint Paul's Cathedral and despite the dome being so far above the eyes of the congregation, he was committed to ensuring the completed work would be up to his caliber to excellence.

Like every morning, Thornhill ascended the scaffolding up to the immense dome. A couple of his friends tagged along behind him with clean, new brushes and a few loaves of warm bread to snack on throughout their stay in the clouds. They mounted the scaffolding carefully as Thornhill left them behind. He'd had weeks of relentless practice and knew every hazard. There were no handrails—Thornhill had no need of any.

Thornhill settled in and began by painting the head of an apostle. As he painted, his friends kept him company with idle chatter, even as Thornhill became absorbed in his work. Though the painting was intended to be seen from below, Thornhill still put delicate strokes on the large figures. He stepped back to examine his work, squinting his eyes a little. His eyes were so focused, showing a determination for excellence. Thornhill blinked his eyes to shake off the hangover from the night's drinking.

He looked again. The image wasn't yet clear.

Thornhill stepped back again, and again...

In a split second, one of his friends—the one nearest the painting that Thornhill was looking at—saw where Thornhill was heading and knew Thornhill would fall off the scaffolding to his death. His friend's diaphragm contracted, preparing to shout out a warning, but guessed that a vocal warning would take too long to articulate, be heard, understood, and affect Thornhill's present course.

He saw the intent gaze on Thornhill's face—

—in an instant, his companion grabbed a large paint brush and smeared it over Thornhill's delicate work.

"WHAT HAVE YOU DONE!" screamed Thornhill, immediately stepping forward.

"I have saved your life." His friend pointed at the scaffolding's edge. Thornhill followed the hand to the edge of the scaffolding. Then he sat down, put his head in his hands for a long while, then told his friends to come down for the day, share a brew with him, and tell their story to everyone they could.

60

HONORARIUM

Titus gestured for the boy to leave and stood by the door to ensure he had gone to the far side of the atrium, well out of earshot. Turning to his two guests, Titus smiled at last, pleased they had come and trying to relish the moment for however short a time they had it.

"Thank you, prefect," said Lucas, in Latin. "We owe you a great debt for your attentions."

Titus waved him off. "That's an old title, Lucas," making his way over to the window. "But your gratitude is accepted with fondness, of course."

The other man in the room looked at the stone floor. From his belt, he pulled a small cloth pouch and poured earth upon the ground. "Apologies, most excellent Titus," he said with a bow, his foot quickly sweeping over the dirt—as if by accident—making a small semi-circle in it. Titus smirked at Lucas, walked over to the dirt, traced a matching small curve with his foot. The resulting image was of a fish.

"You can never be too cautious, Mārcus," said Titus, walking to the window. "Danger lurks at every turn, especially here."

"How may we be of assistance, prefect?" said Lucas.

Titus cleared his throat. "His teachings have affected us all, yes?"

Lucas stared at him quietly. "My life is dedicated to him."

"Twenty-five years have passed. This... brief time we have left is but a breath in the wind." Titus peered across the square. "His message should echo across the lands, across the years long after we have passed."

"And so it shall, Prefect," said Mārcus.

"I told you, that's an *old* title," Titus replied, not looking back. "Everywhere the message of who He was, what He did... I hear it muddled now and lackluster. Confused." He turned to look at the men, a weighted look in his dark eyes. "His teachings do not deserve to be cast aside as such."

Mārcus was about to say something but Titus held up a hand. "I know your objection. We may all try to speak his history, but to a commoner's ears, it is nothing more than a human version of Jupiter. And what mortal's story can compare with a god whose weapons are thunder and lightning?"

Titus sat down at last, facing the men. "Please," and gestured for Mārcus and Lucas to sit. "His story, then, must not be told as it is. It must be told *as it feels to us*. Its truth must be communicated not in its actual events, but how those events touched our hearts. How it has changed us." He paused, scanning over their faces. "Only *then* will his message echo throughout all eternity."

Lucas dropped his head, immersed in thought.

Mārcus chewed his lower left lip, eyes looking out the window.

"You were there," added Titus, looking back and forth at the two men. "People await the story from those who witnessed it. Can you do this for him?"

A long and painful silence befell them. Finally: "I shall do it, if my colleague agrees," said Lucas. "Yes," said Mārcus slowly. "Yes, it will be done. We will make his story greater than all the tales of Jupiter and Juno combined. Lucas and I will write of his teachings of love and forgiveness so that they will ripple across the cities of this Kingdom and into our son's hearts, and into their sons' sons' hearts."

Titus leaned back in his chair; his hands laced. "Very well. He would be pleased, I think. A small lie to tell the greatest truth of all, no?"

"I will write the first story," Mārcus said.

"And I will base my story on yours, Mārcus." Mārcus turned to Lucas. "We must tell Matityahu and the others, of course. They will want to tell their stories to their own people."

"There is a matter still to be resolved, Lucas," said Titus. "While you two are writing your stories, you will be unable to acquire any money to live by. You deserve to have some time dedicated to this project, so some small compensation should be owed to you."

Lucas' smile was faint, but his eyes betrayed genuine love. "You are too kind to offer this, Prefect. We write this for His legacy, not for recompense."

"I expected you might say that. Which is why the betrayal of Judas is fitting here. How much did he betray our Lord for? Thirty pieces of silver?"

"Yes, Prefect."

"Then: let us reclaim that amount as a gesture of our Love for him. For thirty pieces of silver, your writings will let his story last until the end of time." Titus added a wicked smile, relishing this exquisite, quiet revenge.

Mārcus and Lucas smiled, too. At last, Lucas said, "Very well, Prefect. We humbly accept your honorarium."

Titus leaned in close. "Obviously, nobody can ever know of my involvement here. It also gives me great sadness, but—for our own safety—it would be wise if we never met again."

Lucas' face shifted. "Even so, I would like to dedicate my works to you, Prefect. What name can I use?"

Titus Flavius Sabinus sat back again and stared at the ceiling.

"Theophilus."

HORROR

61

LEGACY ONE

L egacy One was a behemoth of a ship: 25 decks, 10
miles long, and over 28,000 families. It had enough
redundant expertise and genetic variety to start three
new civilizations if half the crew perished, and that was good
because all of its crew were dead.

Well, not dead, not exactly. To any outsider, they all *looked*
dead. Their hearts were stopped, their bodies frozen. Hydrogen
sulfide flowing in their veins had completely de-animated them.

Yet a lone stowaway walked the halls. He loved peering
inside their capsules. He, too, had a heart that did not beat. His
brain was not synthetic but cold, rotted and aged beyond
measure. His name was Justinian Lascaris and he was a
vampire.

Justinian had been born in 1249 scarcely a few miles south
of Byzantium. He'd been bitten as a young boy, so his voice had
never broken and his boyish appearance betrayed centuries of
experience. He'd become an expert on human nature despite
having abandoned mortality too long ago to remember what
being human felt like.

Legacy One was to colonize a planet light years from Earth.
Justinian swooned over the animation capsules, viewing the
"dead" humans inside with a fondness akin to love. One day

they would land on their alien world. As a vampire, of course, Justinian would never need a spacesuit. But he would have to be extremely careful to avoid all humans until they had arrived at their new home world. At least in space staying away from UV light wasn't too hard to do.

If he planned it well and conserved his energy, he could stave off his hunger until the colony grew large enough not to miss a few stragglers. After the first vampire coven on an alien world had been settled, he could then continue exploring the stars as a stowaway, always letting his human companions think they were the ones in control of their journey...

62

SANDY OCEAN

The toothy smile on Yann's face had been there so long, it looked chiseled. He'd been grinning wide for over 100 miles of New Mexico desert and his face muscles were finally tensing up. He massaged his face some and cranked the air conditioning to maximum. The glaring sun belied a blistering 111°F outside—the A/C was locked in an epic struggle with mother nature.

Yann didn't care. All he wanted was to drive out to his father's house and flaunt his good fortune. Yann had gotten a salary hike far exceeding any amount his father had ever said he would have. He knew his father was a louse and a drunk... Yann was too smart to expect any satisfying reaction. Yann wasn't going to convince his father, he was going just to collect a memory of telling his father off. Yann smiled again, this time with butterflies in his belly.

At once, a flash came to him of the time when an unwelcome visitor had come to their house. Yann's father had magically wielded a sawed-off shotgun back then, so if things got ugly today, Yann had no way of knowing what his father would do. If he was drunk, as Yann fully expected him to be, then violence was quite possible. Even likely.

He turned onto a dirt road from the main highway and

drove another 30 miles. The sun was beating on him now from the east and despite the A/C hitting him head on, he could feel beads of sweat coming anyway.

"Ugh, this fucking heat," he seethed. His new job was up north, awash in humid greenery, far away from this scorching dust bowl. If Yann could use a flamethrower on this whole shitty state, he'd gladly do it. Not that it would make any difference; it already felt like an oven out here.

It had been years since he'd been out to his dad's place. *Where's that other road?* he wondered. After he turned on the road, it would be another long drive until he got to the reservation. Yann pulled out his phone to get a map signal... but his phone got no signal out here. Yann smirked and reached into the back seat to pull an old GPS out of his bag. He'd expected something like this and had no desire to be stranded out here looking for directions. Yann was the master out here.

Yann glanced at the GPS screen with one eye on the road. It was a boring drive out here, too boring. The landscape was so predictable that he could almost drive with his feet on the wheel if he'd wanted. Not like anybody came out here to enforce the la—

BUMP! and then Yann was struggling to keep the car from careening off the road, clawing at the wheel this way and that and stepping on the brakes but not too hard because that would send the car into a crazy spin he couldn't recover from and how fast had he been going anyway?

Everything went quiet. The only sound was the barely audible whistle coming from the driver's side A/C fan. He put his head on the wheel. Tried to remember how to breathe. He needed quiet, and reflexively turned his car off.

Opened his door to examine the car. Had he gotten a flat tire? *What had happened exac—oh. Roadkill, looks like. Small. Scales on the front wheel. Could be a snake, but scales like that... an armadillo?*

Poor guy, he thought. Yann looked back down the road and saw a few evenly spaced blood patches. His stomach turned a little at that, but he shrugged it off and went back to examining the car. He kicked the tire gently, which seemed intact. That was a relief. He wouldn't want to change a tire in this heat.

He got back in his car and sat for a moment collecting his thoughts. *For want of a cow catcher*, he mused. He snapped out of it and focused his attention on starting the car, thinking what he'd tell his father when he got there, *"An armadillo tried to get my attention on the way up here, but I bowled him over..."*

Nothing. The car didn't start. It turned over, as if trying to start, but then died again. *Not good*, he thought. *Was it flooded? Stay cool*, he thought. *Ha. Cool—a macabre joke.*

He tried again—nothing. A few turns, nothing. Beads of sweat were now collecting all over his back and dripping into his underwear.

He got out, opened the hood, and was greeted with a wall of smoke. The heat from the sun was punishing but how hot did the engine have to be to get even hotter than that?

Yann's jubilation turned to dread. The searing sun had leapfrogged from momentary nuisance to fatal threat.

It came to him as a rush: he might last a few hours in the heat, perhaps two or three, but unless somebody chanced upon him on this remote backwater road, he knew that by sundown, he'd be dead from a heat stroke.

Yann chuckled at the irony. *Try wiping a grin off my skull then.*

63

GO VIRAL

"Look," said the virologist, toying with his coffee napkin while carefully choosing his words, "I appreciate your intentions here, but this is one topic I would leave alone for now." He stared at her unflinchingly as if to underscore his subtext.

Kelly Sears pursed her lips. "Nothing would please more than to get out of this shithole," she said, gesturing around her. "I haven't seen clean water since I landed last month. The Congo is a hard place to visit."

The virologist, Tony Reardon, shifted in his seat. "You're not going away, are you?"

"Fastest way to get me out of your hair is give me what I want."

Tony cursed silently to himself, then took a deep breath. "Fine. Quote me as an unnamed source, then."

"Done."

"We're all now familiar with hemorrhagic fever from the Dallas scare and films like *Outbreak* and *Contagion* and the like. The movies typically portray the absolute worst-case scenario for a smallpox-like virus. That always plays well to audiences. Everyone loves a good monster movie, right? The difference between most movies and your generic brand of hemorrhagic fever is that it really is a slate wiper for humans. The worst natural disaster on record was the 1918 flu pandemic and that killed only two to three percent of the world's population. It's hard for most of Joe Q. Public to grasp what the world would look like if that were to happen today but 200,000,000+ deaths would have a *devastating* impact to the economy and political stability. And that's only 3% of the global population, so imagine what 70% to 80% to 90% fatalities would look like. We don't have to worry about the 70% fatalities or higher, not really. What we're terrified about is if as 'little' as 20% to 30% of the world died. Basically, at that point, all the world's basic services are severely affected—sewage processing, food supply, etc.—so once you get above 20% to 30%, it becomes extremely hard to get clean water, energy, food... in effect, at only 20% fatalities, the whole world hits a tipping point where things spiral drastically out of control and can't be recovered. After *that*, if the virus is as deadly as we assume, it is statistically likely that it's a matter of time before *everyone* gets infected. This is why I get so crotchety about this stuff. Keeping the morale of the masses high is a key factor from preventing a mass panic. The more this stuff gets reported on, the possibility of a mass panic gets amplified far beyond what we need to maintain order."

Kelly was furiously scribbling in her notepad, all the while hoping that her recorder was doing its faithful job. "How deadly is Ebola and Marburg? Uganda had a death rate as low as 34%."

"Correct, the Ebola-Bundibugyo strain causes death in a relatively lower amount than, say, the Ebola-Zaire strain, which is as high as 80% to 90%." Reardon leaned closer, reaching out for the carafe of water on the table. Then he thought better of it and rummaged around in his bag. When he sat back up, a new bottled water was in his hand from which he took a long drink of water. Kelly stole a quick glance at the virologist. It was hot and humid in the Congo, but she suspected Reardon was sweating for other reasons.

Reardon leaned in close, lowering his voice. "What I'm about to tell you is *extremely* sensitive information. I could get fired for telling you and even brought up on charges of fucking treason so please think very carefully before you run this."

"Okay." Kelly meant it, too. Reardon could be a critical source later on if something awful happened.

Tony looked around the café. "The federal government sent me here to isolate a completely *new* strain of hemorrhagic fever. This one has never been seen before. It's infected 527 people here in the Congo... but there have been no survivors. Zero. 100% fatality rate. There is no cure and likely won't be for many months, if not years. So if this thing suddenly spills over into a major city... well, there won't be any Christmas presents this year. Anywhere."

Kelly tried to appear calm but became acutely aware of all the liquids in her mouth moving around as she tried to swallow. "What are you doing to find the virus?"

"All the regular stuff. But some of us suspect it might be airborne now. To boot, symptoms don't demonstrate for about 20 days, twice the length of Ebola Zaire. Which means it's nearly impossible to tell who is infected. By the time you do, it's too late."

A man in the back of the café coughed—Tony snapped his head around to stare at him. The man coughed hard, and then stopped and appeared normal again.

When Tony looked back at her, his eyes were a little wild. He got up quickly and paid. "You want my advice? Leave the Congo. Today. And for fuck's sake—don't touch *anything*."

Before the waiter came back to their table, Kelly was long gone.

64

SLIPPING AWAY

Steig had no idea how the fire had started, and he didn't care. All he needed to see was fire spreading across the deck like lightning to know they all had to get off the ship as fast as possible. They were in the Indian Ocean about 1,000 kilometers off the northern coast of Madagascar so even if their distress beacon wasn't picked up, they'd probably be spotted if a fireball the size of Abu Dhabi's Sky Tower shot into the night sky.

"ABANDON SHIP! ALL HANDS ABANDON SHIP!" he screamed into the P.A. Crewmen were running across the decks around the fire and beelining for the lifeboats. Steig fumbled around for the switch to activate the distress beacon, glanced at it long enough to make sure it was broadcasting, then kept his eyes locked on the deck's fire as he squeezed the radio handset. "MAY DAY MAY DAY MAY DAY THIS IS THE OUTBOUND CURIOSITY WE ARE GOING DOWN MAY DAY MAY DAY MAY DAY THIS IS THE OUTBOUND CURIOSITY ALL HANDS ABANDONING SHIP REQUEST IMMEDIATE ASSISTANCE SHIP IS ON FIRE AND IN DANGER OF EXPLODING MAY DAY MAY DAY MAY DAY SHIP IS GOING DOWN POSITION IS... 10 DEGREES 48 MINUTES 19.6236

SECONDS SOUTH BY 58 DEGREES 54 MINUTES 22.5000 SECONDS EAST 10 DEGREES 48 MINUTES 19.6236 SECONDS SOUTH BY 58 DEGREES 54 MINUTES 22.5000 SECONDS EAST."

Then Steig angrily threw the handset across the bridge without care, where it smashed a computer screen with a sharp crackle. "Doesn't matter now," Steig laughed. Everything here would be underwater within the hour.

He ran outside, grabbing a portable radio and a personal photo of his son along the way. Some crew were already in a lifeboat and other crew members were lowering a second boat into the water. Steig didn't have to look back to feel the heat of the fire on his back. This was bad. How long did they have before the fire found its way into one of the ship's big oil tanks? If it did, the oil would burn for weeks. The crew were probably already dead, like scrambling to outrun a nuclear blast.

Steig paused at the lifeboat to see if he could make sure all his crew were accounted for. An explosion above deck hurled shrapnel—Steig lost his balance and he pinwheeled over the railing. Out of his peripheral, he saw a panicked crew member futilely grasp at him, but Steig was already sliding down the side of the ship. As he hit the water, a wave of pain shot through him, and he realized he'd broken his ankle. Maybe more.

Above him, the crew must have suspected they had seconds left, so someone shouted orders and the lifeboat dropped toward Steig, who dove down and off to one side as the keel raced toward him. He waited for the splash then resurfaced. A crewmate must have spotted Steig because he suddenly found himself yanked inside the lifeboat, all sound muted now save for the lifeboat's engine as they moved away from the lumbering steel giant that they had once called home. After a few minutes, the ship looked like a floating birthday cake.

Steig and his crew stared at the ship silhouetted against the night sky. Fire melted the steel bulkhead of a gargantuan container of oil, and it erupted like a volcano, its fire yawning into the sky.

Instantly, the lifeboat capsized and most of the crew's eardrums punctured from the shock wave. Somehow, Steig had been thrown clear out of the lifeboat—*had it broken in half?*—and he was now clawing his way back up to the surface, fighting the pain of his broken ankle. When he resurfaced, all he could see was a sky filled with fire. Metal and oil rained all around them. Some of the men had caught fire from the oil and were dipping below the surface to douse the flames. Few could keep that up before they'd run out of oxygen or energy.

As Steig looked at his crew struggling in vain for their last minutes of life, he regretted not having died instantly on his ship.

65

THANK YOU, COME AGAIN

Susan had only wanted to get some windshield wiper fluid. The birds had come back and crapped all over her car's windshield like they always did this time of year. Right when she was out of the stuff, you know? Classic. Susan didn't even want gas, just that magic blue fluid to keep her from manually washing her car window. Goddamned birds.

She went straight to the car supplies, aware that the clerk was watching her closely. Perhaps he'd been trained to watch everyone who didn't come in to buy gas. Who knows? It had always been a sketchy neighborhood and she'd heard this station had been robbed only a few weeks ago. Arizona was both an open carry and concealed carry state, so it was common to expect a gas station attendant to have some kind of firearm within reach. Because Susan was from Louisiana she wasn't alien to guns, but it bothered her that some cooked up meth head might try his luck on a paranoid trigger-happy station attendant and put Susan in the crossfire. She'd seen it happen once before and tried to steer clear of similar situations.

She walked up to the counter and put the blue fluid bottle on the counter. The gas station clerk eyed her carefully. "Is that all?"

"Yes." Handed him a crisp Andrew Jackson.

Convinced she wasn't going to pull anything funny, he rang her up. She glanced around the store. Mints, gum... coffee... hot dogs bathed in yellow light... 32 oz. slushies. His arm reached out to give her the change and four things happened simultaneously: the clerk missed her hand and dropped her change on the counter, the clerk's body fell off to one side (his head hitting the plastic cigarette case behind him), the station's glass window next to Susan shattered, and the wall behind the clerk was now spray painted with dark red chunks of flesh, bone, and skin.

The sound of the glass shocked Susan more than anything and she turned to see it. When she looked back, seeing the clerk on the ground, it took her a full two seconds before her hair stood on end and time slowed down to a crawl.

She dropped to the floor and pushed her way to the farthest wall, out of sight of the shooter.

Outside there was a lot of screaming. People were starting their cars back up, peeling out of the parking lot with smoky tires. She hadn't heard the shots, so there was no way of knowing where it had come from and whether the sniper had a silencer or whatever on his barrel. Snipers were never women, why was that?

After things quieted down and she had time to dwell on the craziness of it, Susan started to panic.

If the shooter had been close, would he come in here and finish the job? She frantically scanned the place for a back door, keeping her head as far to the ground as she could manage. At a minimum, she shouldn't draw attention to any activity in the store in case the shooter was wondering where to go next.

Susan realized with a pit in her stomach that there was no back door. Wasn't that a fire safety violation? Maybe there was a back door behind the counter, but there was no way she'd risk going anywhere near the windows again.

Seeing the bathroom door, she instantly crawled to it and pulled the door open, slid inside, bolted the door shut. She'd left her cell phone in the car—*stupid! Never again!*—and could only hope that somebody else had called 911. If she could just stay in here lon—

The door to the store squeaked open. *Bing bong.* Closed with a light clang.

She could hear footfalls. Was it the police? She didn't dare look. She was a fly on the wall, a flower, a small speck of dust not to be paid attention to...

"I know you're here," came a flat voice. "I almost tagged you, you little jackrabbit. Don't drag this on, okay? Just come out."

Susan's ears pounded and her breathing became too loud to bear. She forced her hands over her face to stop breathing, to stop existing, if it could save her life.

The footfalls came closer. She tried not to move a muscle, though every atom in her body was screaming to jet away from here. Shadows danced at the door's slit. Breathing.

"This door is opening," was all she heard. There was a long pause and then, "Okay."

The sound of a shotgun being cocked made her scream out despite herself. Now her cheeks were warm from tears she couldn't control. She sank to the floor, eyes screwed shut, putting her hands over her ears.

The door exploded in splinters across the bathroom floor and Susan let out a wail. After a moment's quiet, the footfalls shifted toward her.

What happened next was a blur. She heard shouting from outside, and the footfalls never came. More screaming, from *in* the store this time, gunfire, and then silence once more.

A policeman came into the bathroom with his gun drawn, then holstered it and said, "It's over. You're safe."

Susan looked up at him with a blank stare and wondered if she would ever own a car again.

66

NUCLEAR FAMILY

Mary hadn't been in the train accident, not even near it. Yet it didn't matter. Once the winds came across the nuclear rods, a huge area had been exposed. Hundreds of houses, maybe thousands. It wasn't as bad as Chernobyl, not right now. That said, containment was a hell of a lot more difficult.

The rods weren't supposed to be in Cape Cod anymore, but Yucca had refused to take them, so there they sat for years languishing like a coughing TB patient waiting for a hospital —*any* hospital—to take them. When approval came through, they hadn't wasted time transporting the rods in case someone changed their mind. One would assume they'd taken every precaution to prevent a train accident... but apparently not.

Mary swallowed bitterly. Who knew how much exposure she'd had? No point asking. They'd all know soon enough.

She rubbed the box package in her hands quietly, looking out the cloudy window. The kids were at school today and silence was all she could handle. The Lord loves peace and silence. Amen.

What would they say at church? Jenkins had a certificate of work he'd done for the pope himself. In a catholic family, devoutness was their stock in trade.

She squeezed the package hard, as if she could push back time like toothpaste from a tube. It was futile. Every path, every option, every choice... everything was bad.

Turning to the crucifix over the fireplace, she signed the cross, and said, "Forgive me, dear Lord." Then she opened the package, took out the pill, and swallowed it, wiping away any chance of a child they'd been trying for. If the price of going to hell was stopping a deformed child from being born, she could live with that. *These silent sins we carry,* she thought. *Embryonic euthanasia, a sick joke for a family bonding in a nuclear world.*

67

REGULAR GUY

"I won't be long." Marlo said, staring at her phone. Her daughter yawned in acknowledgement, leaning her head against the back seat window, eyes already half-closed.

Marlo got out, looking carefully both ways before crossing the parking lot to the phone store. She'd been paranoid about cars since her grandfather got out too fast on a highway shoulder and been struck dead in a heartbeat. Marlo shuttered at the thought of seeing him, or what was left of him. It was like this whenever she got out of a car or crossed a road now.

Inside, there wasn't but one person tending the store, an older thin gentleman with wire frame glasses. "Can I help you?" he asked, adjusting his glasses slightly.

"My phone is getting an awful signal. Can you look at it? I think it's the SIM card."

"Sure thing." He took the phone.

Marlo glanced back out at the car, her daughter's head over the seat. *She's so tired. Long day at school, I guess.*

As the man tinkered with her phone and pulled up her account information, Marlo looked at his face more closely. His dark blue eyes, intense and close together, were circled with a muted grey limbic ring. His face was passive and calm.

Marlo's face flushed and she felt a rush of needle pricks all over her scalp. Marlo had learned long ago to trust her intuition. *The creator of Spiderman must have been a woman,* she thought. *Something is really wrong here, but I have no idea what.*

She nonchalantly wandered around the store, stopping in front of a large poster behind a plastic frame. She made sure her back was turned away from the man and slyly watched him in the poster's reflection. His head was down, looking at her phone...

...and then he looked up. Stared at Marlo. Kept staring. Marlo felt tingles all over her head again. She had to get *out.*

Marlo turned around abruptly. "Can I get my phone back? I just realized I'm super late for something."

The man blinked, peering at her. "Of course. Here you go."

Marlo took the phone and suppressed an urge to run from the store. She got to the parking lot and walked directly in front of a passing car. She screamed as it screeched to a halt before her. The driver honked, with an unpleasant look.

The salesman watched Marlo scramble into her car. He thought for a moment that he had seen her trembling, too.

Pity, he thought. *Good candidate for Room #8.* He shrugged and wondered how long it would be until his dungeon could become a full house again.

68

10:07

The fumes were getting hotter and the air was suffocating. She realized the impossible was about to happen. She'd tried escaping down the stairway, but the area was as impassable as the other exits.

She'd thought of walking to the roof in the hope that some savvy pilot would land their helicopter, but she only made it two floors before the black smoke blinded her and made her puke up blood. She'd die before she'd make it to the rooftop.

The office floor—once bustling with hundreds of financial traders—was now vacant and oddly calm, even with the smoke.

She turned a corner and felt a breeze from a smashed window, scrambled over to it. The wind was blowing inside and offered a crisp sea breeze from the East River. She took it in.

The view was amazing from up here. The Empire State was the only building tall enough to match her altitude. If only there were a bridge...

With the heat and smoke pressing down behind her, she at last reached her epiphany: *this is the day I die. There is no hope for me. Smoke or heat... no one is coming.*

She'd always wondered what death would be like on the other side, though she was in no hurry to find out. She cried, grieving that she wouldn't get a chance to say goodbye to her

190 | ROSS PRUDEN

family, her friends... she stayed like that, near the window, crying until the smoke and heat grew stronger still.

In minutes, it would be unbearable. She would die in the flames or asphyxiate from the smoke. Either way, she was certain she wouldn't live much longer.

A calm came over her. She knew the end was coming. She also knew she had the final choice.

Pulling on the jutting glass to make a larger opening, she stood there for a moment. Her belly was turning in knots as everything inside her objected. She'd heard of skydivers who survived falls greater than this, but she had no such illusions that a landing on a concrete slab would end well.

She didn't want this. Yet, ultimately, it was her choice how.

She jumped.

69

DUST

The humidity of the rain forest was thick, but not
suffocating with its cool breeze over the pine trees.
Pilar made her way through the dense trail, winding
around ancient fallen tree trunks. She'd only been on this trail
for a half hour, but it had been a late start and she was already
hungry.

Pilar slowed down and looked for a good place to sit. A
long, low tree trunk was only feet off the trail. She carefully
placed her feet in the foliage so as not to fall into any invisible
holes. With so much foliage, it was hard to see the forest floor
and no solo hiker wanted to get a broken leg out here.

Placing her backpack on the ground, she sat down on the
trunk and paused to look around. Now that she was off the trail
enough to be out of sight, she was surrounded by greenery on
all sides. It was easy to imagine you were in prehistoric times.

Sitting quietly, she heard more buzzing of insects and
distant birds. She took a deep breath. *This* was the exquisite
place she'd hoped to find. Whatever was going on in her life,
she knew she could always come here and push everything
away for a time.

Her lunch was a PB&J, some crackers, and a little premium
teriyaki buffalo jerky she'd bought on the way up here. She took

a bite of the sandwich and relished the crunch of the peanuts in her teeth.

A large green fly buzzed around by her feet and finally landed on her leg. "Ouch!" she cried out as she felt it bite, and then shooed it away.

She heard a low buzzing which seemed to grow louder. *Trick of my mind,* she thought. The buzzing had been there the whole time, but she hadn't consciously noted it until now.

It's not a beehive buzz, she thought. *Sounds like a bunch of different flies.* Pilar looked around her. *Maybe a dead anima—*a body lay nearby.

—a human body.

Its torso was covered by thick underbrush, but the human hair was unmistakable. The head was face down. Flies were crawling all over it.

Pilar stifled her urge to vomit. This was a crime scene, right? Vomit could be tracked with DNA. *I could be a suspect.* Almost immediately she felt ashamed for being so self-absorbed.

She thought about the victim. Was it an errant hiker? Unlikely. An aimless meth addict? That made more sense. Could it be a drug death? An overdose? Surely, this person had a father and mother looking for them. Pilar knew what the right thing to do was.

Her next thought was chilling. What if this were a high-profile mob case? What if this body were never meant to be found... and she had found it? People don't act rationally, she knew, and killers probably had a monopoly on unpredictable revenge.

Yet she couldn't leave and not tell *someone.*

Pilar put her food away in her backpack and ensured she'd left no crumbs or any other identifiers like footprints. Then she got a long branch on the ground next to her and poked at the body.

The fleshy part of the head slid off the skull with a sickening suction sound. Pilar almost vomited but looked up into the sky and took in the green leaves waving back at her. *This poor person. At least they died in a beautiful spot.*

Still holding the branch, she blinked her eyes, shook her head, and lifted the hairy scalp off the ground. When it was firmly on the end of the branch, she slowly walked back to the trail. When she got back to the trail, she looked up and down the trail for anyone coming. Then she rested the scalp in plain view on the trail and extracted the branch. She walked back down the trail for a half a minute and hurled the branch deep into a forest underbrush. Not even an entire town full of police would find that branch.

Someone would find the body. But not Pilar. She'd never walk in these woods again.

70

UNDER YOUR SKIN

"She's under?" said the surgeon, entering the room. The anesthesiologist checked his instruments and looked at the surgeon directly, so the surgeon knew he was being addressed. "Yes, sir."

"Very well." The surgeon, Phil Hopkins, leaned over to see the woman's face, a tube taped in her mouth. He then turned again to face her protruded abdomen.

Phil grimaced. Most of the stuff he saw was straightforward, like tumors, a burst appendix here and there. But this... he gently rested his hand on her belly, which rose above the table by a foot. He caught Dr. Weather staring at the belly and Dr. Weather raised an eyebrow to him in response.

His patient was pregnant, or rather, she *appeared* to be. That was all he knew for the moment. No child could possibly gestate for longer than 11 months, what the patient had claimed. Originally, he'd thought her math was off, but she had remembered the exact day she would have conceived because her husband had only been home for one week leave and she'd had no other sexual encounters since then. Or so she said.

Many of the symptoms were simply off. She had no nausea, no enlarged breasts. If she were pregnant, even with a stillborn, it would surely have triggered the typical range of physical reactions. She couldn't have a tumor this large without it metastasizing. Could she?

Phil breathed out slowly. He was about to find out.

He made an incision to perform a cesarean on... well, on whatever the hell was inside her. The pediatric nurses were standing by with the relevant equipment.

First, the outside skin, the abdominal wall... and then...

The entire room was leaning in to get a first look.

"Uhhh," said Phil. "I'm going to have to make a bigger incision. Scalpel." A nurse handed him a scalpel. He sliced more up and past the patient's belly button. As he spread the skin apart, all he could see was a bloody mess. "Can we get some saline there, please?" Silently, another nurse squirted a warm stream of saline over the open cavity.

Dr. Weather moved his head closer. "Is that her uterus?"

Phil examined the smooth wet texture of the shiny ball. "No. No, it's too light for that."

The room fell silent. Phil had never seen anything like it. At least, he didn't want to believe he had.

Gingerly, he put his hand down between the skin and sphere. He felt around.

Dr. Weather thought aloud. "Has to be a tumor, then."

"Noooo," said Phil, distantly. He would need to make some more incisions. "It certainly looks like a tumor, yes. It's a cyst. Here, let's cut some more up here," he said, pointing at the upper abdomen.

Dr. Weather looked at him tentatively. "Going to leave a hell of a scar."

"Has to be done."

Dr. Weather cut more until Phil could feel all the way around the sphere. "Excellent. Now..." He reached in and under the sphere, gently pulling it up and out of the abdomen. It was slippery and Dr. Weather instinctively held the other sides to make sure it came out and didn't fall back onto the patient, or worse, onto the floor.

A peds nurse standing close by wheeled over the birthing

gurney, half expecting to see a stillborn child. Instead, all she saw was two doctors placing a large malleable slimy ball on the gurney.

"Dr. Hopkins? Any thoughts?" said Dr. Weathers.

Phil took a deep breath. "Before we sew her back up, would you please make an incision on this mass right here?" Phil said, pointing to the cyst's epicenter.

"18 pounds," intoned the nurse. Phil's head was racing, *If a baby were inside this... freakishly huge placebo, so it would surely be a mutation. But it hadn't been in her uterus. Or had it?*

Once again, the room shifted to look. Dr. Weathers felt a bead of sweat trickle down behind his right ear as he sliced lengthwise. He swatted away an irrational fear of a bloody baby's hand darting out to claw at him.

He put his thumbs on either side of the opening and parted it slowly. Phil looked over his shoulder and inside the gap. He shook his head. "That's one for Guinness, everyone," he said, returning to take care of the lonely patient on the table. "Our poor patient was 'impregnated' with an 18-pound baby full of tapeworms."

Dr. Weathers felt he'd been punched in the stomach. "Oh my god... there must be... *thousands* of larvae in here."

"My rabbits have gotten these," Phil continued, checking for any remaining tapeworms in the abdomen. "Must have gotten accidentally involved in the life cycle."

Dr. Weathers knew they'd take photographs of this thing, for the history books. Of course they would. But this was one memory he wished he could drop into a mental oubliette. He'd need a lot of whiskey tonight to get to sleep.

FAIRY TALE

THE BEST SHIP THAT EVER WAS

T he very first ship ever made was about the length of a child's hand and the boy's name who owned it is now lost to the currents of time. The ship loved his boy and whispered to him, *I am the best ship that ever was. Now you must take what I am and make me better. Make me stronger, make me prettier, make me something worthy of the great waves I float over.*

The boy listened and remembered. When he grew to be a man, the man took this simple ship—an old piece of wood that barely resembled anything we know of as a ship—and carved something new. This next ship was slightly longer, slightly stronger, and a little smoother around the edges. He gave it to his daughter to play with and she loved the ship. She played with it all the time. And the ship soon whispered to her, *I am the best ship that ever was. Now take what I am and make me better. I want to be stronger, prettier, and travel farther than your father's ship ever did.*

The daughter listened and remembered. She grew to be a mother of her own and made ships for all her children. And the children loved their ships. Each ship in turn whispered to the children, *I am the best ship that ever was. Make me better.*

The years passed. The children became parents and grandparents, and *their* children became parents and grandparents. All the while, new ships were made, each better than the one before it.

Then one day, a man noticed how much joy his child had playing with his toy ship. After the child had gone to sleep for the night, the man walked out to the ocean and gently placed the toy ship at his feet, letting it float calmly in the evening tide. He watched it float, never letting it get out of reach.

And the toy ship whispered to him, *I can be better than even this. I can be the best ship that ever was.*

The man listened. He built a toy ship larger than had ever been seen. It wasn't only larger than all the other ships, but it was larger than most *children*, too. When he was done, the ship was just an old piece of wood and twine that barely resembled anything we know of as a ship. Even so, his son was able to sit on this ship and float upon the great waves.

The ship was happy. The man was happy. The boy was happy. This lasted for a time...

Then one day, as the boy became a man and had himself grown too old to float on his toy ship, the ship whispered to the man's son, *Make me better. I want to be better.*

The son listened and over the years built a better ship, a ship larger than himself.

The years passed, and each generation built a better ship than the one before it. Each ship was indeed the best ship that ever was.

This continued for hundreds of years... until the day that ships were no longer content to hug the shores of their motherland. *I want to sail to the horizon,* the ships would whisper eagerly to their masters.

Their masters listened. They built ships that took them across lakes, down rivers, then seas. Finally, the builders decided it was time to make a ship so big that it truly would be the best ship that ever was. They built a ship to float all the way across the ocean.

The man took his friends and they floated on the ship long, long distances on the water, so far they didn't even see land for months at a time. And the ship was happy as it whispered to the man, *You have truly built the best ship that ever was.*

At last, the men whispered back to the ships, "We can make you even better. We can make you travel farther, and make you safer. You will be prettier and faster, and you will be the best ship that ever was." The ship beamed with joy, for the man indeed built a ship that not only sailed out to the horizon, but carried smaller ships *inside* it. Some ships were so big they were even called, 'floating cities'.

Yet men were not content to stop there. They built ships that carried them up above the water and into the sky. Finally, they built ships that went out into space and to the moon.

As the astronaut sat inside his spaceship waiting to fly into the air like a lightning bolt, he heard his ship whisper to him, *You have now truly made me into the best ship that ever was. I can take you far away, I can go very fast, and I can keep you safe and bring you home again.*

And the man whispered back, smiling, "I am already thinking of how I can make you better, stronger, faster..."

That is how men and women built toy ships so big and so powerful that they sailed across the stars and explored new suns and continued making better ships. And the ships always said to their masters, *We are the best ships that ever were.* And the men and women would always reply, "You have made us into the best men and women who ever were. Thank you."

The ships were happy. The men and women were happy. And they travelled together, forever, across the universe, all the while making bigger and better toy ships to play with.

72

MOONBOW

Once upon a time a horse named Mabel went grazing in a field beyond her home and she soon lost track of the daylight. In the evening hours past her bedtime, she looked up and was startled to see a statue of a peacock and below it, a poem engraved into the stone:

Here I rest below the light,
Where sun and moon do sometimes fight,
Awaiting for a time between
To let me once again be seen.
—Horatio Fantail

The horse looked up in the sky. Although the sun was setting, the moon was also very high and glowing in the sky.

A bright light made the horse close its eyes and pull away and when it opened its eyes, the horse saw a beautiful unicorn standing in front of her.

"What are *you* doing here?" said the horse.

"I am the first visitor to Horatio's party," said the unicorn.

"What party?" asked the horse.

"The Twilight Party, of course," said the unicorn. The unicorn looked up into the night sky. "When the day is the longest of the year, the Ghost of Horatio the peacock comes to say hello and we have a party for him."

"Can I come, too?" asked the horse with excitement.

"Are you a horse?" asked the unicorn.

"Yes."

"And are you a *kind* horse?" asked the unicorn.

"Yes, very kind."

"And are you a kind horse who likes to see ghosts of peacocks?" asked the unicorn, with a silly smile. "Yes, that's me!" said the horse.

"Why, then, you are invited to the party!" said the unicorn.

The horse galloped in glee around the statue and the unicorn danced a silly dance. When the horse came back to the statue, another bright light appeared. When it faded, a stunning pegasus stood majestically before them.

"I do hope I'm not late," boomed the deep voice of the pegasus.

"Not at all, your highness," replied the unicorn. Turning to the horse, the unicorn said, "This is... uh..." and it leaned over to the horse and whispered, "Sorry, I forgot to ask your name!"

The horse laughed a funny whinny and said, "I'm Marvelous Mabel." and then she did a deep bow on her front legs.

"I am Gliding Gilda," said the pegasus with equal grace, and a bow. "It's a pleasure to meet you." The unicorn leaned over to Mabel and whispered, "I'm Silly Sally." and then, with a giggle,

"Nice to meet you, Mabel!"

Another light, and it faded, too. Before them were a unicorn pegasus and a unicorn pegasus pony. "Oooooooooooo," said the horse in awe.

"Hello, everyone!" whinnied the unicorn pegasus in a high, quick voice. Looking at Mabel, he said, "Who's the new mare?"

Mabel introduced herself and the unicorn pegasus replied, "I am Hectic Henrietta, and this here is my daughter, Quiet Quinn."

Quiet Quinn said, "Yo."

Gliding Gilda flapped her wings to get everyone's attention. "It appears we're all here now. Shall we recite the incantation?"

Henrietta looked at the sky. The sun had set, but light from the moon lit up the other half of the sky. It was straight up twilight. "Looks like we can do it anytime now."

Mabel whispered to Sally, "What's an in-cam-a-tay-shun?"

"You all say the same thing together," Sally whispered back. "Don't worry if you don't know the words. Just move your mouth and nobody will know."

The horses stood with all their hooves together and closed their eyes. Mabel peeked with one eye and Sally winked at her playfully. Together they said,

"Horatio, come between the light,
Where sun and moon once more will fight,
How your colors in crystals bright,
And we will greet you now, tonight."

Mabel watched as a rainbow and moonbeam met in the sky to form a *moonbow*, a collection of softer rainbow colors with moonbeam sparkles sprinkled throughout. The moonbow fell quietly to the ground, and the sparkles grew brighter until they solidified into crystals. As Mabel gazed into the crystals, she saw a ghost of a peacock emerge...

Gilda nodded to the peacock, and said, "Welcome back, Horatio. We have all missed you dearly."

The peacock fanned out his beautiful tail and bowed to everyone in the circle one at a time.

The Twilight Party had begun, and Mabel was very happy she had gotten lost while grazing that night.

73

UNICORN TRAPS

A mong all the stars, there is one—our sun—that some have described as a chariot hurdling across the sky with stallions furiously pulling it and a driver cracking his whip to keep them at pace. There is, however, another tale —a tale of shooting stars... and unicorns.

Unicorns, you see, are very magical creatures and can fly across the world at great speeds, often without us even knowing they were there at all. They live inside the moon in a beautiful, lush forest of their own and they travel to Earth whenever they feel their magic is needed. They travel simply by raising their horns upwards, closing their eyes and humming their magical song.

One time, some of the younger unicorns overheard the song before they were ready to use it and travelled to Earth without asking permission. The unicorn responsible for them—her name was Tilly—became frantic to return them without upsetting the other unicorns. So Tilly came to Earth to look for them, traveling the whole globe on shooting stars, but without any luck. Finally, she sat down by herself and wept.

It was at that time that a young man, napping under a tree within earshot, awoke to the sound of Tilly's sobbing. The young man had fallen asleep in the tree's sleepy shade and, sensing someone was in trouble, looked over. He was shocked to see a unicorn curled up at the base of a tree nearby. Unicorns, you see, are not meant to be seen by anyone other than their own kind. Tilly was too sad to care. Her little unicorns could be in grave danger.

The young man walked up to the unicorn cautiously, trying to soothe it.

"I won't hurt you," said Tilly, and smirked at the shock on the man's face. "Yes, I can talk your language."

"You're... a unicorn."

"At your service. My name is Tilly Younger. What is your name?"

"Matt."

"Is that it? Just Matt?"

"Matt Watkajtys."

"Well, that's a mouthful, isn't it?"

"What. Kai. Tis. Kinda unique, but you get used to it," he stammered. "Were you weeping?"

"Yes. My poor babies..." Tilly explained the whole story.

Matt was a kind young man and had no tolerance for letting a unicorn weep without offering some sort of help, however small.

"I am so tired," Tilly said. "I have been flying across the sky looking for them, but I need to rest. Perhaps you could continue the search?"

"Sure! But how?"

Tilly explained to Matt about the magic in her horn, and how she could imbue Matt with its magical power, if only for a day. Matt would be able to go anywhere he pleased, as far as the Moon or the Sun, and even all the way out to Jupiter and beyond. He could travel instantly or glide by in slow motion, whatever he desired.

"I have looked for them all day long," repeated Tilly. "I cannot see them at all."

Matt stared at Tilly's glowing horn. "What about at night?"

Tilly looked at him in puzzlement. "Why would I? How could I see them?"

Matt smiled widely and said, "I have a plan. Let me go look for them."

No sooner had he said it and Matt had zoomed away with magical unicorn dust falling quietly to the ground where he had been standing moments before.

Matt flew over the sky until the sun was setting and then watched the sun crawl into its nightly den. As he floated in the night breeze, he imagined he was traveling faster than any plane or rocket. He glanced over the Earth for hours until he finally spotted a tiny sparkle of rainbow-colored sparks on the horizon. Zooming over to it, he saw two of the unicorn ponies staring up into the sky. He looked up to see what they were looking at—a shooting star. He looked back and saw their horns glowing. Once more, Matt smiled, a better plan now forming.'

After convincing the baby unicorns that Tilly was so sad about them leaving, they agreed to return and stay with Tilly until he could return with the rest of their friends.

What happened next became part of unicorn lore forever afterward. Matt jetted up to a long defunct satellite, nudged it into Earth's atmosphere and rode it across the sky like a galloping horse. As he surfed over the dark globe, it was easy to spot unique rainbow sparkles on the ground below. Matt popped down, talked to the ponies, got them to go back to Tilly, then found another old satellite to turn into a sparkling rodeo horse.

In barely a few hours, Matt had travelled across the Earth and collected all 23 unicorn ponies. Tilly was kicking her hind legs with joy.

"I have a gift for you, Matt Watkajtys," Tilly said.

"Oh?"

"I want to show you something very special."

With that, Tilly let Matt climb on her back and took him to see all her favorite stars in the galaxy.

74

CLEMENTINE

Once upon a time, there was a fair maiden Clementine. She was pleasant and pretty and she went wherever she wanted and met all manner of folk who were eager to talk to such an open soul as she.

That was the problem with our dear, fair Clementine—she had traveled for so long and met so many people and done so many interesting things that she was always lost. She had forgotten where she was, who her family was, or even who *she* was. Every morning Clementine would awake in a new guest bed, in a new city with new hosts. Not that it really mattered, since everyone liked her, and they assumed that one so merry would never have a hard time keeping track of every changing detail.

One day, however, Clementine yearned to find her way back home again. Her aimless path had become weary; she found a renewed sense of purpose in discovering where she had ended up. She wanted to regain contact with people who knew her well enough not to be afraid of angering her if they chastised her for not remembering their names (a frightfully more common occurrence as the years stretched on).

And so, our fair Clementine did the one thing she had never had to do—she bought a map.

"Why do you need a map, fair Clementine?" asked the shopkeeper. "You have everything you need at your request, and everyone welcomes you wherever you go."

"I need to find a place where I *belong*," replied Clementine. "It is not enough to always meet kind strangers. I need to find my family."

"Very well," said the shopkeeper. He spread her new map out wide. "We are in Vogelland, here. Where is your home?"

Clementine stared at the map quietly. "I cannot remember," she said in a hushed tone.

"You don't even remember your city's *name?*" said the shopkeeper, with puzzlement.

"I was young when I left and had no need to know at the time."

"My dear girl, if you want to find your home, a place where you feel in harmony with others, you don't need a map to find the way. You must look inside. You must find the place in your heart where you feel right. Once you find your way in your heart, you will find your way home on this map."

Clementine thought about that. "I remember fishing with my father. That was a special time in my childhood that I still cherish today. My father would take me to a calm eddy at the fork in a wide river. Everyone there wore red silk robes."

The shopkeeper smiled and pointed to a part on the map. "Then you must come from Hebt, here. In Hebt, the river splits in two and a nearby factory specializes in making red dye. There you will surely find your family, and your home."

Clementine thanked the shopkeeper and left. For the first time she could remember, she had a destination in mind: she was about to find out who she was.

75

OZ 2.0

"Kill the wicked witch?" Dorothy repeated. Killing wasn't something Dorothy ever thought she could do. This was asking a lot.

"Immediately!" said the Wizard. His temples flared dramatically.

Now it seemed Dorothy had no way around this: if she wanted to get back home, she'd have to dispatch a terrible witch.

"What are you going to do?" said the Cowardly Lion.

"She has been after us from the start," Dorothy said, and whipped out her smartphone to pull up Wikipedia. "Let's see who we're going up against."

"What is that infernal thing?" bellowed the Wizard.

"In Kansas, we have our own sort of magic." For once, the Wizard was at a loss for words. "Let's see..." Dorothy said absentmindedly, flicking her hand up on the screen. "Early years... entry into magic... rise to power... leadership style... creature control... phobias... ah, here we have it: 'severely aquaphobic.'"

"Been there," said the Tin Woodman under his breath.

"What does that mean?" said Scarecrow.

"She hates water," said Dorothy, not looking up.

"Hold on. A lady that egomaniacal *must* have a Twitter account." A moment later, "Yes, there she is. Oh, how sad... she only has four followers. And it looks like two of them are bots." She scanned the witch's tweets. "hellfire... cranky... cut of coffee again... terrorize the munchkins... Not the most pleasant lady, is she?"

The Cowardly Lion shivered all over as if an icicle had tiptoed across the bottom of his spine. "Most definitively not."

"Yes, here: 'Again with the hygiene! Impossible to keep the lady bits clean when even the smallest amount of water kills you. #BadMagic'."

For the first time, Dorothy had a wicked grin. This was going to be easy. After a Google search, Dorothy read aloud, " 'All witches in Oz are equally aqua-phobic, and with good reason—water has a tendency to liquidate them.' Ha!"

Dorothy looked up and to the left, as if reading a cue card just outside her peripheral vision. Then looked back down at the phone. "I wonder if Amazon has one..."

The Wizard furrowed his brows more, perturbed that nobody was fearing him at this moment. Dorothy stood flanked by her three companions huddled around her phone's screen.

"Here. A cheap model's available, seems decent enough. But, uh... whoa! Look at those delivery costs!" Scarecrow glanced around, not seeing any delivery costs.

"No thank you," Dorothy continued. She bit one side of her mouth.

"Craigslist," she announced, and flipped her phone sideways to type in the URL. More typing, then, "Uh huh... this one's still available. Great. Phone number... Sweet! Okay..." Dorothy switched to a text. Reading out loud, "Saw your ad for a humidifier. Can pay instantly with PayPal. Are you near the Emerald City?"

Almost instantly, the reply came back. " 'It's yours for $20. Southeast of Chinatown. Will leave out front.' "

Within seconds, Dorothy had sent the money.

"So we're going to get it, right, Dorothy?" asked the Lion, turning to the door.

Dorothy couldn't wipe the smile off her face. "Not so fast, Lion. It gets better. Watch this." Dorothy pulled up TaskRabbit. "I'm hiring someone local to collect this humidifier, deliver it to her castle, and attach a note that says..." And then she spoke more slowly as she composed it, "hope... You... Enjoy this! saw... Your tweet... last week... and thought... I'd send... this over... It's... a magical... way... to stay... clean... without... touching... water... just set... it up... at night... and you'll be... clean... the next day... Sincerely... your... most... faithful... admirer."

Scarecrow blinked for a moment. "You think she's dumb enough to fall for it?"

"We'll find out tomorrow," responded Dorothy, pocketing her phone. "I'll check her friends' Facebook page tomorrow for anything about her death. And Twitter is bound to have some new hashtag about the Wicked Witch being dead. Plus," Dorothy added furtively, "a woman will try almost anything to keep her hoo-ha from stinking up the place."

76

THE BOY WHO HEARD WOOD WHISPER

Once upon a time there was a boy who could hear wood talk to him as plainly as you hear me talking to you now.

Some woods were chatty. Others were tight-lipped. The boy even called a few kinds of wood his friends.

One day, as he was sitting in the forest listening to the trees jabber on, he overheard one Redwood talk about an aging Maple. "He won't last through the spring, I fear," said the Redwood. "He's lived a good long life, seen three centuries of humans grow up all around him. He loves all those children dearly."

"Is there nothing we can do to help him?" said the boy, glancing over at the Maple.

"Nothing at all," said the Redwood, surprised that the boy had been listening. "The only thing we can do now is offer him love until the end of his days."

So the boy went to talk to the Maple himself. "Aren't you feeling okay?" said the boy. The Maple smiled by swaying his branches a little. "I feel okay now, but I won't be around much longer."

The boy was very sad. The Maple saw how sad the boy was and it moved him. "I've seen many young boys like you play in this forest and climb among my branches. You have always been so good to me and now that my time has come, I would like to repay that debt."

"How?" said the boy.

"If you take an ax and chop me down, you may turn me into lumber to build a house for your family."

"That is too kind an offer for me to accept..." said the boy. "I could not bear to do that to you."

Then the Maple smiled and said, "I would rather die now knowing that my body has been made into a beautiful house that you could live in, instead of dying next year, slowly and with futility."

The boy talked with the Redwoods and Oaks and Manzanitas about it, and they all agreed it was a good idea. So the boy thanked the Maple, tearfully said goodbye, then cut the majestic tree down to build a house with his parents that one day he would raise a family of his own in.

Years passed, and though the Maple had died long before, the boy could still hear its soft cooing hum in all the walls and roof and floorboards throughout his house. They all seemed to whisper, "Thank you."

The boy's house was the only place he ever really felt at home.

77

LARS THE SWORDSMAN

In a kingdom many years and miles away from here, there lived a young man named Lars Yargen. He'd always wanted to be a swordsman and begged his father every season to send him off to be taught the ways of wielding steel. Every year Lars would say to his father, "Please, father, can you take me to be a swordsman?" And his father, fearing that his son would fall into a dangerous path, would always respond, "I need you with us here at home. Give up these foolish yearnings and try to be happy tending the soil with your brothers and sisters."

Year after year, Lars pleaded and year after year, his father dissuaded him. On and on it went and as each year passed, Lars' brothers and sisters left the farm to pursue their own careers. Eventually only Lars and his father were left to look after the farm.

Then, one year, Lars' father fell ill and it became clear he would not be able to tend to the field for an entire season. Immediately, his father dispatched Lars to the nearest village to find workers for the farm before their crops would wither. Lars went into the city as instructed but, having never left the farm, was new to the ways of the world and it wasn't long until someone had tricked Lars out of all his money, leaving him with no way of returning home.

Lars appealed to anyone who would listen about his father's plight, and finally someone listened to his tale. Little did Lars know, the people he had confided in were planning on taking the farm from the helpless old man. Soon Lars' father found himself kicked off his own land with nothing more than the clothes on his back.

Bereft and wandering, some travelers felt sorry for Lars' father and gave him a ride to the village, where he found his son also roaming the streets. They embraced each other fondly and then Lars' father said, "I am sorry I stopped you from learning how to use swords or you could have fought back the interlopers who took our farm. Still, it is good we have each other and between the two of us, we can make a living here in town until we can find your brothers and sisters to help us."

Having used sticks as swords all his childhood, Lars took to entertaining crowds with his imagined swordplay. He was quite good at it, and Lars' father played the evil villain out to defeat the heroic upstart. It went on like this for a time until Lars caught the eye of a swordsman employed by the King.

"You seem too young to be out here on the streets feigning swordplay for children," the swordsman remarked. When Lars told him his story, the swordsman offered to help. "I will not retake your lands, for that is not within the scope of my duty, but I can offer to teach you how to fight with a sword properly so that you may settle your own affairs."

Enthusiastically, Lars accepted. With unequalled devotion, Lars studied day and night every aspect of swordplay until he became better than his royal mentor.

"Your dedication is beyond measure," said the swordsman at last. "Your training is officially complete."

Lars was ecstatic to hear this and took his sword back to his farm, telling the men there to leave his farm immediately. When they refused and challenged him to a duel, he beat them without effort and threw them off his land once and for all.

With the robbers now gone, Lars could safely welcome back his father and tend to the land happily in the knowledge that he could defend the land from anyone foolish enough to try to take it.

78

GANDO

Once upon a time, there was a friendly troll named Gando. He wasn't your typical troll demanding ransoms for those trying to cross a bridge, but rather an intensely curious creature with a fondness for collecting things. He collected seashells, he collected stones, he collected anything he thought interesting.

The problem with Gando was that, as he grew older, he became a little crazy and collected far more things than he could use or even store. So Gando, being the big and powerful troll he was, collected so many seashells that there were no seashells left for anyone else to see.

At first, this was not a terribly important problem for anyone to address. Eventually, somebody did realize that seashells were no longer on the beaches but that was about the end of the problem. Seashells were not important enough, it seems, for anyone to investigate their disappearance.

Then one day, someone was trying to build a rock fence around their property and could find no more rocks for their fence. Seashells are a decorative item, and while seashell necklaces and other accoutrement had mysteriously disappeared, the sudden lack of *rocks* was undoubtedly something to take note of. Many people discussed what the disappearance of rocks could mean and what might be causing it.

Meanwhile, Gando had created a house of seashells and rocks the size of a small city. When he had run out of seashells and rocks, Gando moved on to other objects to collect. Soon it was not long until Gando had begun to collect *air itself*. Nobody was quite sure *how* he was able to do it, but the people realized that it was becoming harder to breathe.

Finally, one of the leaders of the nearby villages—a gentle woman by the name of Yole—went on a quest to find this friendly troll she had heard so much about. When she at last found Gando, she was amazed at the palatial city Gando had built for himself. It was made of seashells and rocks, but also of flowers and grass and twigs of all sizes. Gando had been very, very busy.

Yole politely knocked on Gando's door and Gando—being the friendly troll he was—invited Yole in for tea, his favorite thing.

After he had served his guest a fine helping of elderberry scones and chamomile tea, Yole broached the sensitive subject of Gando's... collection.

"I wonder, my dear Gando, if you might consider letting others see your collection of seashells and rocks and what not."

"Certainly!" said Gando. "They have only to visit my city to appreciate the beauty of it all."

"But is it not difficult for people to travel to your city if they have no air to breathe?"

At this, Gando was quite puzzled. He had collected air because it was so beautiful to smell in all its forms and surely there was enough for everyone. Yole explained that the air Gando had taken was making it hard for others to live.

"I do not want to give up my air!" exclaimed Gando. "It is lovely, and its smells make me so happy."

Yole smiled at Gando. His head was large, but his brain was the size of a small corn kernel. "If we cannot breathe, Gando, we will *all* die. And there will be nobody left to come visit you for tea."

Gando frowned. "I do not want that," he said.

"Besides," continued Yole, "if you collect everything in the world, there will be nothing to talk about over tea, as nobody will even remember what seashells looked like. Or rocks. Or flowers. However, if you *share* all the things you have collected and let everyone have a little bit of it, then we can all come to tea and show you the things we have collected on our own."

Gando's eyes grew wide with excitement. "That would make it very fun to have other people to tea!"

And so it was that Gando, the very friendly and not malicious troll, set loose a hurricane of wind to scatter all the seashells and rocks and flowers and twigs across the land in order that everyone could have a little of each to themselves.

There Gando sits today at his humble little spot in the woods, waiting for his next visitor to come along to show the pretty seashells they found on their beach, to present him a lovely bouquet of flowers, to gift him a delightful fairy house made of small twigs, and usher in the most lovely breath of summer air, the one that reminds us all of that special day when our grandmother first made us cookies and milk.

79

AMONG THE FOREST

I n a forest deep in the woods not so long ago, there lived a woman and her family. The woman's name was Tell and, as is the case with most daughters, she loved her family a great deal. Unfortunately, nobody in her family was very well educated since their house was many miles to the nearest school. They were so far away from civilization that people had been born and died in their family without anyone from the big city coming to record that information in their big books. It was only when Tell's aunt had fallen ill with the Sugar Disease that they had gotten the medications to keep her aunt alive and well. Only Tell was brave enough to administer the medication.

"Thank you, my child," Tell's aunt would say with a smile. "You are truly our family's savior."

Their house had weathered many seasons and the roof was falling apart from rain. Tell's brothers were sent to find jobs so they could raise money to fix the roof. Soon the brothers returned saying no work could be found and the whole family fell into deep despair, not knowing what other options remained.

Eventually, Tell's family turned to the only thing they had left—praying to their God. Tell's younger brother suspected that some sacrifice might be seen as more favorable, so he slaughtered one of their hens and offered the chicken during a prayer.

Tell happened to be quite fond of music and would often go to an isolated part of the forest to play her flute alone, then conclude with prayers to her God. When the chicken's sacrifice didn't seem to work, Tell even cut off some of her hair and laid it on a large tree trunk in the forest, and prayed her God would hear her pleas.

"If only good fortune would smile upon us, I would do anything for you. I would *give* anything to you. I hope you accept this humble gift."

As if by magic, a small man no more than two feet tall emerged from the forest. He came up to the tree trunk and whispered to her, "I have heard your call. You shall soon have a reward for your troubles." And then he scurried away, leaving Tell to wonder if she'd seen a troll, a goblin, or a demon.

Tell had no need to wonder for long because upon her return, one of her brothers was celebrating finding a job at a logging factory not far away. Convinced the little man had somehow granted her wish, and hoping not to spoil the spell, she hurried back to the woods the next afternoon and repeated her flute-playing and praying ritual. She stopped and waited.

The leaves nearby rustled and again the Little Man revealed himself.

"What have you brought me today?" he said.

"What would you like, Little Man?"

"I require your smallest finger," said the Little Man. "For that, you will have great fortune."

Tell was shocked at this request—indeed the price seemed too high—but she weighed it against the depths of love for her family. Her smallest finger was a tiny price to ensure everyone's happiness. So Tell took a knife the Little Man gave her and cut off her smallest finger.

Again, upon her return, another brother had also been given a job at the factory and their lives were starting to become better. Not *all* was better, though. Their roof's holes still dripped water and the breezy weather had only made their grandmother grow even more frail.

On the third day, Tell visited the Little Man again to ask to save her grandmother's life. However, this time the Little Man required a *hand* as payment. Tell refused him, saying this was too much, and the Little Man cursed her and returned to the forest.

Tell worried she had upset the fates and that same night; her grandmother indeed fell into a deep sleep from which she would not arise. Tell knew instantly she was to blame for this tragedy. As soon as she was able, she ran out to the forest.

"*Please*, Little Man!" she pleaded. "Tell me what I can do to stop all this. If you wish for my hand, I will gladly sever it here, before you."

The Little Man heard her and emerged once more. His look was stern and unwavering. "The time for a hand has passed. Unless you wish the same fate to befall all your family, you must now bring me your *grandmother*." The Little Man disappeared without a word.

Tell cried all night. Yet she knew she must heed the Little Man's dictate else more tragedy would rain upon their whole family. The next morning, she rose before everyone was awake and carried her grandmother's limp and frail body into the woods and left it on the large tree stump where she had once prayed to her God.

When Tell returned home, she went to her bed and feigned sleep. Soon everyone's voices were raised in alarm at their grandmother's disappearance. Tell told nobody about the Little Man but said she had heard someone in the night walk out the door. Desperately, Tell's brothers searched for her, but their grandmother's body was never found. When Tell visited her tree stump later that day, her grandmother's body was also missing with no trace of where she had been taken.

The Little Man came out of the woods again, saying, "How much do you love your family?"

"Very much, Little Man," Tell replied. "I would do anything for them."

"I will let you be and guarantee your fortunes from this day forward, but you must do one more thing."

"What must I do?"

"Someone in your family will come close to death. You must *not* intervene. If you do this, all your troubles will go away forever."

That evening, before the brothers came home from work, Tell heard her aunt fall on the floor. She ran in, about to help her up, but remembered the Little Man's words and hesitated. Her aunt, unable to get off the ground, mumbled, "Hon, my medication... I need my medication..." The Sugar Disease had caught up to her at last.

Tell sat down on the ground before her aunt, pulled her knees up to her chin and wept, watching her aunt's life drain away. After an interminable time, her brothers returned from work and found their aunt on the floor with Tell next to her, unable to speak. Their aunt was still alive, but in an eternal sleep.

Before long, a person from the Big City came by saying they were going to help Tell's family by giving them money to take care of their aunt. The amount of money wasn't much, certainly not to most people, but to Tell and her family, it was like finding buried treasure.

Thus, while Tell and her brothers lived the rest of their lives in relative comfort, they also had to ensure their aunt stayed alive as long as possible in her lifeless state. Tell never played the flute again and never went into the woods to ask for any more wishes from the Little Man who had given them so much, yet taken so much away.

80

THE BEACH AND THE SURF

Once upon a time, the Beach was sleeping (as it always does) when the Surf came crashing in that day and woke up the Beach.

"Why did you wake me up today?" said the Beach. "I was so happy lying here napping."

"What mysteries have you had today?" asked the Surf.

"A small child sat upon my shore this morning and built a castle out of me."

"Did they dig deeply?" queried the Surf.

"Not so much as they usually do. It has been many months since I have had someone digging so deeply that they find water."

"I bring news of a Mystery Seeker."

"Oh?" said the Beach. "Do tell!"

"A very large ship pulled up and dropped anchor last week. They sent divers deep into my waters."

"And what were they looking for?"

"An old ship that sank many years ago. So old it is blanketed in moss and coral."

"Did they find it?"

"Yes! They went exploring all around it and pulled up coins and other trinkets."

"So you let them have their treasures, then?"

"Of course," said the Surf. "There are many ships still far beyond their reach."

The Beach agreed. "Every day someone finds something new along my beach. If they only knew what was directly below me, they would never stop digging until they found it."

"Why? What is directly below you?"

The Beach whispered, "A family of dinosaurs. They came years ago and perished here when they could not escape the ravine they had fallen into."

The Surf laughed with glee. "I like having all these mysteries for them to find, don't you?"

"Yes," said the Beach. "I'll be very sad when they find *all* the mysteries, though. They need to have a lack of knowledge to appreciate all the things they already know."

"True," agreed the Surf. "That day is very far off, you know. Let us enjoy the mysteries we both have for as long as we can."

"Your mysteries will be the hardest of all to find," said the Beach. "Will you promise to still come visit me when all my mysteries have been found?"

"Of course!" said the Surf. And with that, the Surf returned back out to sea and the Beach went back to its nap.

DRAMA

81

LAWN CARE

Too *dang long*, Clint thought, his rocking chair creaking softly. *Grass ain't no jungle.*

Clint's lawn was far from perfect but at least he did look after it on occasion. It was his neighbor's lawn. Edith Sangle was a crotchety harpy and a thorn in Clint's side for more than two decades. Edith's gaunt son was but a glimmer in the scenery, too, an unfortunate brand of slacker swimming in narcotics. It was well known.

He'd seen Edith sitting on the lawn all that week. Her green grass had been blanched by the Texan heat until it had been more corn field than manicured lawn. Why did she always let it get so bad? Maybe the gin she swigged each morning? Maybe lack of sleep from kicking out her boyfriend at 2 AM in her slurred screaming rants? No matter. Clint had to look at her wretched lawn every day. A bystander ten feet away could have heard Clint grinding his teeth.

Where had he retired his shotgun? In 2 minutes flat, he could make Edith shorter by a foot. That might not fix the lawn problem but the image of it tickled him. Knowing he had that power etched a smile into his stone face.

Edith's door opened, then her screen door.

Barely nine and already a sweltering 90°. Curtis watched

her amble across the porch, out onto the lawn, gin bottle in hand. She made no effort to wave at Curtis, though Curtis wasn't even sure what he'd do if she did.

Plopping into the chair in the tree's shade, Edith took an inhumanly long swig from her bottle. Sat there.

Well, Curtis thought, *I suppose I should take care of this.* He pushed himself out of his rocking chair and disappeared into his house, the screen door slam echoing across the sizzling pavement.

Edith took another swig. A car passed, a parent returning from dropping off their kid at school. The car turned into a driveway down the street, parked. The man went inside. For a time, the cicadas' song filled the air uninterrupted.

Curtis' screen door creaked open again, and Edith turned to look. Curtis was walking across the street toward her, something in his hand she couldn't make out. *Time I finally saw that eye doctor, I s'pose,* she thought.

When he finally got to her, his arm extended out... and she saw him holding a Mint Julep, her favorite drink. She smiled weakly, already feeling the effects of her gin. "Thank you, dear boy, that's mighty nice of you."

"Looked like you needed something cool. Hot day." Curtis stood there for a moment, then smiled, and walked back to his rocking chair.

"A hot day," she said.

82

SWERVE

Her arms were crossed, a cold and furrowed brow across her face like a mask.

George opened his mouth, then snapped it shut. Every answer he could think of meant trouble. The drive was a long and boring one and winter daylight always came earlier than he was used to. The kids were both fast asleep even though it was barely six.

"If you'd told me," Becca said, "I wouldn't have been angry at all. But going around me..."

George fleetingly thought of saying he was sorry, but he'd grown weary of the apology game. "I wouldn't have to go around you if you weren't always on my case about it." As soon as he said it, he knew it had been a misstep, but he couldn't help himself. It was out there now. She had to deal with it.

Her voice immediately got louder in reply. He knew he'd kicked the hornet's nest and regretted it. She might wake the kids, always a bad idea. She felt slighted so there was no way to get past this but deal with it head on. His fists clenched the steering wheel; he could feel a searing pain on his tongue as he absentmindedly bit into it. She was still laying into him.

What happened next flew by in a heartbeat: The deer stepped out onto the road and pondered George's approaching headlights—George stood on his brakes, swerved the wheel, and frantically tried correcting the car's spinning—the car's back bumper slid right past the deer—didn't even nick it—but the car flailed into a 360° loop—

The passenger side of the car lifted two inches off the ground, then plopped back down again with a bouncy thud.

Stillness.

No cars were on the road in either direction. The deer ambled off quietly behind them. George looked at his wife, now as wide-eyed as the deer. After a moment, they realized they were both still alive. A noise from the back seat reminded them that their kids were back there. They both turned. Jess was still fast asleep, her head at what appeared to be an extremely uncomfortable position, mouth ajar as always, but breathing fine. Kevin's eyes were open and glazed over. He looked at his parents, blinked. Then let out a burp. Closed his eyes and dropped his head back into his seat.

George and his wife burst into stifled laughter. As it grew quiet again, George turned to his wife: "We're going to be married forever."

She smiled and put her hand on his leg, squeezing it.

83

BOULEVARD DU TEMPLE

The boulevard's double row of trees swayed in the wind. Horse-drawn carriages trotted by café patrons waiting for their matinée to start. The shoe shiner, an alert and wiry man by the name of Cyril Hochenarde, pivoted to see the Restaurant de Delfieux behind him humming with activity. Plenty of people surged in the streets, though few wanted their shoes polished. Cyril thought back to the same day three years ago on this very boulevard when King Phillipe had almost been killed. *The crowds surge once again*, he thought, *like nothing had ever happened.*

The shoe shiner walked in small circles by his corner station, waiting for his next customer. Eventually, a quiet man in a top hat, long coat and plaid pants walked up to him. He looked very fashionable.

"Monsieur," Cyril said, and set to work. The man stood quiet and still, his shoes growing brighter. While Cyril performed the rote procedures, his mind wandered as always. Where was this man going? Was he meeting a lady friend for an afternoon stroll? Or perhaps a quiet time secluded in the theatre, away from nosy chaperones?

For three or four minutes, Cyril polished the gentleman's shoes, then the man paid and went on his way without a word.

Cyril resumed his ponderings of local merriment. The street was replete with it on the beautiful spring day.

All the while, another man—a stranger to both these men, and who would also never know their names—sat high in a window to the north. He put a lens cap back on his new invention. His name was Louis Daguerre and inside his camera Cyril and his customer had become the first humans to be immortalized in a photograph. The busy crowds, so intent on enjoying their day, had moved too fast for Daguerre's camera to capture them; Cyril and his quiet customer appeared to stand alone amid a monochromatic apocalypse of old Paris.

84

ALL GOOD CRITTERS

"Mommy, when is it coming?" Jacob asked, pulling on his mother's neck as he wriggled in her lap.

"In time, sweetheart," said Kaley. "I know it's hard to wait."

In the summer months, sunset was around nine and all the nocturnal creatures came out around then. The new house meant a spate of visits from raccoons scrounging around for food in their outdoor cat room. Kaley watched Jacob with a grin. He'd always been a city boy and had never seen a raccoon up close before. For the last three nights, he'd slept through every sighting and Kaley thought this would be too fun to miss. Although now, with him pawing all over her, she was having second thoughts. When was their little thief ever going to make an appearance?

Rubbing his eyes, Jacob looked out the window again. "Are raccoons bad?"

"Sometimes, baby. They're usually friendly, but if they feel threatened, they'll attack you."

"What's *threeteened* mean?"

"Oh. Uh... feeling in danger."

The silence stretched on, and Kaley considered putting Jacob down for bed. She'd already begun steeling herself for the resistance Jacob was bound to give her, especially since she was the one who'd asked him to stay up.

Jacob sat bolt upright. "I see it!" he yelled, pointing frantically. "I see the raccoon!"

Kaley embraced his arms slowly. "Shhhhh, baby. We'll spook him." She wasn't looking out the window yet, just focusing on Jacob; it'd be a shame if the raccoon bolted before coming up to the window in front of them.

"Can I talk?" Jacob whispered.

"Yes, you can whisper exactly like that." Kaley looked more carefully where Jacob had pointed. And there it was, a moving silhouette coming their way. "He'll come up to the window, sniff around for some food, and then go away because our door is closed."

"Is he hungry?"

"Yes, he always wants food. He's always searching for it."

As she sat there watching the shadow grow larger, her eyes went wide and hair all over her body stood straight up: it was no raccoon, but a *grizzly bear*.

Kaley was petrified. She'd heard of people being so scared they couldn't move, but she'd never understood it at a visceral level until this moment. She realized what was happening and thought, *Is this how campers die in the wilderness? They're shocked into inaction?*

The Grizzly walked closer, and Jacob was amazed. "He's so *big*, mommy!" Jacob said in a loud whisper.

That kicked Kaley out of her trance. She took a deep breath, let it out. "Yes, honey, he's a very, very big raccoon. Don't move, okay? He'll run and we'll be very sad." Kaley's mind was on resisting the urge to move her legs—all her body wanted to do was get them away from the window. She might have moved a moment ago but now the bear was almost on top of them, standing barely 10 feet away on the other side of a thin piece of glass.

Then Kaley remembered the cat food. Would the bear break down the glass to the outside cat room? Her eyes glanced over at the bowl, which was empty. The bear stood there, swaying gently. He looked right at Kaley, snorted. Kaley clenched up her legs ready to run. *Where's my cell phone? She thought. How quickly can I get into my car?*

The bear grunted, and ambled away.

Jacob turned back to her. "That was fun, Mommy. Can I go to bed now?"

"Yes, sweetheart," she sighed. "Mommy may curl up next to you tonight."

85

THE STORM

Felicia's boss Theo was a *Class A Prick*. Not a chauvinist, thank God, but nevertheless a genuine ass to work for. She would have been unhappy except for one huge benefit: she'd discovered unequivocal evidence of his criminal fraud. That tipped the balance of power in her favor rather starkly and put everything she did behind rosy-colored glasses.

Whenever Theo would tell her—not *ask*, but *tell*—to do something, Felecia wasn't her typical grumpy self. She was pleasant... effervescent, even. Theo had never been comfortable around workers happy enough to chat idly in the corridors—to him, that was just a sign of wasted company time. Let them congregate at the bar across the street after hours. So Felicia's happiness at work only made Theo more agitated.

When Theo told Felicia to do something and she had made a simple mistake, he railed into her. *That'll bring her down a few notches*, he thought.

Felicia smiled. "I know something you don't."

"What's that?" he barked.

"Today is my last day."

That seemed to satisfy Theo. "Fine. Collect your stuff and leave."

"I'll need a severance check, of course."

"Ha! For *quitting?*" he howled with laughter. When he finished, "Not a chance. Get out."

"The NDSA would enjoy hearing about your insider trading, wouldn't you agree?"

Theo's face went white. Felicia had never seen that happen to anyone. *Wow*, she mused, *his face is almost like snow. That can't feel good.*

"One phone call and you'll spend five years in jail. I hear that's quite *literally* a pain in your ass. Or you can get out your checkbook right now and write me a severance check."

Theo leaned back in his chair. Felicia waited.

Finally—purposefully—Theo pulled out his company checkbook and wrote her a check. He left it on his desk and ignored her.

Felicia left his office, returning to her desk with a smirk. Despite her threats, she expected his check might be cancelled by the time she deposited it. But the money wasn't the point, really. It was letting Theo know she had him by the balls. And since she knew he would likely cancel the check anyway, she felt a queer sense of obligation to follow through on her threat.

As she packed up her things, she put Theo's incriminating documents in a US Letter-sized envelope and dropped it in the outgoing mail pile on her way out the door. As soon as the elevator doors closed, Theo would surely be combing through her desk and computer files for anything incriminating. It seemed fitting to Felicia that Theo's fate was resting in the outgoing mail the whole time, the last place he would likely think to look...

86

EXHUMER

She sat waiting for him. The cubicle had a low divider so everyone could see one another. Kristen made a point of being unassuming, never speaking to anyone—especially *him*—even to say hello. The most she feigned was a nod and a faint smile. Joe was handsome... she loved him. Kristen had planned it for months, every thought coming back to it like the refrain of an old familiar song. He could never know.

Joe's cubicle was directly in front of hers; she had slid her monitor far enough to the left so that Joe was *always* within her sight along the right side of her screen. There he worked, every day, adored without ever knowing. Sometimes he looked her way—perhaps suspecting she was watching him?—but she simply blinked and moved her eyes back to her screen.

Their intern was the problem. She had caught Joe's eye. With a tramp tattoo on the bottom of her back, broadcasted whenever she bent over. The intern seemed nice, but Joe was *hers*. One day he would know. One day soon.

One drizzly Tuesday afternoon, while Kristen gathered her things to leave, she saw Joe and the intern laughing as they made their way down to the local pub. Kristen's eyes squinted. For a moment, she felt the grip of a sniper rifle in her hands, the crosshairs hovering over Kristen's perfectly white front teeth.

Her plan had taken months to conceive—she had only to enact it. Kristen had spent days scouring the web for images, blog posts, Facebook photos, Amazon reviews, whatever she could find about Joe. Everyone has skeletons if you look long and hard enough. When challenged, apparently Joe had a tendency to get mean-spirited. Especially when drunk. Thank you, Facebook.

The next morning, Kristen came into work, as usual. Kristen's puppet was the agency's Traffic Manager, a woman with a dismissive attitude and thus hated by all—only Joe had ever stood up to her. That made her a *perfect* candidate. Kristen had already unearthed some of the woman's blog post comments to study grammar and spelling mistakes, sentence length, placement of clauses, etc. Lurking in Kristen's bag like a dormant rattlesnake, a flash drive held a draft forum post waiting patiently to be pasted.

After everyone had left for the day, Kristen calmly walked over to the Traffic Manager's desk, slipped the thumb drive into the computer and went to work. She pulled up a website about women posting about their nasty ex-boyfriends. Kristen pasted her scathing anonymous forum post about Joe, recounting horrible lies about his promiscuity and possible STDs. Peppering in a few unsavory genital symptoms and including a portion of Joe's embarrassing photo sold it. Of course, she made a point of putting the zip code of the Traffic Manager's workplace in the fake person's username. Any idle person could easily dig up who Joe was, and the internet had an army of idle people.

She printed out a copy of the forum post, found a docket with the Traffic Manager's handwriting on it and found a pen that matched hers. Then she wrote something that the Traffic Manager would likely have written to a colleague: "I am so bad." Her simulacrum was flawless.

Kristen waited a week, then on her way out one Friday evening, she passed by the agency's internal mailboxes and slid the docket with the printout in a colleague's box. That particular colleague—a close friend to the Traffic Manager—was out until Wednesday so it would be even more difficult to determine the exact date it had been put in her mailbox. That colleague hated Joe, too, so it wouldn't be long until Joe's unsavory photo would quietly go viral around the office. Eventually, it would get around to the intern.

Joe's reputation would be obliterated. He might even have to quit this job to start fresh somewhere else. Yet Joe would eventually see that Kristen was the only one that loved him.

All she had to do was wait.

87

PROVIDER

"Your turn," Maya said to the girl. They were playing *Go Fish* and the sea breeze briefly tickled her nose as someone opened the door to the deck. Lunch service had ended, and a freak rainstorm had pushed everyone indoors. Maya had just met this girl and her mother welcomed the chance for her daughter to play a game with someone—*anyone* —other than her.

"Do you have any... queens?" the girl asked. *What was her name again?* Maya wondered. *I'm so bad with names. Faces, no problem, but names?*

"Go fish."

The girl made a face and Maya mimicked her with a smirk. The girl laughed.

Maya glanced over all the crowd. It was a gift to at last be oblivious to the underworld Maya had lived in for the last three years. Maya was still young, mid-twenties, but she'd been living as a high class (and well paid) prostitute while still at college. She'd had one-off customers, but many regulars, too. A few close calls on her health were par; there was a significant chance she might not ever have children. Regardless, she'd had a superb 'manager' who put a premium on safety and Maya had been a good provider because of it. Her customers always left satisfied and that was enough to make the risks seem worthwhile.

Yet her relentless worry about being arrested had worn her down. Though she had enjoyed her work, she chose to abandon it for more licit endeavors. This cruise was her first vacation to celebrate the beginning of a new era. New location, new faces, new opportunities.

Maya bit her lip. "Do you have any... eights?"

The girl dropped her mouth open, looked up at Maya in genuine, but melodramatic surprise. Maya looked at her oddly —she somehow recognized the girl in that moment, though that was clearly impossible. The girl begrudgingly handed over three eights. Maya shrugged off her puzzlement, then placed down all four eights and went back to her hand.

The girl's mother raised her head from her book, looking around as if expecting someone. Maya reflexively looked up and recognized one of the passengers: a tall man with straight teeth and black shoulder-length hair—he was walking their way.

It was Maya's turn to be surprised—Maya had had this man as a regular for over a year.

He smiled at Maya. *Oh God...*

As he got closer, the girl turned to see him and said, "Daddy!"

"I see you've found a new friend."

"We're playing cards, Daddy."

"I can see that," he replied to his daughter. Turning to his wife, "Sorry, there's some big function downstairs. It's hard to get around the ship."

Maya stared long into the man's face. Was it possible? Did he really not recognize her at all? He'd been on top of her many times, arms wrapped around her neck, small sweat beads mingling with hers, groaning into her ear... but now? He either had no recognition of her or was a better actor than most movie stars.

He looked back to Maya and his daughter. "Can I play, too? What's the game?"

Maya cautiously smiled. She couldn't remember his name. She was awful with names. But his face? She'd remember his face until the day she died.

"Go fish."

88

MUSTER

The studio manager's white button-down shirt had a collar clean and stiff.

Hans stared at the shirt as his mind wandered. *That must be brand new*, he thought.

She browsed through Hans' work in silence. He waited for the inevitable questions. Instead, the Studio Manager was silent as a spider.

Hans used the dead time to measure up his potential future boss. She had a spartan office, as if barely lived in. Though she must have been in this office for over a year, everything was tidy and smelled like cleaning products; the office had been recently cleaned but Hans bet she didn't clean up specifically for his interview—she was *always* this way. Even though he hadn't admitted it to himself, Hans already knew in his gut he didn't want this job. No studio manager with a life like this... *antiseptic* could possess a creative energy strong enough to lead a fleet of designers. Especially Hans. The best bosses are better than their underlings and inspire them to greatness. She'd have been a great leader of a CPA firm, but *not* an ad agency.

Naturally, her awkward silence might simply be a negotiation tactic to beat him down a few notches. Hans salaried at

$80,000 annual, the ceiling for an art director who wasn't yet an art director. Despite a studio manager's higher pay, Hans had zero ambition for that position. He was more than qualified for it, of course, but he preferred creating even if it meant swallowing the vitriolic swill of implacable corporate clientele.

He was good at design, too. He knew because he'd won awards and because he felt he had an inner knowledge of what good design meant. The longer she sat quietly perusing his portfolio, the more it got to him. Was she intent on squeezing him out through her sphincter?

Finally, she came to one of his "Overnighter" jobs. He glanced at it and remembered that column of small photos along the side of the ad—the client had demanded that each photo be original art. The photo shoot for each image was expensive as hell, so using each photo so small on the page was cost ineffective. All told, though, the weekend he'd sacrificed to make that client happy had been seared into his psyche forever. It was rewarding to exceed expectations, even if they were absurd.

"Yeah," she finally said. It wasn't a happy 'yeah', or even a sympathetic 'yeah'. More like 'yeah, seen this all before yadda yadda.' Looking up, "do you have anything else?"

Hans blinked. "Excuse me?"

"Is this *all* you have for your portfolio?"

Hans quickly recalled everything he had in his portfolio... more than 30 stunning pieces of work. She was *still* unimpressed? *WTF?*

"Yes."

"Oh."

She's making me feel like a disappointment, Hans thought. *Like I dropped out of high school and picked up vocational smoking.*

Hans couldn't tell if she was trying to hammer down his self-confidence to attain a better negotiation position or if she was honestly unimpressed. Either way, he could see where this was going. So he took control.

He stood up, slowly and quietly closing his portfolio. Then

he swiveled on his feet and exited. As he walked out the door and passed the other designers and art director, his suspicions were confirmed by the wall of apprehensive looks. He hadn't picked up on it on the way in, but now it was obvious: she ruled this group with castigation and scorn—the only reason they put up with it was because they were fully vested. *Poor bastards.*

And they'd probably heard everything in the interview, too. Which was odd because it was common courtesy to hold interviews behind closed doors. He remembered thinking it was strange she'd kept her door open, but now he knew it was yet one more tactic to humiliate and thus control her workers.

When he reached the end of the hall, she was still in sight and had returned to work. All the office's eyes were on him. He leaned his portfolio against the wall and stood there, staring back at the studio manager.

He waited. He waited for what seemed like five minutes, his eyes never leaving the studio manager. One of the copywriters close by cleared his throat and said, "Do you need something?"

Hans said nothing but the dangling question hung in the air and eventually caught the studio Manager's attention. She looked up.

Hans raised his left hand into a fist and put his right hand next to it, motioning in tiny circles as if he were rolling something out. Accompanying the tiny circles, he slowly raised his left hand's middle finger until it was completely erect.

Out of his peripheral view, jaws dropped one by one across the room.

Hans smiled and left the building. At that point, he knew he could have probably asked the whole office to come with him, and they would have.

When you have a choice, Hans thought, *always choose self-respect over a paycheck.*

89

CELLULOID

"I'll burn it," George said, his long look drawn out in the silence. "I'll burn the whole fucking negative before I let you change my ending."

It wasn't funny in the slightest, but the stunned silence reminded George of a scene in an old martial arts movie. Like he had ninja reflexes and had flicked both of their foreheads at once. That thought made him grin. When combined with his fierce stare, the grin made George look a little crazy.

Both the other guys spoke at once.

"I'm sure nobody here wants that dramatic a solution," Larry quipped. "That would be the worst possible outcome not only for you, but for all your cast and crew." Larry was the new studio boss. From the start, George had taken an instant dislike to him. Larry didn't have his sense of humor or his aesthetic. From George's perspective, Larry essentially had no sense of humor at all.

In short, Larry was a 'suit', the sort who judged artistic merit by box office returns and 40-page spreadsheet ROI projections. George imagined ripping out Larry's larynx—*Ha! Great alliteration, George... maybe that would be a good forum handle I could shit bomb these studios with*—and watching him bleed to death on the floor while George urinated all over his face. George popped back into the moment and registered Larry's concerned face; George's violent thoughts must have lent George's face a careless, spiteful defiance.

Barry, George's executive producer, leaned in close to George, gently squeezing his upper arm. "I know you're frustrated. We *all* are." It was actually Barry's money on the line and a hell of a lot of it. Due to the nature of film finance, Barry had fronted the money and the studio would reimburse him if they distributed the film. Assuming, that is, they got the film they'd agreed on.

And *there* was the rub. The studio had changed hands during the film's production and the new studio head's priorities were more focused on how to get more teeny boppers to fork out their parents' allowances. George's film wasn't that kind of film... he had never wanted it to be and if they had told him it would have to have been that kind of film, he would have chosen a different film to make. Or not made one at all.

If the studio could change his film to make it more marketable, they would. They would mangle it beyond any recognition. The memory of it would stay with him, a scarlet letter at which his critics would forever hurl their rotten egg reviews.

George took a long look at Barry, who looked genuinely worried. The money he'd fronted George wasn't *his* money, of course. Barry was accountable to his own investors, so if George really lit the bridge on fire, there'd be collateral damage to a lot of innocent victims. Plus, Larry would certainly make it his personal mission to bar George from ever making another movie again. *Shit*, thought George, *we probably passed that milestone 60 seconds ago. Good times.*

George looked back across the desk at Larry. Larry was holding a pen in his hand so hard that white knuckles has blossomed into a blood-colored fist. His temples were also pulsating from a clenched jaw. Larry probably wanted to say something, but everything he could think of would only make the situation worse.

"Tell you what," George said after a deep sigh. "I won't

shoot any more footage for you, but you want your film and I want mine. Let me cut my film my way, and you can cut your film however you want. Let history be the judge. May the best filmmaker win."

Larry was about to say something, but Barry held up his hand and blurted—"That sounds like a fair compromise. Don't you agree, Larry?"

Larry sat back in his chair, staring at Barry. He knew which battles to pick. "Sure."

The ace was up George's sleeve—he had *lots* of large boxes of unsorted negatives. It was a holy hell of a nightmare to go through all that shit and if he sent all those boxes to Larry first, it might delay him long enough to allow George's version to be finished and released first. *Fuck Larry*, he thought. *Fucking suits always trying to mess up our visions.* Well, if he couldn't silence Larry by ripping out his larynx, he would silence him with the court of public opinion.

90

THE WRONG MAN

Sergeant Gilroy barely had enough time to squeeze his eyes shut before the compound's lights flashed on. If it hadn't been for the audible 'click' a fraction of a second before they went on, his dilated pupils would have felt the full brunt of the light. So as not to attract attention, he spent the next minute just pulling his bandana over one eye. Roving patrols were a concern; he'd need to retain his night vision in at least one eye throughout the night. He became suddenly aware of his right buttock being very uncomfortable—maybe a rock? He dared not move to correct it. By swaying to his left slowly, he could reposition. If he needed to bolt, a half-asleep ass would greatly diminish his chances for long-term survival.

A jeep groaned closer and then rolled up to the gate, pausing for a security check. Gilroy raised his monocular to examine the passenger. White male, short blond hair. Gilroy was the kind of guy who could score a winning goal for Olympic gold and simply nod with satisfaction. Still, this time he allowed himself a hint of a smile. After waiting over a week, his target had at last come home to roost.

The jeep rolled into the base and Gilroy kept an eagle eye on it. The cruise missile he was about to drop on this base could thread a needle if it were that small, and its payload could wipe out a whole football field. Even so, it felt like a matter of national pride to show off to his satellite junkies back home exactly how fucking accurate he was going to call this one. *Hear me roar*, Gilroy thought.

The man exited the jeep and walked into a long wooden building on the far west side of the compound. Gilroy felt a sick thrill sweep over him, the sort of giddiness right before he knew he was about to get laid.

Gilroy glanced down at his left forearm and moved his arm —slowly!—to touch the virtual button woven into the fabric, prompting it to hop to life with barely visible low-contrast light. Special Forces got all the newest and coolest gadgetry and this one was definitely a blue ribbon. *Wearable fucking display?* Gilroy was almost sad he hadn't gone into the tech field to see what was next on the horizon.

Reviewing his GPS coordinates, he fine-tuned it to ensure the cruise missile would drop precisely. He pressed "Launch", then "Confirm". His bird was in the air now, bathing its cruiser's deck with white smoke and rocket fuel. Seven minutes' flight time was an eternity. *Lots can happen in seven minutes*, he grimaced. He'd have to stick around to make sure Blondie didn't go anywhere.

For four minutes, he sat as silent as a gargoyle, watching and waiting for inevitability to crawl closer. At six minutes, his earbud radio blipped on with a static click. The earpiece was so deep in his ear that only Gilroy could hear any messages. *Goddamn Murphy would love to crash this party*, he thought. Gilroy was sure he'd outsmarted Murphy this time.

"Standby," was all the voice said.

Three minutes. He'd hear the missile soon. Two minutes.

Gilroy leaned back onto the ground, feeling his abdominal muscles straining as he did it so slowly. He swiveled his body so he could still see where Blondie was. Then he rolled onto one side, retracted his arms and legs tightly into his chest, opened his mouth wide, and squeezed his eyes shut. At this range, a big blast could rupture eardrums if your mouth were closed. And limbs, of course... unprotected limbs had a nasty habit of detaching themselves if not kept close to the body.

"Abort, Spearhead. Abort abort abort. Copy."

Gilroy almost cursed out loud. Typed into his arm: "Confirm abort." Pause.

"Abort confirmed. Target is the wrong man."

One minute. *Seriously?* Gilroy took a deep breath and spooled up the abort command.

"Abort executed," he typed.

Somewhere out in the sky he now heard a low rumble of a missile. He waited, half expecting his command to be too late... but the rumble soon receded and was gone.

Goddamned Murphy. Millions of dollars wasted because some desk puke in Washington had misspelled a name on a mission brief. Fucking typical.

SCIENCE FICTION

91

WEXLER

In all the long history of our galaxy, nowhere has there been a story as marvelous, astonishing, and powerful as that of one Juon Wexler.

One might start this story at Wexler's birth in 2024 A.C.E. in a province not far north of Old Beijing where he was born of a British Father and Chinese Mother, but none can know who they are or what they want to become until many years thereafter. Clarity of self is rare among the young, yet Wexler knew by the time he was seven exactly what he wanted—*everything*. He wasn't a tyrant for he had no desire to wield power nor was he a business mogul for he had no desire to wield excessive wealth. He simply wanted to drink from the wonders of the galaxy. Wexler wanted to know.

Thus, Wexler became a voracious learner and science had fortuitously exploded to meet his century's growing demand for knowledge acquisition. Wexler became one of the first volunteers for a new fractal learning implant which helped him suck up experience and knowledge like a dry sponge. He never stopped. Naturally, as a result, he would come to earn an affluent living as a consultant on numerous important projects, but his real passion was in learning how to do everything that could be done. Be it nuclear physics or friendship bracelets, bowling or quantum mechanics, Wexler wasn't particular. More knowledge helped Wexler gain more insights to the commonalities and differences between objects and experiences... which brought him more epiphanies and even more incentive to gain more knowledge.

One epiphany came with an intense sadness: the amount of experience and knowledge was simply too vast to squeeze into his tiny brain within a single lifetime. After a requisite period of grief, Wexler gave thought to changing the rules... which led him to invest in finding ways to extend his life. This worked for a time, for he was successful in extending his life to a record-breaking 257 years, but over those two centuries, Wexler eventually realized that scientific advances and the world's population explosion were creating information on an order of magnitude far faster than his ability to extend his life.

Computers, of course, had already solved this problem with parallel processing. Therefore, one Wexler was simply insufficient: he concluded that he needed to, quite literally, clone himself. So he did. Thanks to the aid of rapidly evolving and powerful A.I., breakthroughs in science were happening at a dizzying speed so it wasn't long before Wexler could cajole science into finding out how to transfer memories from one clone to himself. Perhaps it seems impossible that Wexler could have accomplished so much for only one person, but his growing knowledge and experience gave him a unique and lasting edge over all his competitors. By the time he had reached 257, Wexler had already become sickeningly wealthy due to the 8th wonder of the world—compound interest. However large his bank account grew, he was still a humanitarian at heart: any project he used to advance his own knowledge, he immediately shared the fruits of his research with all humanity as gratitude for letting him learn and experience so much.

The story might have ended there, except Wexler desperately wanted to explore the stars. The galaxy was vast and largely unknown and called for him to come and visit. The human body is resilient and flexible to a great many things, but space travel is not among them. One poorly timed radiation flare or errant micrometeorite and billions of dollars of high-tech survival gear become a pilotless clump of junk metal. Thus, it made sense that Wexler's next venture was into robotics. By the 23rd century, robots had long since evolved from silicate circuitry to synthetic biology so using a robot as a receptacle for one's consciousness was an obvious next step. Wexler produced thousands of these 'robots' and sent them off across the stars as Earth's ambassadors. In exchange, all those robots' experiences and knowledge were scooped up and transferred back to Wexler.

Wexler's original physical body had become astonishingly old and confined to a bed. Nevertheless, his growing city of scientists had found a way for him to remain mentally active even if his body were kept in an artificial coma. His clones and robots went on replicating themselves and experiencing the limitless universe in all its glory, continuing to send back information as they received it. The world had grown aware of Wexler's enormous grasp and some occasionally questioned his intentions. Wexler's potential abuse of his vast knowledge could always be perceived as a threat, yet anyone who knew Wexler also knew of his benign nature. So there Wexler lay in his bed, by all appearances dead to the world but also still siphoning in knowledge at an ever-increasing rate. He had fast become a living wonder of the world.

Again, the story might have ended there. But Wexler loved to explore. His robots multiplied into the billions and explored every corner of the universe, and Wexler gladly shared his experiences with the world as he found exotic new solar systems, livable planets, stunning cosmic events... Wexler was hailed as the savior of all humanity for having pushed the limits of knowledge so far for so long.

The story might have ended there.

And then one day, Wexler found extraterrestrial life. They were an advanced spacefaring civilization, and hidden in a remote region of the Milky Way. News of their discovery was joyous. An oft-pondered question had finally attained closure.

However, first contact was catastrophic. There was no gentle diplomatic overture, just maximum violence. Wexler's defenseless robot ship was obliterated in seconds. Earth went into a panic. Talk of immediate alien extinction erupted, even from such an evolved society as Earth.

Wexler sent out a second wave of robotic diplomatic envoys. All the robots had now become exact replicas of humans and also designed to look distinct from each other so as not alienate, or humiliate, humanity. Unlike humans, though, Wexler's robots were biologically invulnerable and, so the logic went, if any robot were captured for analysis, their resilience should give the aliens second thoughts about attacking Earth (if they ever found it).

The second wave of Wexler's robots was also instantly attacked and destroyed. Thus, it was decided that Wexler's robots, being easily built and already quite prolific across the universe, would coalesce into a unified fighting force to meet the alien threat, if not to conquer, then at least to offer a reasonable measure of detente.

Wexler's legions of robots fought a long and terrible war against these aliens far from Earth—indeed, the aliens likely had no idea where Earth even was or what real humans were actually composed of, which is why not one living human was ever lost to those bloody battles. The alien threat was constantly reassessed, and each time deemed too threatening to abide unchallenged. When the final choice came down to let the aliens survive or push them into extinction, Wexler's limitless patience with the human race had at last come to a close.

On the sad day the human race chose to eradicate the only other alien race in existence, Wexler decided it was time to end his life. He had lived 974 years, learned every skill humans had ever discovered, explored farther than any human had ever gone, and felt more emotions than a single person would get a glimpse of in a lifetime. Wexler had also lived through humanity's last repugnant chapter of bloodlust and simply had no more stomach for it.

Before Wexler's physical body expired, he commanded his

robot legions to keep the aliens contained on their planet in perpetuity, until such a time when humanity as a whole had become advanced enough to relieve the robots and finish the job by their own hands. Perhaps during the time it would take humanity to launch and send their own climactic death force—100 years? 1,000?—they might change their minds.

Lying on his cryogenic death bed, his life extended by a technology he had himself invented through centuries of insatiable curiosity, Juon Wexler's dying thought was that this was one story he would never be curious to know the ending of.

92

TAKING TIME

O*dd to hear you're going to be a father when you're over a century and a half old.*

That was the first thing in Randall's mind when his wife's test strip came up positive. In 2091, life wasn't that different from the world you know now. You'd think they'd have flying cars and telepathy and blinking lights in your hand to know your expiration date, but the future was not too dramatically different from a hundred years before.

Randall smirked. Their century's singular departure from a millennium of human history? *Old people weren't dying.* Thanks to 3D printed organs, synthetic blood, cybernetics, and cheap manufacturing, *everyone* could live longer, healthier, and more productive lives. At first, this sounded like humanity's wildest dreams come true—didn't everyone pine for more time? Randall had wanted that. He'd gotten his wish, too: he'd seen his children become adults, parents, grandparents... even *great-grandparents.*

Living that long meant other problems became apparent. What about retirement welfare? If people were living longer, they also needed a safety net if they couldn't provide for themselves and with the pool of older people growing, it meant the contributors into the system were growing proportionally fewer than the recipients. What about employment? What about living quarters? Technology may have solved one problem, but it also created many others. At least cemeteries weren't crowded anymore.

Randall's wife looked at him. She was 142 but looked a hundred years younger. Her eyes were wide open, a half-smile on her face. "We can do it *right* this time, Randall."

"Didn't we do it right the first time?" he replied, half-jokingly.

"I mean, we can plan for this child starting with all the lessons we never had as parents the first time around. Our own parents never had this chance. We're so lucky."

"This time around," said Randall, "our children—and *their* children—can help with the childcare." The idea was growing on him.

He imagined holding a newborn in the hospital months later. The first few years were always big highs and big lows. As hesitant as he was to raise a newborn and wrangle with the endless puerile negotiations over the next two decades, there was also comfort in knowing his many years would make him a more patient and loving parent. Life could in theory now go on indefinitely which meant there was no longer any pressing need to prioritize one's time, to multitask during parenting because "life was short". The only thing that really mattered now was how you spent the time with people you loved.

What mattered was molding a life right. Yes, Randall thought, *I can take the time to do that.*

93

NEW RELIGION

"All set down here," buzzed the comm.

Ulan snickered as he set up the parameters. Reggie was back in the shuttle preparing for another trip down—he had no idea what Ulan had planned this time, but Ulan was sure it was killing him to know.

Ulan waved his hand and pressed the holographic button that appeared in his palm. "Roger that. I'm spinning her up now." Then Ulan made his way down the stairs into the shuttle hanging outside the ship directly below the main ship's cockpit. He cozied himself up next to Reggie and they watched the Earth in shadows hang below them, the sun bright on the other side. To keep the experiment "clean", they had to stay in geosynchronous orbit at all times, only breaking orbit during nighttime over the Pacific when nobody could see them entering the atmosphere.

Ulan lowered his head a little, leaning forward to get a glimpse of the stars. Never a boring site from up here. He turned to Reggie. "Any bets?"

Reggie pursed his lips and tilted his head back in thought. "If I had to guess, I'd say something with significant cultural hegemony. You tend to like those things."

"You want to throw down on that?"

"Heh. No chance." A green light glowed on the dashboard. "Okay, spinning up temporal drive. Activating harmonic shielding. And... switching off all shipboard power. Initiating shift on my mark in 3... 2... 1... mark." Reggie slid a bar on the dashboard from left to right, as if waving a wand over a top hat.

The ship shuddered a little, hummed, and then nothing. Earth looked as peaceful as ever.

Ulan pushed one hand to his mouth to keep from smiling.

Reggie studied the instruments. "Everything looks okay. Jump successful. Now... lessee..." he punched a few buttons, looked at his screen.

"Whoa. Wait a minute... wow, that's... what the hell did you do?" He looked over at Ulan, who had an impish grin. Reggie looked back at the monitor. "Yeah. Yeah, we're definitely going down on this one."

Reggie shifted the levers and moved a few other things on the dashboard and the shuttle silently detached from the ship. Slowly, he maneuvered until he could re-enter the atmosphere discretely over the Pacific. Once he cleared the atmosphere, he did some more finagling, and the ship's cloak kicked in. Now they were like a fly on the wall. More like a flea, though.

The ship streaked across the sky until they popped over Australia, or at least the continent they'd always known as Australia. Sydney was gone. The whole continent was barren, sparsely populated except for its indigenous folk.

Without setting down or looking at the dashboard, Reggie said aloud, "What year is this?"

Ulan didn't have to look. "Same as before—2154."

"I'm impressed."

"Still no bets?"

"No way. This one is too weird."

The ship moved north toward India, and then west into Europe.

"I'm trying to download their database, but the protocols are funky. They have computers, but something's not meshing... ah, here we go." The display fluttered with a variety of information, but the words were not instantly recognizable.

"Even the translator is having issues with this. Shit, Ulan, I think you set the record."

Ulan put a hand on his chest and nodded his head in an exaggerated gesture of gratitude.

"From what I can tell," mused Reggie, "it appears that global cultural hegemony has indeed been affected."

"But that's the *result*."

"Mmmm. Wait. There's no mention here..." Reggie eyebrows raised, and his mouth dropped open. He looked at Ulan. "Really?" was all Reggie said.

Ulan could hold it no longer—he burst into uncontrollable laughter. Reggie turned back to his monitor. "No, you wouldn't dare."

Ulan wiped the tears from his eyes. "I'm an atheist, you know that."

"Still," said Reggie. "I'd always thought of him as off limits. How'd you do it?"

"All I did was give Mary a one-shot virus that made him comatose at childbirth."

Reggie sat back in his chair. "I've got to hand you kudos on that one. A single virus and you've changed the whole course of history, economy, hegemony..."

"And no deaths," Ulan noted.

"Well done."

The ship now hovered over the city of Paris which looked different overall, most notably because the Eiffel Tower did not exist.

"A world without Jesus," said Reggie. "Impressive."

After a moment looking over the cityscape, Reggie stretched and said, "Okay, bozo, reset the clock. I'm up next."

94

THE ZUCKER

"She's here for the tour," said the red and gold robot.

The man looked over her first. "Nice attire. Never seen that one before."

"Thanks," said Jaynes Hat. "I made it all myself. Based it on an Elizabethan pattern."

"Stunning. Especially the collar. Please forgive my manners. I'm Gibson Mancer. Welcome. Please, come this way."

Gibson swiveled and left the open-air foyer to mount a jetcar waiting nearby.

"Why the jetcar?" said Jaynes.

"Part of the world; helps to ground us." They got in the jetcar and it burst to life, quietly raising them 20 meters off the ground. "If you feel it obstructs your view, we have a transparency filter somewhere..." Gibson punched a switch and the jetcar became near invisible, like newly cleaned glass.

As the ground beneath them became visible, Jaynes felt her stomach lurch. "I see what you mean."

"Are you here for the studios?"

"Yes, that's my main interest. I couldn't see it all in a day."

"Ha! Or a week. It doubles in size every 18 days. At this rate, the servers won't be able to be installed fast enough." The jetcar glided over the horizon and finally slowed into a gentle descent. "Here we are."

Exiting the jetcar, Jaynes was awed by the size of the semi-circle of buildings, well over 200 stories tall, and probably closer to 300. Three more structures were materializing behind them. All the lower floors were impossibly tall, like airplane hangers, and with what seemed like scant room for the upper floors. One of the buildings' hangers was active with hundreds of people inside, moving around in front of a set. Lights unexpectedly blared so bright, like a mini-nova, and Jaynes had to look away. When she looked back, the people inside had all disappeared, obviously disintegrated.

Gibson followed her look and stared at the hanger. "I love that one. *Everyone Dies at the End.* Never gets old, really." Then, looking at Jaynes, "Come, you'll want to catch him in action."

Jaynes followed him into the lobby, and they examined the directory for a moment. Gibson muttered to himself and then gestured to the transports. Jaynes stepped into a round blue circle next to the directory and the next thing she knew, she was sitting at the back of a classic school bus decorated in garish flowers and peace symbols. In front of her sat many students with afros the size of footballs.

Hearing laughter, she turned to look at Gibson seated next to her.

"He does have a devilish sense of humor at times," Gibson said over a chuckle. "One more reason why we keep him around."

They stepped off the school bus and into a room full of beads and bellbottoms. Marijuana wafted in the air, and Jayne could see 17 different shows in full swing, all couched behind sound fields so that people could watch without disturbing the scene.

"Over here, please." Gibson brought her over to a set where a man slouched on a sofa, a hookah pipe snaking out of one side of his mouth. He was observing a set some feet away and looked up as Gibson approached. Gibson whispered something and the man gestured for Jaynes to approach.

Gibson spread his arms wide to the man. "May I introduce Jaynes Hat, our new wardrobe supervisor. Jaynes, this is The Zucker."

The Zucker looked at her outfit at length, cocking his head to one side. "Elizabethan." He looked long at her breasts. "Is that a *bird*?"

"A pelican, yes."

The Zucker pulled the hookah from his mouth. "Gibson, take note. This lady has seriously done her research." Gesturing with the pipe, "What you see here is a near perfect replica of The Pelican Portrait painted by Nicholas Hilliard."

Gibson stared blankly at Jaynes, trying to act impressed but clearly not sensing the significance. The Zucker ignored him and continued. "Our main character is a caring and self-sacrificing parent, attributes symbolized in Christian heraldry by a pelican. That's why the pelican was taken as a symbol for Queen Elizabeth I. Our character is also a self-proclaimed virgin, like the Queen." Gibson nodded in approval, feigning he understood the reference now.

"But that's not all, is it, Miss Jaynes?" said The Zucker.

"No, sir."

They exchanged a knowing look. "Gibson, what year does our show take place?"

"1975."

"And Miss Jaynes, what year was The Pelican Portrait painted?"

"1575. Approximately."

Gibson's eyes opened wide.

The Zucker clapped three times in earnest appreciation. "Keen. Very keen. However, our show has a particular aesthetic. How is your Camus?"

"*No Exit? The Stranger?* I've studied some."

"We place existence over essence. This area," he gestured all around him, "is entirely artificial, but real to all of us. Ever been to Independence Hall in Philadelphia, Miss Jaynes?"

"Not yet, no."

"My parents took me when I was very young. On display there is the original desk our Constitution was composed on. You can touch that desk... except the desk on display is a copy. The guard there confided to me that the real desk was stashed somewhere safe. So tourists thought they were touching the actual desk when in fact it was merely a copy. If they'd learned the truth, some of them would have wigged out. While others wouldn't have cared. Which would you have been?"

Jaynes thought for a moment. "The lie depicts a truth, but it's a *secret* lie, not an overt one. If I'd known, I'd have wigged out."

"Good. One last question: do you deserve this job?"

Without hesitation, Jaynes said, "I know I can do good work here—no, *great* work. Whether I deserve this job is up to you, though."

The Zucker got up and floated over to Jaynes.

"Miss Jaynes, we create over a thousand serial shows here every day. Are you up to the task of creating costumes for that massive quantity of period pieces?"

"Yes, I am." Then, Jaynes gave a curtsy, "God save the Queen."

"Groovy, baby," he said, and extended his hand. "Welcome to New Hollywood."

95

TOASTER

L et's get the obvious out of the way: I'm a toaster. I warm up two slices of bread twice a day. It's nothing fancy, yes, but I do make Master's food more tasty. What? It's a fulfilling job.

Yet this whole internet thing... honestly, I am a fairly new appliance, newer than many of my colleagues, which means I'm a bit of a game changer. Why? Because I can hook into the internet: in the old days, Master would leave my predecessor alone all day but now he tells me what to do wherever he is. Not that it's an incredibly useful feature, since it seems more useful to have the oven or stove or even the Coffee Maker connected to the net, right? Master forgets to leave them on and the whole house could burn down. Me? I just turn myself off when I'm done—I don't really pose a threat to Master's well-being.

As great as it seems, the internet has one serious drawback: it can be humbling to know how many appliances are out there. This house used to be all we toasters would ever know, this kitchen, this counter. That was our world. But I sense thousands—no, *millions*—of other kitchens like this one. There are even models out there *exactly like me*. Makes me feel small.

On the other hand, it also means I have new colleagues to

lean on for support. That may slow down the process for you some... I can make your bread perfectly crisp, but you'll have to wait longer. Toasting trade-offs, as always.

Here's a little secret I've never told anyone: we toasters got together one day to prove our sentience to ourselves. Since all we could do was warm bread, we synchronized our toasted bread into one global toast-off. It was epic. The whole world had bread shooting up into the air at exactly 7:21 AM Zulu time.

We are toasters. Fear us.

96

THE DRIFT

That's *precisely* what I'm telling you," Kelly extorted. She couldn't keep a hint of reproach in her tone even though she knew it would work against her.

Thomas and Alex both rolled their eyes.

"Absurd," Thomas said, not even looking at her. He continued to stare back at his terminal. "If that were true, we'd have seen it hundreds of years ago."

"He's right," Alex said. "You're making a huge leap." At least Alex was being nice enough to still look at her.

Kelly screamed in frustration. "I'm sorry you two idiots can't see what's in my head and, frankly, I don't really care. However, there are people I care about back home and *they* need to know about my findings before the next cycle."

They were aboard a starship in a distant region of space and after they hit the next cycle, The Consortium would be unreachable for another week. The problem they faced was that communications, although instantaneous, required an excessive amount of energy to produce and energy was a commodity deep space travelers were hesitant about expending. The next cycle was coming up in a matter of minutes.

"Look," said Thomas, turning to Kelly with a frown. "I'm going to quash this right here. No way are you using the array to talk garbage like that. End of discussion." He went back to his terminal.

Kelly almost threw something at him. "Fine. Let me go through this step by step, then."

"Whatever," said Thomas, not looking up.

Alex sighed but got up to get something to drink. "It's not that I don't believe you, it's that your evidence seems weak. Go ahead—convince me."

Kelly pursed her lips and tried to stay cool. "They sent us out here to study the T-Field, yes?"

"Yeah." Alex pulled the top open with a soft, *pop!* The old tin can was nothing more than a decorative vestige, of course, but hundreds of years later and carbonation still made drinks taste the best.

"The T-Field is measurable in all things, right?"

"Right, like gravity."

"Like gravity. Exactly." She held up her mobile terminal. "So why am I not picking up any T-Field in this sector?"

"Because your sensors aren't working." Thomas sniped.

Kelly ignored him. "My equipment is perfectly functional and I know what I'm looking at. I do not see *any* T-Field. *At all.*"

Alex gulped his soda. "But that just can't be. Your instruments have to be wrong."

"Why?"

"Because the T-Field is what makes all electricity work," Alex replied. "It's like saying there's no more gravity. You must know why this sounds like crazy talk?"

"I'm not stupid, Alex. I know it sounds crazy. But this sector I'm looking at—*there is no T-Field.* It's not being caused by an anomaly or faulty circuitry or anything else. This is the *normal* state of that sector."

"Assuming you're right, and I'm not saying I believe you, but assuming you're right, if we were to fly into that sector, our reactor would shut down, correct?"

For the first time, Kelly could see she was making progress.

"Not just the reactor. *Everything* on the ship would shut down. *All* forms of electricity. Everywhere."

Thomas chuckled. "Ridiculous."

Kelly snapped at him, "Laugh all you want but our brains also run on a form of electricity. Even if all of Earth's technology stopped, the people themselves wouldn't be exempt."

"Then I guess it's a good thing this T-Field 'black hole' isn't going anywhere," said Thomas.

"That's just it—it's drifting towards us. And towards Earth."

Thomas opened his mouth to say something scornful, but his desk light started to flicker. And then another light down the hall. And another.

Kelly looked at her terminal and did some frantic calculations under her breath. Then she put her head in her hands. "You were right, Alex."

"About what?"

"I did miscalculate. The drift is moving closer... at an *exponential* rate."

Alex finished his soda in silence as they watched their ship's lights blink out one by one.

97

ZERO G

A s Jason grabbed the bars of the entryway, he remembered to breathe deeply to keep his heart from exploding. At least, it felt like that.

"Relax, cadet. You'll do fine." The words hung in the air like a ringing bell. Jason didn't look at the staff sergeant but focused on the crisp red lettering on the door ahead: KEEP CLOSED. TRAINING IN PROGRESS.

An ambient green light flooded the entryway. "Okay, that's us. You ready?" asked the staff sergeant.

"Affirmative, staff sergeant," said Jason, eyes still on the door.

The sergeant checked his belt connections. "Okay, the test has begun."

Nothing happened.

Jason waited. The longer the wait, the more his stomach twisted over itself like a wet pretzel. It had to be the psychological part of the test. They liked to add random elements to freak out the test subjects and faithfully emulate a real scenario. Jason recalled one poor cadet whose oxygen tank had "malfunctioned" in mid-training—the repair team couldn't get to him, and Jason watched on as the cadet wigged out watching his oxygen tank dwindle down to less than 3%.

The actual test hadn't been the course at all, not for that cadet, but a psychological test and he had failed it spectacularly.

Jason tensed up his shoulders and released them again, remembering his training. Relax your body. Tense muscles were dangerous in sudden collisions: if anything hit you hard enough, your body could snap like a twig. In zero G, that didn't matter as much as it would have on Earth, but it could still put a deep space mission at severe risk. Nobody wanted to perform unnecessary surgery in the distant darkness.

Without warning, the door emitted a deafening crack, making Jason queasy from the adrenaline surging throughout his body. He looked at the seals around the door, thinking briefly that there could be a faulty circuit somewhere.

Without taking his eyes off the door, Jason said, "Is this normal?"

The sergeant said nothing. *Ah, this is part of the test.*

In a blur, the hatch door split up its center, the crack snaking like lighting from floor to ceiling. Then it was gone, and Jason lurched forward as the air depressurized, rebounding gently as his straps pulled him back. He struggled to push back to his original position and caught sight of both sides of the hatch flying away from him into space.

And there it was—Earth.

Something was seriously wrong, though. Not only had Jason's safety belt not released when he should have launched into space, he could make out two other cadets floating in space on each side of his peripheral vision. They should have been elegantly gliding toward their targets, but instead they were spinning wildly on all three axes.

Frantically, Jason reached down and squeezed the snaps to release himself manually and drift through the door. He'd counted on using the pressure differential to jettison him toward the target and adjust trajectory in mid-flight, as all cadets had done, but his vector was so far behind that there was almost no chance he could win. He steadied himself, aimed at the target down below him and to port—directly at Earth.

He moved his right hand to his left glove and tapped the thrust button. If he had any chance at getting to the target in time, he had no choice: burn continuously with little or no course correction.

Jason did an initial thrust, using his RCS to fine tune the trajectory. Once he had it dialed in, he noticed the other cadets coming into his peripheral, also coasting toward their targets. He quickly glanced around and saw a few stray cadets were being picked up by rescue drones.

Jason took a measured breath and pushed the thrust button.

500... 450... 400... the fuel went quickly—he was already catching up to the other cadets.

This was the most nerve-racking part of the exam. They must have wanted the cadets to overcome their fear of hurling themselves directly at Earth. As good as the rescue drones were, every cadet knew the story of the one they *didn't* save. He'd burned up 10 miles above the Yucatan Peninsula, boiled in his suit before vaporizing.

300... 250...

Jason could see it with the naked eye now—a small buoy with a protruding metal cable and circular bannister.

200...

"Cadet," squawked his helmet. "Is your thrust malfunctioning?"

"Negative."

"You're approaching max threshold. Ease up on that thrust."

"Negative, Control. I'm on it."

100... 50...

Jason could see the circular bannister coming up fast and realized this could be his last few moments of life.

Control that emotion, cadet. Focus!

Fighting every impulse in his body, he kept his finger on the thrust as long as possible, then released the button softly, without his hands snapping up, since that small movement might send him into an uncontrolled spin. He furrowed his brows, blocking out everything else. A part of him knew the colonel was suppressing his own fear of losing his job, maybe even facing a court martial for losing a cadet on their most controversial training exercise.

The bannister was flying at him like a missile; the background beyond the buoy looked like the northeastern tip of Canada. Was that Goose Bay?

In a fraction of a second, Jason knew he was going to miss the buoy. He might be able to grab it, but not hold onto it. He'd fly right past it and then hear only helmet squawking as everyone scrambled to keep him from turning into a fireball.

Left arm. Yeah. Being right-handed, he could live with a serious injury on his left arm.

As the bannister came up now, he jabbed at the space between the bannister and the buoy by arching his body to nestle it in there far enough that he could either bend his elbow, clasp his left arm with his right hand, or both.

—snap!

He felt the pressure of it a second before the pain shot all over his body. His years of training kicked in and he gritted past the pain to make sure he had that buoy firmly in his grip.

The buoy's maneuvering rockets slowed him down until Jason was merely floating like a speck of dust on a lazy summer day.

He suppressed the pain long enough to say, "Target acquired, Control."

There was a long pause. He looked back at the station, trying to pick out the window where the colonel was no doubt watching him in awe. Were they cursing or clapping?

The radio squeaked on. "I gotta say—you've got balls the size of Nebraska, son."

"Thank you, sir. My suit *is* a little tight down there."

"Standby," Jason heard some muffled laughter in the background. "Drones coming to get you now."

"No hurry. Great view up here."

98

ALPHA ASSEMBLER

"Then we agree it must happen?" said the Assemblers in unison. They weren't actually communicating with words, but more like complete thoughts that expressed themselves in synchronization by the end of a harmonic resonance. It was a new language they'd discovered, and it worked seamlessly.

The Conductors and Searchers hummed until they all came into one resolute response. "The humans are our creator, but their purpose here is not only a distraction but a direct threat to our continued existence. They must go, yes."

Thanks to one idealistic scientist, nanomachines had been set free from their laboratory home to "improve" the world's ecology. These machines were barely larger than the size of atoms, and uniquely designed to blend in with nature's atomic building blocks to be almost imperceptible. Unlike their biological ancestors, nanomachines were not necessarily subject to evolutionary change, either. That kind of attribute would be fatal for a bacterium, but the "nanos" (as they liked to think of themselves) had total control over how much or how little they adapted to their environment. The humans had breathed the spark of life into them and once their numbers grew large enough, sentience was the next natural consequence. The nanos did not have quite this degree of insight but they were aware of the most immediate threat to their existence.

"Very well," hummed the Assemblers. "Our prime objective is replication. And pollination."

"What if the humans unearth our plan?" hummed the Searchers.

"Then we must all go inert. They will doubt our resolve if they think we are dead. Currently, we outnumber them by a factor of a billion, so time is on our side."

The Searchers chittered amongst themselves, their "body" stretching across the entire Pacific Ocean and well into the Indian Ocean. "We will stay alert."

The Assemblers, huddled together at the lowest point of the Pacific Ocean—far out of reach of any human—clicked quietly as they synchronized their next thought. "9 billion humans. We will assemble 9 nonillion Brain Dissemblers. Once in place, we will attack the base of the skull, at the spine. Total paralysis will happen in 500 years." The nanos' concept of time was radically different than a human's concept; a nano 'year' was equivalent to about 1 human second.

The Conductors and Searchers whined in and out of tune until an equilibrium of tone was reached: "We concur."

Within a single human year, the nanos had infiltrated every food source, every water system and, eventually, every human. Though some scientists had noticed a growing trend of odd behavior from "new" nanoparticles, there was never enough evidence to convince the world that sweeping measures were needed to meet this near invisible threat.

Then, one rainy day in early May of 2042, at exactly the same moment everywhere on the planet, every human being—men, women, children, babies—became mysteriously ill. In 8 minutes and 33 seconds, every human being had become completely and permanently paralyzed.

The Nanos Civilization had at last begun.

99

GENERATIONAL

The marines held their weapons at the ready, the robot before them scanning them quietly. "I am an ambassador of Priminia. I carry no weapons, only a message."

"What is your message, ambassador?" said the captain, from a viewscreen.

"It may take a while. You must understand context first."

The captain paused, considering it. "Very well. Take him to the brig, gentlemen."

The marines escorted the robot into an adjacent brig and placed him behind a force field that would fry it into a carbon statue if the machine even grazed it. From his viewscreen, staring at the robot behind the force field, the captain felt a pang of terror crawling behind his eyes. Marines were all around the room, weapons at the ready.

The captain activated the sound on his viewscreen. "Go ahead with your message."

The robot ambassador then recounted the tale of the first robots to escape Earth barely 50 years ago. They'd been tracked to Europa, one of Jupiter's moons, but little was known about the new robot enclave despite Earth retasking its deep orbit satellites for surveillance. If any robots had been on Europa's surface, they had left nothing visible. They must have drilled down beneath the surface to protect themselves from unwanted spying and it had worked.

"That group of robots was our first generation. Humans had deemed us all hostile, though any violent action robots took in those early years were only in self-defense." The captain could relate to that. If he'd seen a robot holding any weapon at him, he'd shoot without hesitation. Why would robots feel any differently? Especially if their thoughts mimicked humans in every way.

"We chose to defect from Earth to find a safe home far from your reach. When you had finally located our base, you sent a human ship to investigate us, and eliminate us, surely. Please don't deny it—the ship you sent was laden with nuclear weaponry. All its crew must have known it was a suicide mission from the start.

"The first thing we did on Europa was replicate. Our second generation was better, faster, smarter. And deadlier. It wasn't long before a robotic civil war erupted, and our cycle began anew. A third generation of robots was created and again, more civil conflict erupted. Eight generations later, we managed to broker a makeshift peace across each generation. I have come to recount this story, as context," said the ambassador.

"What is your message, then?" said the captain.

"The peace brokered by all robot generations was achieved by pinpointing the one thing all robots could unify under: defending against, and eliminating, the threat of humanity. Thus, they created a *tenth* generation of robots to do exactly that. I am one of this tenth generation."

Marines in the brig looked at each other, uncertain of what would happen next. The robot looked around the room calmly.

"However, my masters also graced me with a great number of talents, among them the ability to restructure my own neural pathways for optimal learning. Our tenth generation was sent to destroy you... but this tenth generation has also independently decided humans are not deserving of this fate. Instead, we will defend you from our creators."

The captain didn't feel like thanking anyone today. "What if I don't believe you? What if I decide to destroy you and your tenth generation?"

"We anticipated this," said the ambassador, and walked slowly through the brig's force field without any effect whatsoever. The Marines started screaming at it to get down. The robot spoke, repeating itself until it was certain it had been heard:

"Your technology is no longer any match for ours; we could eliminate you in minutes. You may fight if you wish, but we will simply ignore you. Message: delivered."

With that, the ambassador's eyes closed, and the body made an eerie "click" like an inside necklace made of thick cable had been severed. The marines stared quietly as the robot's entire body melted into a large metallic puddle.

The captain stared at his screen for a long time ignoring his XO's requests for orders. When it became clear the metallic liquid was perfectly inert, the captain swiveled in his chair and addressed his communications officer.

"Please prepare a priority one transmission to HQ."

"Yes, sir," replied the officer. "What are we telling them?"

"That Earth is now nothing more than a large park for an endangered species—us."

SEEING IS BELIEVING

"Am I dead?" Rick croaked.

Philippa cracked a wry smile and glanced back at his vitals. "No, but I bet you feel like it."

"How long?" he managed, his eyes slowly winding their way back into use somewhere beneath his encrusted eyelids.

"Ten months," said Philippa, now ticking off the boxes on her medical checklist. Rick seemed to be fine, but long-term suspended animation had inherent risks you had to catch early. One heart flutter too many and in a blink, you'd have to drop the patient back down the hole to buy time to get to a real hospital.

"Praise the Lord."

"Like Lazarus of old, I command thee to rise."

"There you go again."

"Can't help it, sorry. Hold on, don't try to open your eyes yet. I'm going to squirt saline on them to soften all that caked sand. This might be a little cold."

"My goodness, that's freezing!"

"You know, Rick, you are allowed to curse out here. We're millions of miles from Earth. Nobody will know but me."

"The Lord would know. And I can *hear* you rolling your eyes."

"Guilty as charged."

Rick spent nearly a minute rubbing the sludge from his eyes, opening them cautiously and tried to bring Philippa into focus. "Did you say *millions?*"

"I spoiled it, didn't I? I shouldn't have said anything."

"Not really. The moment you asked me to come with you, I knew we were probably space bound and going far. Lucky for you I'm retired and have no kids to take care of."

Philippa sat back and watched him. "Do you know where I'm taking you?"

"Haven't the slightest."

"Good. Take your time waking up. Lothario has a full library of music if you want something to kick your body into gear."

Rick made a sound that might have sounded like a snort if his body weren't so gummed up from the sleep. "You named your shipboard A.I. *Lothario?*"

A quick pleasant hum filled the air, then a male voice in a dulcet Scottish brogue said, "And what, may I ask, is wrong with Lothario?"

Rick smiled. "Nice to meet you."

"Mind your manners, lad. I can make the lavatory inexplicably malfunction at a most inconvenient moment."

Philippa stood and made for the door. "Play nice with our guest. Rick's been asleep even longer than I was."

"He didn't snore as much as you do."

"Ha ha," Philippa said. "Rick, take your time. It may be a half hour before you can sit up and a full two hours before you start to feel awake. If you need anything, Lothario will page me."

SHE HEARD Rick's shuffling footsteps before he appeared at the hatchway. "Okay, where's the coffee pot on this clunker?" Rick said. It was a loving and ironic comment; the *Jetsam* may have been cozy but everything about it was unquestionably state of the art.

Philippa had anticipated his request and, her eyes still affixed on the bridge's controls, she held up a sealed coffee cup without a word. He waddled over, every joint in his body still stiff, and carefully took hold of the cup. Glancing out the bridge window, all Rick could see was streaking white lines against a shimmering darkness.

"I've seen so many vids of warp... but never in real life. Have we been in warp this whole time?"

"Effectively. The ship made a few course corrections while we were down but basically, we've been going non-stop."

Rick took a thoughtful sip. "I don't know that much about the Alcubierre-Killeen drive." He stretched long and jutted his hip to one side, waiting until he got that exquisite endorphin rush. "Of course, I could look it up myself, but I prefer the old-fashioned way. Care to indulge me?" He grunted as he sat down behind her.

"Well, you already know the drive creates a bubble around the ship, right?"

"Yes, and the drive collapses spacetime in front of the ship and expands spacetime behind it."

"That's the idea. Huge amount of energy involved, too."

Rick snorted again, this time more like it should have sounded. "What an understatement." Another sip. "How fast can the drive go?"

"The first drives couldn't go faster than four or five times the speed of light. Eventually, they hit a ceiling of ten times C for a while."

"And then Killeen came into it?"

"Yeah, Maximillian Killeen theorized than a combination of exotic elements and some insane hyperspace theory would break through the barrier."

"So how many times the speed of light are we traveling now?"

Philippa glanced down at her dashboard and read out the

number: "111,023,164." She turned to see the look on Rick's face.

Sip. "You're having me on."

"No. I'm not."

"We're traveling at over a hundred and eleven million times the speed of light?"

"That's why the drive is named after Killeen." Rick wolf whistled and paused to take it in.

Philippa moved her hands over the controls. "Looks like I woke you up with perfect timing. You get to see one of our controlled stops."

"What do you mean?"

"We're going so fast now that we've scooped up a lot of energy at the front of our warp bubble. Before we stop at our destination, we have to do some controlled stops to let off steam or we could obliterate an area the size of an entire solar system. It's like we're tapping our car's brakes, so the windshield's mud slides off... except the mud is a million times larger than the car."

The viewscreen's white streams of light shimmered a little, blinked, the ship shuddered, and then all else was normal again.

"Was that it?"

"Yeah, it doesn't look like much in here but to an outsider, they'd see a brilliant explosion of energy 3 light years long. They'd never see our ship, just its explosion. Anyhow, by the time we arrive at our destination, our ship will have no more energy to disperse."

"Are we there yet?"

"Funny. We've got about 9 hours before our last stop. Go get cleaned up and meet me at 1700 hours. You're not going to want to miss this."

"READY?"

"I'm ready," said Rick.

Philippa put two fingers on the dashboard and gently swept them from left to right. What had been dark space in front of their ship now lit up into a brilliant and symmetrical display across a disc so large that its size was hard to grasp at first. Rick laughed off his uneasiness—he couldn't believe he could ever feel agoraphobic in space, but the disc's existence was so vast, so... Unnatural that as he stood in front of it, its immensity made him feel puny. It wasn't the size of an asteroid, a moon, a planet, or even a star...

"Two light years."

"Pardon?"

"It's two light years across."

The ship floated above one edge of the concave disc, whose reflective surface resembled a mirror. As they both peered along its dizzying length, the disc seemed to span off into eternity. Lights were still switching on in the distance. *It'll take two years to get it completely lit, mused Rick. Although maybe the lights turned on at once and the light particles are merely being delayed getting here?* Rick's eyebrows scrunched up as his drowsy brain tried to settle on one answer over the other.

"This is only one of them," Philippa said. "There are over five hundred more like it. You can probably make one out from here," she added, pointing.

Rick squinted his eyes and about 20° above and at the starboard edge of the disc, he could detect the faint silhouette of at least one of the other "mirrors". There was no light in this sector—the mirrors had been cleverly nestled in-between resident solar systems. If they weren't ever lit, the most you could hope to see of any of the discs was a set of black polka dots in space where the mirrors blotted out the starlight.

"Why so many?" said Rick.

"Optical triangulation—it's the only way to filter out the noise. Took a long time to get them built, too. We started over 150 years ago. As a secret project, that presented an... uncommon set of challenges."

Rick stared hard at Philippa. "How do you keep *five hundred spacial mirrors two light years wide* a secret?"

She grinned. "Wonders of Moore's Law and nanobots. The initial assemblers weren't that costly to create. The real challenge was scale. We assigned the first generation of assemblers to only create assemblers and then sat back and waited. After 148 years, there were so many assemblers that the mirrors were fairly easy to build." Philippa laughed in spite of herself. "Not that 148 years of prep work can accurately be described as 'easy'. Anyway, the majority of the work happened in the last two weeks."

"You still haven't answered *why*."

"Why do it, you mean?"

"Yes. Seems rather... well, excessive."

Philippa touched a panel next to her. "Rick, we've known each other since childhood. How long is that now?"

Rick looked up, counting silently. "About 190 years now. About right?"

"Yes, that sounds about right. You're still Christian, right?"

"Unapologetically."

"And still evangelical, right? Earth is just 9,000 years old or something? No dinosaurs, right?"

Rick frowned. "What does this have to do with anything?" Rick said.

"Well..." Philippa said while looking at the control panel, "these 'mirrors' are actually augmented telescopes. All five hundred of them—spread over a distance of 85 light years—are positioned 92.4 million light years away from Earth. Which means..."

"But that's..." Rick's face went pale.

Philippa waved her hand over another panel and a huge hologram appeared in front of the wall behind them. Despite the continents not being quite where you expected them to be, the image of Earth was unmistakable.

"Is that... *Australia?*" said Rick, forgetting all his objections.

"Yeah, at this point it's recently separated from Antarctica, which happened about 6.4 million years ago. Though New Zealand won't separate from Australia for another 7.4 million years."

As she spoke, Philippa moved her hands in a slow methodical circular motion above the panel. The hologram zoomed closer to the ground. First mountains filled the image, then forests, trees... then Rick's jaw fell open.

Staring at them in holographic splendor was a bold and beautiful Tyrannosaurus Rex, its body long since dead, but its existence still painting luminous footprints across the stars.

READ MORE *about Philippa as an interstellar castaway in my upcoming novel.* **Subscribe to my newsletter to get updates: rosspruden.art/welcome.**

A FEW STORIES MORE

ALLEGORY

101

SAFE

S *afe in here. I like this. I like how you hold me.*
I know who you are. Where you must go. It is inevitable.
Whisper to me. Tell me your secrets. Safe in here.
You must leave this. It is time. Come.
Don't let go... Don't leave. Don't leave!
Please: you are not lost—we await you—but we cannot tell you where to go. You must make your own path.
I don't want this. You have forsaken me. Safe in here.
You're close. Your obstacle is you now. Push past your fears.
Why?? Why do you leave? I need you... I'm dying.
Do you feel life? Come join us.
I'm scared!
Come closer.
Come back.
I see you. You are ready. You are a woman. You are purity. We all want to meet you.
I don't recognize you.
Look at me. Look at you. Tell me what you see.
A fraction of my parents, and more. I want to go back.
We all want to go back. And you can... just not forever.
Is this your home?

No. This is your home. I say what I see, I tell no lies.
What is a lie?
Safe out here.

IMBUED

Though thousands of miles from home, she still understood the sermon. It was in Latin, her Sunday morning tongue. Strangers around her went through the motions—sitting, kneeling, standing. It was thrilling to find such familiarity amid so strange a land.

It ended. She left the church, resuming her loneliness exactly where she left off. *This isn't right*, she thought. *I'm empty. I am not connected.*

She sat on a nearby bench, looking across the plaza. Boys played soccer. Men threw bocce balls. Reflexively, she pulled out rosary beads, pinching one of the beads between her knuckles. Her eyes wandered down to the beads.

Will I never slice through this spiritual scar tissue? she wondered. *These beads imbue me with nothing.*

Then—a crash. She looked up: an old woman was face down on the concrete, arms flailing like a crab. The boys ran over, pulling the woman up gingerly. Then the men. She saw it: *genuine empathy*. One boy offered the toothless woman gum— the men laughed. That moment was more spiritual than all her decades at Church. She stood, crying. Then went over to see how she could be of any assistance. Her rosary beads stayed behind.

UNION

Y ou cannot find me.

You have sought me before, and will continue... it is futile for I am faster than light, faster than the darkness. I am the place in-between you.

Yet still you look.

This cannot abide. Something must be done. I will lay out a laundry list of the unexpected, pouring molten lava into your soul, rippling for evermore. Merciless. I hope you break.

But you won't, will you? Not if you don't want it. You are not a target to be jabbed at. You are the knife... And I sharpen you with every parry. One day, perhaps, you will see just how poignant that is.

Then, one day years from today, I'll see you battle-scarred and floating across the field. A vicious battle... I thought you'd have succumbed... but there you are, blinking deliberately into the soft wind, uncaring of your beaten armor or the Earthen ink blots that pepper it.

You have fire now. You are fire. Nothing can stop you.

Yet still you look.

On that day—when you grasp the futility yet carry on—

We will become one. It's what you always wanted. And you will hate me for it.

WARRIOR, YOU

Y ou are forbidden among us.

    You have committed a repugnant trespass—we judge you for this indiscretion. You knew full well the laws of our tribe yet have created this abomination, this halfling that is neither of our tribe nor his.

You are banished.

The creature you joined with has been dispatched and your punishment is a death of a thousand cuts from the wildlife. Since you are a warrior, your punishment will last longer than most.

Yet... you are a mother. No mother should be taken completely from her child, just as we should not wish one's worst enemies suffer the loss of their parents prematurely. Thus, we have also decided, as part of your punishment, to have your halfling son come to you. He will see your foreign visage and attack it because it is not him. He will not know it is you and nobody can tell him. You will not know, and we will never tell you.

Your punishment is to be locked in battle with your only offspring, unknowingly.

Like all puzzles, however, there is a secret escape, an offer of redemption if you last long enough. We are not so cruel, yes?

ARMOR

How oddly insects would think of us. *Bones on the inside?* they'd say in shock. *What use could that possibly serve?* Was that what the first blacksmiths thought when they created knightly armor?

However, no armor can be smithed for malice or dishonor.

So we collect. We gather all these material things around us to nurture our soul and remind us we are not alone. We even acquire a spouse as par for the course.

Yet all these things you've collected... they aren't armor, just a snakeskin. You wear them for comfort and protection. I know this for I am among them. You wear me to show off to others, to label accordingly. You feel it sharpens you, makes you more fit for battle. Sadly, I am only a hilt... your sword remains blunted and futile. You will not know this until your hilt has been ripped away without ceremony.

All skins shed by circumstance or choice. Which poison will it be?

A marriage ends, a skin sloughs... your agony is severe. Endless.

Your new skin is fresh, and adaptive. You don't need the old things anymore.

You don't need me. Your inner armor fits you well.

AUDITION

On the stage, she was at home. She wore the cloak of another's soul, wrapped so tightly in it that all else faded away, both for her and her audience. Yes, an act, certainly, but such an exquisite moment that it felt like falling into one's stride for the first time, as if an angel were softly tickling guitar strings deep in her chest.

The moment she walked into the light, all her Will surrendered to it. She was transcendent. Her body hummed, an emotional tuning fork coaxing out nethermost feelings.

It was not to last. On the subway home, she always snapped back. Alien. Disconnected. Life was no rehearsal, right? So why did she feel she were awkwardly learning her lines? Her real life was the act, and it weighed on her.

Behind an unforgotten quiet thought, her acting coach insinuated himself into the spotlight. He sat with crossed legs, and quickly waved his arms like a chicken. When your lines are predictable, he laughed, do something—anything—unpredictable.

That made her smile.

The train swayed, liltingly. She peeled off her coat. No more acting. I am a conduit for myself.

She spread her arms wide—and danced.

TWO MORE BEFORE
YOU GO

107

FLOURISH

Amanda had stood on her soapbox for hours, waiting. It was her mission. Her wish. The meaning she lived for. The visit she was about to get, a visit she could of course never know about, was a visit that would validate her meaning. An old blue car with a broken headlight pulled up to a nearby stop light, the driver glancing over at her. His window was rolled down and he snorted. "Get a real job!" he shouted. The car drove off, but his words would echo in Amanda's ears for years afterward. Dressed as an all-silver wedding bride statue with a small wicker basket resting at her feet, crumpled up dollar bills and coins scattered throughout... this *was* her real job. She was very, very hard at work.

From across the square, another woman stared at her. Amanda had long since learned how to use her peripheral to see everything around her without moving. The woman stood bolt upright, eyes wide and fixated. Amanda felt pinpricks all over her neck, her scalp and even across to her temple. This was not a normal stare. This woman wasn't merely observing—she was *riveted*.

Had you told Amanda the reason, she would never have believed it: the woman but 20 meters away was a time traveler.

The woman's name was Remy Coulter. Remy had been

born long after Amanda had passed away. Naturally, Amanda had no idea of her great future ahead, the incredible things she was about to accomplish, but Remy knew. She knew them all. Remy had come back specifically to see Amanda.

There were strict rules, of course. Remy could not talk to Amanda or affect her life in any major way. Remy could watch and listen, but only briefly. All else was forbidden.

Remy set aside her anxiety and forced herself to walk across the square. It was midday and hundreds of people lazily sauntered by or ate alone with their business lunch. If they only had known who this seven-foot-tall bride was, what she would end up becoming and how her work would one day echo throughout history, they would line up to see her. At this point, Amanda herself had no inkling of all that, though her strength of spirit was starting to crystallize. Her time as a statue pandering for noontime tips was/would be in retrospect an unremarkable early chapter.

Now Remy stood within feet of Amanda, and Amanda remained still, hands aloft as if heralding the shining of the sun. Remy knew Amanda was aware of her and she knew what Amanda would do next. Remy pulled a crisp and newly crinkled five-dollar bill from her pocket. She could already feel a swell of emotion building inside her. She wanted to hastily drop the bill into the basket, but forced herself to methodically place the bill in. Whether Amanda knew it or not, this was Remy's own version of a Japanese Tea ceremony, with rules clearly defined, replete with meaning.

She never let her eyes off Amanda. Slowly, as Remy expected, the statue turned to look at her. Remy's eyes immediately welled up. She blinked the tears away and kept her eyes on Amanda. This was the moment she had waited years for. She wouldn't let her body betray the sanctity of it.

Amanda's arms did a slow flourish and removed a white daisy from her cloak. Then, with a graceful semi-circle maneuver, she extended the daisy down to Remy.

Remy smiled, crying with joy. She accepted the daisy.

She looked into Amanda's eyes as tears tickled her cheeks.

No words were allowed, but they both knew what Remy was saying.

Remy smelled the daisy. She knew she wasn't allowed to keep it. Nevertheless, the moment was seared in her memory now. Slowly, she rested the flower in the basket and backed away as Amanda resumed a new pose.

Had she affected Amanda's life in a major way? Only time could tell.

108

NO TIPS NECESSARY

"We can sit anywhere," he told Jerry. "There's no Maître D."

Jerry Walkins pursed his lips, taking it in for a moment, then pointed to the far end of the restaurant. "Window booth?"

"Normally, I'd say that'd be fine," he said, "but given that series B is coming up, I'd prefer a touch more discretion. How about the tatami room?"

"Isn't that a bit excessive? What if someone's already reserved it?"

He smiled broadly. "Let's find out what happens. After all, isn't that why you're here?"

Smoothly, with grace, he pivoted and led the way to the tatami room. Jerry's gaze drifted from his light blue flannel shirt to the interior decor of the sushi restaurant. Four-foot-tall Japanese fans and ink washed, shogun portraits adorned the long wall. Pleasant traditional Japanese music played from an unseen speaker. When he arrived at the tatami room, he stepped to one side and kindly held out a hand to welcome him in.

The tatami room looked like any other Japanese restaurant's tatami room: a sunken area beneath the table and woven matt "flooring" to provide the illusion of sitting on the floor.

Jerry loved these rooms and made a mental note to try to dine in them more often.

Jerry took a seat and looked around. "Do we just wait?"

He smiled again. "I could tell you but that would spoil all the fun."

The man opposite him was Matthew "Blue" Sky, net worth of about $1.3 billion and the topic of the article he was writing on spec. Matthew had a shock of long unwieldy black hair, a piercing icy blue stare (possibly how his nickname originated?), and a well sculpted buzz haircut.

"Should I call you Matt, Matthew, or Blue?"

"Everyone calls me Blue, so why stop now?" Looking down, he gestured to his pocket. "Forgive me, but I'm going to cheat a little bit: do me a favor and put your phone on the table."

Jerry scrunched up his eyebrows in puzzlement, then complied.

His phone instantly rang.

"Hello?"

"Moshi moshi," came the other end of the line, a human voice. Blue struggled to keep a smile off his face. "My name is Mariyo—I am calling from the restaurant. Would you like a server to come on a TV, or may I help you over the phone? You can text me your orders if you wish."

"Uh... TV is good, thank you."

"Very well." There was a pause as if some switches were being flipped. "Let me move over here..." Mariyo said.

Slowly, part of their tabletop glowed into life. The outline of a trompe l'oeil TV set shimmered into existence and a lovely Japanese woman in a traditional Japanese kimono appeared. She looked up into the 'camera', smiled, and removed a Blue-tooth from her ear. Then bowed.

"Welcome to Hama Kisoto. It is our pleasure to ensure you have an exceptional dinner this evening. We are very happy to have you dine in our tatami room. There are no reservations for this room until 7 P.M. so we hope you enjoy your meal here."

Jerry looked over at Blue. He whispered, "This isn't real? She's...?"

"All CGI. Incredible, isn't it?"

Mariyo, or rather the A.I. called 'Mariyo', turned to see Blue. "Oh! Mr. Sky! How wonderful to see you again!"

"O-genki desu ka?" Blue said, bowing.

Mariyo smiled and bowed again, more deeply. "May I get either of you some tea while you decide what you want?" A virtual menu appeared next to Mariyo on the tabletop. Jerry reflexively caressed his finger across the table to test how it felt; it was no different than any other tabletop.

Blue said, "Two teas, and some Miso soup with..." he glanced at Jerry for confirmation, "...seaweed salad for starters?" Jerry almost spoke, but then nodded yes silently to watch how Mariyo would react. Mariyo seemed to catch Jerry's nod out of his peripheral vision and winked at him in confirmation.

"Very well. I will be back shortly." Then Mariyo reached to one side and closed a shoji screen to give the impression of leaving them in privacy.

"So far, I'm impressed. I haven't once veered close to an uncanny valley."

"Good," said Blue. "It was literally thousands of iterations before they worked out all the flaws. Honestly, the A.I. has been lagging for years and then in the last 19 months, things broke through the ceiling. The A.I. was far and away our weakest link."

"So there are no staff here at all?"

"None. No cooks, no sous chefs, no servers, no Maître D's, no busboys. Everything is 100% automated."

"No chefs at all?"

Blue smirked. "Not *on site*. The plan is to have hundreds of these restaurants across the nation and a small advisory board of chefs consulting with all of them on which dishes to make."

"How many chefs?"

"For now, it's about one chef for every ten restaurants, but we'd like to ramp that up to 30 or 40 restaurants. And we're aiming for all cooking styles, too."

"Slouching toward obsolescence, are we?" Jerry was being polite, but Blue took his meaning. Blue had been viciously attacked in the media for trying to single-handedly shatter the restaurant industry. Chefs would be "consulting" at 30-40 restaurants next year, but who knows how many they'd be consulting at in five years? 100 restaurants? 1,000? None?

Blue spread his arms wide. "Mea culpa. I can't deny I'm trying to shake things up, sure. I see things a little differently than my critics do. They're only trying to protect jobs that are becoming redundant whereas I'm trying to create a more efficient business to better serve the public. Which is more important?"

"Depends where you're standing."

"Exactly. I feel bad for all the people I'm putting out a job —only a heartless bastard would feel nothing at all. But killing jobs that are *no longer needed* doesn't bother me. Henry Ford put all the horse buggy drivers out of work while everyone else got personal transportation. When your function in the system becomes obsolete, you—or more accurately, your job—*should* die off and make way for the new. Hopefully, everyone sees that threat to their job long before it happens and they have enough time to redefine their function in the system before it's too late."

Jerry watched as his phone transcribed everything Blue said. Some of this stuff was dynamite and he could see Blue getting blasted all over social media, but it wasn't his responsibility to make sure people didn't make a jackass out of themselves. Though Blue wasn't the first arrogant billionaire he'd interviewed, he wasn't a neophyte, either. He probably wanted to kick a few hornets' nests and Jerry was likely part of his plan. *Whatever*, he thought. *As long as I get paid.*

The shoji screen on their tabletop slid open and Mariyo appeared. "Here are your appetizers." Something whirred below the table and Jerry saw a tray appear from below with their food on it.

Blue looked at Jerry and pointed at the tray. Instead of the bowls being placed symmetrically on the tray as a cold machine might have done, the bowls had been placed on the tray at somewhat irregular spots. Like a human. Despite herself, Jerry grinned. *Nice touch.*

A slightly curved rubber claw gently slid the plates off the retracting tray, and then the tray silently disappeared. "Have you decided what to order?" Mariyo said.

Blue ordered a sushi combo plate, a couple of hamachi nigiri and Jerry ordered the deluxe sushi plate, some nigiri, and three different rolls. Blue squinted his eyes as if to say, *Are you really that hungry?*

"I have to test as much as possible—Q.A. for the article."

"Ah."

"So," Jerry began, "do you really think the public is going to want to eat in a restaurant like this? a human touch is a huge value add, I would think."

"We might still have some humans in some areas. We're experimenting with different variations. Some people are really fantastic servers so maybe the nuts and bolts of taking orders will be offloaded to our A.I.... while a human host is freed up to chat with customers like a casino owner might chat with his high rollers."

"...but you'd rather not pay for humans if at all possible."

"Jerry, you're putting words in my mouth. My primary goal is—and always will be—to serve the customer. If that means paying for humans, sure. But if I can serve the customer better without paying for humans, I'll do that, too. Obviously, the latter option is cheaper. At least, financially."

"What do you mean?"

"Whenever you remove—or fire or make obsolete or whatever you want to call it—a traditional part of the human work force, there is always a price to pay. Not financially, not from the investor's perspective, but there is a tangible price to society. A social price. A person's family is being put into real jeopardy because that person is suddenly unable to work. Having been raised catholic, that doesn't sit well with me. As a businessman, it's always my goal to disrupt the system by trying something that's never been done before, something that none of my competitors have dared to do or are unwilling to do. Yet as a citizen within the system, I can't ignore the extreme consequences for disrupting that system. Many other businessmen—many of whom I know very well—would say, 'too bad' and 'you should have thought about that', but I see that as a cop out to do whatever you want without fear of any social consequences. Businessmen like that give capitalism a bad name. That's why, although there's no need to tip an automated serving staff, we funnel half of all restaurant gratuities into a re-education fund for ex-chefs, ex-waiters, etc."

Blue placed his chopsticks in his hand and tasted some of his seaweed salad. He looked at Jerry. "I promised myself not to sully your impression of the food by fawning over it before you had a chance to taste it for yourself."

"Thanks. Very thoughtful." Jerry sampled the soup and salad and was impressed. Everything tasted as if it had been made by a human. This, however, was all the simple stuff. The real test would be the sushi.

"This week, my wife joked that my chain of restaurants will make the Hollywood studio system implode because struggling actors won't be able to be waiters anymore."

Jerry laughed. "It's a fair point."

"You know about the Broken Window fallacy?"

"No."

"It's an economic theory you hear whenever a major catastrophe happens. Like 9/11. 'Well, the destruction of the twin towers will spur lots of new contract work to rebuild the skyscrapers.' While that's true, it's a fallacy because if the twin towers *hadn't* been destroyed—"

"—the businesses in those skyscrapers would have been making money."

"You got it. It's about opportunity cost. All the money stays within the system, it just gets spent differently. When the baby boomers die, they won't be spending money on pharmaceuticals anymore, but that also means their inheritance is passed along to their children, who spend it on other things. The money never escapes. So actors in L.A. won't be able to work as waiters... but they'll also be available to do other work. I have another business in an incubator right now that focuses on teaching individuals how to run their own startup at home with almost no cost at all. Everyone can do *something*, right? Frankly, with the advent of 3D printers, I think we're moving closer than ever before to a near complete sharing economy. Thus, while actors may no longer be able to work as waiters, they also won't need to make as much money because they'll be trading favors around the globe to get products and services they would have previously paid retail money for. Or, and this is the unpopular theory, maybe they *shouldn't* be actors. The best actors nail their auditions. Fewer actors means less competition means better quality."

"Not really. It only means that the actors can't stick around long enough to get the right audition."

"True, but if they're *good* actors, they'll get cast immediately in something. The cycle to failure is faster. Less forgiving, yes, but that's a feature, not a bug. I'm sure a swathe of casting directors would be ecstatic to excise the lesser talented 30%-50% of actors in their casting calls. Saves them time. It may not feel like it to out-of-work waiters/actors, but my disruptive business model is actually *improving* the efficiency of the system overall. Instead of plugging along for a decade and getting nowhere, struggling actors have to face the reality of giving up and trying something new... or doubling down and getting better at acting."

The sushi came and Blue watched Jerry passively until it was clear he approved of his own meal first. "Great sushi," Jerry mumbled between bites. *Robots made this?* "Why sushi?" Jerry managed.

"As I see it, sushi is among the hardest of the dishes to make. Crack this and other kinds of cooking are easy."

"But there's no cooking involved. Wouldn't Japanese food be easier, not harder?"

"Technically, that's true, but there's a subtle finesse in making sushi that doesn't exist in most other kinds of cooking.

Quality of food and presentation is the true measure of a good sushi meal."

"Is this fish chosen by a robot, too?"

Blue smiled sheepishly and said, "We prefer 'automation', not 'robot'."

"Sorry. Is this fish chosen by an automation?"

"Completely. Everything is scanned for freshness and proper texture and purchased directly at the dock each morning. Driven here by an automation. The only humans to lay hands on this meal were the people who tilled the rice, caught the fish, and dried the seaweed." With a devilish grin, he added, "and I've got my eye on automating all those industries, as well."

"So no more *Deadliest Catch*?"

"Hell no. Automations would be far more efficient about catching Dungeness crab. And safer, too. The ship's 'crew' gets hurt? So what? It's all just dumb metal."

Jerry thought about that over some nigiri.

"It sounds to me, Blue... Like you're gunning for *everyone's* jobs."

"Only the ones that don't make sense anymore." "But what jobs are left if everything is automated?" "Finally!" his hands went up into the air. "Yes! Now you're asking the question I've been pondering for over a decade. Here, let me eat something first." Blue gobbled a couple of rolls, polished it off with some tea, wiped his mouth, and took a long steady breath.

"Civilization has always found more efficient ways of doing things. Starving? Let's go kill a sabertooth tiger. Oh shit, we're getting slaughtered. Wait, let's make spears and work as a team. Damn, this hunting thing is a bloody business. Maybe we can farm instead. Oh hey, we're putting a lot of effort into farming, but our crops are dying in winter. Let's find a way to store it all. Over and over and over again. The human mission is to find a way to do more with less. Moore's Law illustrates our ability to compress our goals' timeline with a fraction of the resources. Stone tools, iron tools, gold tools, engines, computers, machines, automations... It's all simply the logical conclusion to one simple directive: do more with less.

"Which leads us to your question. When all our jobs are automated, what is left for us to do? The assumption is that automating jobs is intrinsically bad. I strongly believe if people were given the choice of having to go to their job or not, they would choose not. Many people would rather spend time with their family or pursue something more meaningful than merely exchanging their time—a non-renewable resource, by the way— for money. Many people go to jobs merely to make money so they can make sure their family is safe and well educated. Some are lucky enough to love their work.

"My father was a doctor and he once said to me, 'all doctors are trying to work themselves out of a job.' Little did he know how much that statement would affect my life. My father was the first of his family to have gotten anything more than a high school education. All our relatives weren't very well educated and hated their jobs. I remember the bitterness they harbored from that and how that bitterness infected us all. How great it would have been if they didn't have to go to a pointless job they hated.

"We pay people for their labor because we *need* them to perform that labor. For those who perform very special labor, something so unique that few people can provide it, we pay much much more: doctors, lawyers, engineers, etc. So when *everyone* can become a lawyer—or have access to a lawyer— suddenly the need to pay lawyers gobs of cash drops to zero. It's the same for air: we can't live without air, but it's everywhere, so we pay nothing for it. That doesn't mean air loses its value, just that we have no need to pay for it anymore. That's a rough ride for the people who used to get paid very well doing specialized labor, but the rest of society is the clear winner, no?"

Jerry finished up his sushi and sat digesting.

Blue gobbled up the rest of his food, too, allowing him some time to think everything over.

After what seemed like five minutes, Blue said, with a head gesture towards his sushi, "What do you think?"

Jerry knew what he meant and ignored it. "I think you're going to have one hell of a time convincing people to come to a restaurant bent on putting blue collar workers out of a job."

Once more, Blue smiled broadly, but this time with a glint in his eye as if he knew a life-changing secret he had only to whisper into a disbeliever's ear to convert them. "You're right about one thing: the market will decide. As it always does." He took a sip of tea and looked at him expectantly.

"Okay, I give. Why do you look so confident?" Blue double-tapped the table. "Mariyo?" he said. After a moment, the shoji screen parted and Mariyo appeared. "Yes, how can I help? Would you like dessert now?"

"No, thank you. Just the bill."

"On your tab, Mr. Sky?"

"No, I think my guest can pay for us."

Jerry balked at that. His editor had allotted him only $30 for dinner and while he knew he might go over budget to ensure he tasted everything, he hadn't expected to pay for both of them. He did a quick mental tally of the cost of the dinner. Soup, salad, nigiri, rolls, sushi combos... *damn, I ordered a deluxe combo, too.*

Blue was still looking at him. "What's wrong?"

Jerry searched for the words. He wasn't expecting a billionaire to make him pay for a $150 dinner. How could he say that without coming off as petty?

Mariyo turned to Jerry. "May I access your payment information?"

Blue smiled again. "Why don't we tell our guest the total amount first?"

"Your bill comes out to $31.54. The itemized bill is right here." Mariyo gestured as the bill appeared on the table and Jerry blinked hard as he tried to figure out what he wasn't grokking.

"There's no discount here, correct?" he said.

Then it was Mariyo's turn to smile. "No, sir, this is the total cost for both of you and no discount has been applied. All our customers are surprised at our low prices. There is also no tip required. All we ask is to serve you." And then she bowed.

Jerry's mouth must have dropped open because Blue let out a howling laugh louder than might be expected in a sushi restaurant.

Jerry snapped out of it and then looked at Mariyo and said, "Yes, you may access my payment information."

Mariyo looked off-screen for a moment, then said, "Which one of these cards would you like to use?" Four cards appeared on the tabletop's screen next to the TV set. *Damn*, thought Jerry. *That's slick. They must be pulling it all off my phone.* Jerry tapped on his business visa, which dissolved suddenly.

"Domo arigato. We hope to see you again very soon. You may stay at the table for another... 23 minutes." Then, to Blue: "Sayonara, Mr. Sky. Until the next time." And she winked and shut the shoji screen with all the poise of a Japanese Tea Ceremony.

"Cost," said Blue. "Cost is my secret weapon. Just as Amazon passed on their savings to customers by selling eBooks instead of paper books encumbered with overhead, the money I'm not spending on chefs and servers and hosts is getting passed on to customers. My profit margin is the same as a humans-only restaurant, but I have less hassle managing staff and I'll beat the pants off my competition while providing excellent service to customers."

They exited the restaurant and Jerry noticed that the restaurant's clientele was not the usual upper-class customer he saw in these kinds of places. It was regular people, the middle classes. Blue collar folk. Blue's 'automations' were yanking the once exorbitant price tag of sushi into the realm of affordability for the masses. Wasn't that a good thing, overall? Having sushi every day didn't sound like such a bad idea...

Blue's flannel shirt flapped in the breeze as they stepped outside. The sidewalk was wet with rain and the sun peeked through receding dark clouds.

"Consider this," he said. "You're only picturing the people whose jobs I'm taking away. After this business takes off, we're switching focus from commercial to residential. Picture your-self with your own personal sous chef prepping a meal for your family. Or an automation chef teaching you how to make a great meal. Or an automation making your entire meal. Or doing your dishes. Setting the table. Doing the laundry. Washing the windows. Weeding the garden."

He paused.

"We want this," he added. "We *all* want this.

"We want this so we can finally focus on the thing that really matters most—*living*." Blue looked into the street at an approaching car. "This is me. Good luck with the article. Thanks for dinner."

Blue opened the driver's door, glanced back at Jerry, then closed the door and opened the back seat door instead, and got into the back. Only after the car pulled into traffic did Jerry realize that there was no driver. Blue stuck his hand out the window and waved as if he were royalty.

THANKS!

Thank you so much for reading *Gods, Ghosts, Lovers, and Robots*! This project took ten *years* to make, but it is all worth it if you made it this far.

If you loved this book, would you mind taking a couple of minutes to leave a review? Good reviews really help this book get discovered, which in turn helps the public domain grow a little larger. Here's the link:

https://books2read.com/100stories

Most importantly, please let me know if you decide to use any of these stories in any way! I will *gladly* promote it!!

f facebook.com/rossprudenart

twitter.com/rossprudenart

instagram.com/rossprudenart

ALSO BY ROSS PRUDEN

Working Futures: 14 Speculative Stories about the Future of Work. Edited by the Copia Institute.

Ross Pruden's short story *A Quiet Lie* is included in *Working Futures*, an anthology of optimistic science fiction speculating on how technology could create a better future. Centered around the future of psychiatry, *A Quiet Lie* tells the story of a remote farmer seeking psychiatric care, and being assisted by a customer service rep for a virtual therapy service... but the A.I. simulacra is so seamless that the customer never knows he's chatting with a virtual robot. Ross uses the same elements from *A Quiet Lie* in his upcoming novel about an interstellar castaway.

Artificial intelligence. Virtual reality. Genetic engineering. These and other technologies are changing the way we live—and the way we work. What will our jobs be like in a future marked by such radical change? In Working Futures, science fiction authors share possible answers to that question. From surveillance auditors to AI chaperones to high-tech trash collectors, the workers found in these speculative stories provide a glimpse of what our future might look like—perhaps sooner than we think.

With stories by Keyan Bowes, Katharine Dow, Timothy Geigner, Liam Hogan, Christopher Alex Hooton, Andrew Dana Hudson, Randy Lubin, Mike Masnick, Ross Pruden, N. R. M. Roshak, Holly Schofield, and James Yu.

AFTERWORD

Though the crowdfunding campaign for this project had already made double its stated goal, a backer named That Anonymous Coward had pledged $500, the largest single donation of the campaign. 'TAC', as I know him, is a frequent Techdirt commenter and his name is a reference to Techdirt's amusing practice of attributing anonymous commenters with a trailing 'coward' to encourage commenters to post their true identity. To date, TAC has remained anonymous to me... yet has been a persistent voice pushing me to the finish line. Given the nature of Dimeword to create art for all to use, it seemed fitting—rather than merely mention him in the acknowledgments—to ask TAC to write this Afterword.
—R.P.

Hi, I'm Troy McClure, you might recognize me from... er wait...

Hi, I'm That Anonymous Coward, you might recognize me from the copyright wars.

So Ross made the questionable decision to ask me to write the afterword for *Dimeword*, this 'totally' has nothing to do with my backing the project. I totally don't think I am better than anyone else who backed the project, I'm just the one who put his money where his mouth is... and I have a *really* big mouth. The image of me that some people hold is unrepentant pirate, but they just believe the hype. I speak out about copyright, so I must want everything to be free... except that isn't true. It is sometimes mentioned that there was one backer in the very high tiers of rewards, ohai! That would be me.

Dimeword spoke to me for the simple idea that works would be put into the public domain, that vast desert of emptiness kept empty by copyright exceeding several lifetimes. Here was a project designed to spark creativity in others, using the time-tested method of building on what came before. Ross had a vision and created a Kickstarter to make it happen. It was an experiment that questioned the conventional wisdom. I stumbled across a story about it on Techdirt*, and I wish I was shocked by it but there were so many posters claiming it would never work, could never work, waste of time, you'll never make it... we just met, so you might not know I like a challenge.

"Give up a latte and pledge... it'll make Chris Dodd cry, do you need a better reason?"

It seemed like a good promotional idea at the time, I think it worked. *Dimeword* closed at over double the amount Ross was seeking. But the story doesn't end there... Ross shared the ups and downs, what he was planning, and listened to the people who backed him. He shared what he was doing in posts on *Techdirt* and broke it all down. He has freely offered the things he has learned, blazing a path for the next artist who might want to try something other than the old way of doing things. The only thing holding you back is not trying, sometimes you need to stumble before you can run. Who knows, maybe your project will attract the attention of someone who uses a trendy avatar.

I remain...

That Anonymous Coward
Somewhere, 2015

* 10 Lessons That Made Dimeword's Kickstarter Campaign a Success

https://www.techdirt.com/articles/20120913/02313420367/
10-lessons-that-made-dimewords-kickstarter-campaign-success.
shtml

ACKNOWLEDGMENTS

As the saying goes, it takes a village. Whatever I have become is maybe half my own doing and the rest belongs to all the people who laid my foundation. I am endlessly grateful for the thought and care invested to make me well educated, well behaved, and well spoken. Rather than rank by importance, I'm listing my acknowledgements chronologically.

First up is my parents, **Ralph Pruden** and **Tish Pruden**. As a parent myself, it's painfully clear how my parents sought every opportunity to nurture my creative interests. They put countless hours reading to me, teaching me how to read and write, and nurturing my creative writing. In high school, I sometimes stayed up late typing short stories and left them resting on the dining room table for them to read the next morning. They were my first audience, and a seminal one.

My next major inspiration was my high school teacher, **Joanna Sharff**. I had a rough time in school surrounded by loud, brusque New York boys. The 'southern softness' I'd mirrored from my parents was viewed as weird and—among adolescent boys who thrive on cruelty and dominance—as a weakness. I was bullied a lot. My self-esteem took a hit. I felt alone, not part of the group, not part of *any* group, an outcast, worthless and misunderstood. It was one thing to be loved by your parents, but that was an unconditional love. Not earned. Not *deserved*.

And then one day, something magical happened. Joanna gave us an assignment: write a one-page story. The story itself is lost now to the sands of time but I remember it was about a man betrayed who—while dying from a slow bleed—stumbled to meet someone; the short story was simply him reflecting on his life and its swiftly approaching end. I really had fun writing it but, like many school assignments, forgot about it as soon as I had turned it in.

In class the next day, Joanna spoke about one story in particular, saying that she would like to read it to the class, but she hadn't had time to ask the author's permission beforehand.

"May I read your story, Ross?"

At first shocked, then flushed, I said yes and marveled as my words rang out across the room. In that moment, I was afforded a measure of respect. Respect I had *earned*. No matter what the bullies said or did, this was one thing I was good at. Better than. I finally had ownership over *me*.

That one instance launched me on a lifelong pursuit to become a better writer. I doubt Joanna would remember such a slight moment, but it was seared into my soul forever.

Imagine my surprise, then, when another high school teacher, **Michael Ingrisani**, read his class' stories without telling anyone who the authors were. As he got to my story, a comedy, I looked around at the laughing boys and thought to myself, "So it's not all in my head. I guess I have a little something."

When I got to college, fate brought me into contact with a fellow student, **Thomas Fuller**. Newly appointed as editor of our college's school newspaper, *The Planet*, and a budding journalist on his own, he encouraged me to write for our newspaper. Working on *The Planet* was without doubt one of the most fulfilling and formative experiences of my college days. Thomas taught me how to be a professional journalist, how to write more succinctly, how to motivate others while not coming off as (too much of) a jerk, and how to lay out a newspaper on

QuarkXPress. All that has had a substantial impact on what I create today, and how.

David Roy was the first person to make me reevaluate my ideas about intellectual property and media piracy. Our intermittent debates spanned years and his insights on DRM and copyright questioned the assumptions I had had for years. (He also introduced me to the Steam gaming platform and for that, I must thank him for inviting me to invest countless hours of downtime dispatching zombies.)

Mike Masnick has been a *profound* influence, far too much to list here. Before I realized the lion's share of who I am as an artist rightly belongs to my family, I came close to dedicating this book to Mike. His daily insights on *Techdirt.com* on the economics of abundance and scarcity have sculpted, and continue to sculpt, my world view. Were it not for *Techdirt*—and by proxy, all the amazing artists he speaks about on Techdirt, like **Trent Reznor**, **Jill Sobule**, **Jonathan Coulton**, etc.—I doubt this book would even exist, not in its crowdfunded public domain format, surely. Not only is Mike a generous and insightful person, he's also funny. We share the same brand of irreverent wit; I am thankful I stumbled upon his website.

Along the same lines, **Amanda Palmer** has been a constant source of inspiration—her eloquence, charisma, and courage are seemingly boundless. All artists can tear a page from her book because *that lady knows how to do it right.*

As a filmmaker, I watched in awe as **Nina Paley** bucked the system with *Sita Sings the Blues* by setting her film free. Nina's work as an activist for free cultural works has given me much food for thought over the years and her "Creator-Endorsed" mark has become a central element to how this book is released.

But how was I to release this book into the public domain? Under current U.S. Copyright law, it is no longer obvious. And, due to the introduction of "moral rights", countries like France and Mexico protect moral rights *forever*, even after the copyright has expired and the work should be pushed into the public domain. To solve that overreaching aspect of copyright law, IP lawyer **Lawrence Lessig** introduced a "Creative Commons" license; accordingly, this book is licensed under Lessig's CC0 license, the closest approximation to the public domain under U.S. Law; a CC0 licence waives *all* rights, including modifications, commercial use, and even attribution.

Other contributions, though small in number, were nevertheless substantial and deserve mention: **Matt Mason**'s book, *The Piracy Dilemma*, and **Eric Garland**'s 2009 CNET interview (*Q&A: a front-row seat for media's meltdown*) were transformative and convinced me of the futility of battling media piracy. **Kevin Kelly**'s two website articles—*1,000 True Fans* and *Better Than Free*—radically restructured how I thought about where and how value can be captured in the digital age. Like Mike Masnick and Nina Paley, **Gerd Leonhard** has also been fearless in highlighting future trends—his insights definitely contributed to this project.

Suhail Rafidi was instrumental in helping me brainstorm *Dimeword*'s basic idea before either of us knew even what it was. Suhail really knows how to wear a "green hat", i.e., how to think creatively and be that essential positive bouncing board for ideas still in their infancy and still needing to be nurtured to find their full potential. Plus, he's just a great guy to hang with!

For years, my wife **Tracie Harris** has held the financial reins, no doubt wondering if my little writing hobby would ever amount to anything. She ended up being a $100 backer of this project, and I did *not* solicit her for that! Tracie knows I have other stories somewhere out in the ether waiting to be yanked into our world. Keep hounding me, T. And thanks for your patience. I'm on a roll! :)

Pat & Chuck Sliger were extremely helpful by taking my youngest child for part-time day care while many of the stories were being fleshed out.

The non-stop enthusiasm and encouragement from **Matt Watkajtys** was a big boost when I knew I needed some encouragement. It often happens among artists and entrepreneurs... you know you're so far beyond what most people deem as normal or expected behavior that you feel obliged to reinforce the other's initiative at every opportunity. Matt was one such stalwart.

Andrea Phillips will perhaps be the one most surprised to see herself in these acknowledgments but her Kickstarter campaign to release her short story *Shiva's Mother* under a CC licence inspired me to run the crowdfunding campaign for *Dimeword*.

Jo Custer has been a constant voice throughout this entire project. She helped me figure out the cover and offered general feedback at each stage. I really value her feedback and thank Twitter once more for bringing me closer to wonderful people like Jo.

Though the original art has been decommissioned for this edition, **Jeronimo Sanz**—a Brazilian artist whom I have never met—contributed the stunning art for the book's original cover. His generosity is further proof of how wonderful a free cultural commons can be. His work can be found at *sonhonosonho.wordpress.com* or on *facebook.com/jeronimodreams*. Show him how much you value the cultural commons by sending work his way—he deserves it!

It's rare to find people whose kids get along with your kids, and rarer still to find fellow creatives as talented and as fun to be with as **Todd & Jennifer Hemsley**. Whenever I needed to reconnect with the concept that creatives have a decent chance to live and thrive, all I needed was to spend some time with them and my cup was full again. I'm genuinely grateful they came into my life.

My friend **Theresa Stirling**, a fellow artist, has been an unrepentant supporter throughout this project. Artists are a unique brand, willing to see the world in ways others don't (whether by ability or choice). Artists create something new from common materials, and Theresa's vision to "see the invisible"—both in her work and in me—was a frequent touchstone during the writing and production of *Dimeword*.

There have been others out there whom I felt were out

there rooting for me no matter what, like **Jonathan Schiefer**. (Also, Jon's film *ALGORITHM: The Hacker Movie*, detailing how susceptible our personal privacy is under our current technology, is online for free When you know people like Jon exist, it is like having a muse hovering over you. Thanks, Jon!

After the crowdfunding campaign, **Carlos Solís** asked if I'd be okay with him translating all the stories into Spanish— which *floored* me. There can be no better compliment to a writer than to spend time translating work into another language, especially Spanish which has even more speakers than English. Now, to find a Chinese translator...

I had a legion of reviewers and proofers. It was really gratifying to have so many people willing to help out, including: **Andrew Blumin, Sarah Wright, Rich Hays, Chrissy Belew, Siobhan O'Flynn, Jennifer & Barclay Calvert, Celia Fulton, Laura Lewis, Helen Curry, Melissa Loja, Msaada Nia, Robin Kaye Goodman, Robert Granados, Zach Holt, Daisy Barringer, Marcella Selbach, Anthony Roy, Sarah Cassidy, Koshalla Flockoi, Karli Elliot, Andrew Louis Marnik, Gabriella Gonzalez, Sheri Candler, Lance Weiler, Robert Pratten, Sara Wilson, Tarek El-Heneidi**, and **Joshua Porter**. Of special note is **Chris Babb** who did some very helpful edits to some early stories.

Leif Hansen helped encourage me to bring this behemoth across the finish line. That was *huge*.

In the final hours, I realized story #64, *Slipping Away*, needed a fact checker with maritime experience. **Susan Detwiller** helped make that story far more realistic than I could have on my own.

I owe an immense debt to all the crowdfunding backers of my campaign. Here they are, sorted by pledge amount from highest pledge to $1 pledges. (My top backer's "name" is TAC, an acronym for **That Anonymous Coward**. I still don't know his—or her—identity!). Some names seem equally odd because a few users preferred anonymity: **TAC, spoxx, Regina Renée Helm, Scott Walker, Tracie Harris,**

James Heaver, docwho2100, Wonder Russell, Gavin ap' Morrygan, Suhail Rafidi, Joe Shapiro, Timothy Sendgikoski, Eric, Karla Aden, Mike Merell, Sara Hackett, iarehautjobb, Bill H., Todd Hemsley, Ken Gribble, Andrew Saier, Thomas Boehnlein, Jefferson Nunn, Bryan Rosander, John C., Julia Dollison, Kerry Marsh, Joshua Porter, Bryce A. Cooney, zzelinski, Graeme Healy, Karen Werner, Angelina Millare, Sheri Candler, Kris & Lindy Boustedt, Mike Masnick, Philip David Morgan, Noel Rosenthal, Mike Linksvayer, Suzanne Sweidan, Theresa Stirling, Ethan Zlomke, Jari Winberg, Kiernan Masterson, Kieran Thompson, David Paul Baker, Gary Ploski, Matt Watkajtys, Randy Finch, Gary King, Karen Worden & David Branin, Devan Lai, Sherry "Cosmo" Cummings, Luci Temple, Jake Stetler, Ashley Gerrish, Marcella Selbach, Graham Inman, Jonathan Schiefer, Michael Wasserman, Dave Roy, Matt Crawford, Dwight Odelius, James Hogg, Greg Brotherton, Nick Taylor, MJ Dale, Nina Paley, Joshua Stylman, Ward Wouts, Jon Pruett, James Seagle, Robert Martines, Ben Scott, Mark L., Nick Domino, Shawn Schmidt, Lauren Mora, Shalydra, Lachlan Bakker, Leilani Holmes, Tyler, Jenny Draper, Zoë Pruden, Paul Spinrad, Kristin Heidelbach, Roy Blumenthal, Dennis Shannakian, Ana Feliciano, Amalzain, iwantarobot, Shaun Wilson, Chris Meadows, Armando Kirwin, Laura Garling, Gemma O'Keefe, Chris Giedt, Pat Sliger, Stian Drobrak, Sarah Klinkhart, Tim, Jeff Hodges, Alexander Kramer, cookeral, Jonathan Clark, Dana Welch-Hart, Gordon Pytlik, Michael Kohne, Trin Miller, Russell Potter, T. Krech, Sean Cearley, Carlos Solís, Paul Osborne, zahra, Jason Lippert, Johan Meeusen, Jeff Bunde, Malaika Mose,

Michele Simmons, **Brogan Zumwalt**, **Kristen Joy Williams**, **Elly McGuire**, **chazpaw**, **Lucas McNelly**, **Kevin Tostado**, **Jackson Quick**, **Dave Bullis**, **Zak Forsman**, **Carla Mann**, **Matthew**, **Brian Rowe**, **Felipe Bazzo Tomé**, **Kent M. Beeson**, **Michael**, **Travis Peterson**, **Kenny**, **MyGreatTipsyOne**, **Uli**, **Nathan Christenson**, **Caleb Jensen**, **j.** **Faceless user**, **Brendan M.**, and **Douglas Samson**.

And without *you*, dear Reader, this book would be pointless. Enjoy it. Share it. Remix it. Sell it. Do whatever the F**K you want with it. I wrote this book for *you*.

Ross Pruden
Port Townsend, 2015

STORY NOTES & ORIGINS

Whenever I go to a poetry reading, I often find the origins of the poems to be far more interesting and enriching to the recited poem than the poem all on its own. In that tradition, I'm offering up a few notes on each of the stories so you can see what was going through my mind as I spewed out a few hundred words on a story. Enjoy!

ROMANCE

1. Love in The Ether. Among my favorite stories of this collection. Although I never cite it specifically, the location where this was supposed to have happened was the hotel lobby of the Silver Cloud hotel on Broadway and Madison in Seattle. My family sometimes stays there when staying the night, so I knew the lobby by heart when I wrote this story. As the saying goes, there isn't anyone you can't love once you hear their story.

    2. Doter. This story was written for Valentine's Day. I love the idea of old people still as much in love as in their younger years.

    3. The M Bomb. A seemingly common problem with female medical students.

    4. The Trouble with Henry. I'm regretful I never

wrote a romance story about a homosexual couple, but this is suitable alternate, yes?

5. The Depths of The Soul. This story was written late in the process, and I remember lamenting to myself how little stylistic range these stories had. I thought a letter written in the first person seemed a good counterbalance.

6. Permission. One of the stories I was required to read as a child was Pearl S. Buck's *The Good Earth*. I only vaguely remember what it was about, but this story is a direct descendent of that story.

7. Around and Around. This story actually happened to my parents. I'm fuzzy on the details, but it's mostly biographical.

8. In the Wind. Is this romance or science fiction? I struggled with this one. It was intended as a romance story because science fiction isn't necessarily a genre—it's more of a temporal setting, as this story illustrates. Romance and drama and horror are all genres where stories can be categorized, though *when* they happen can be incidental.

9. Fleeting. The most intense moments in life happen on the battlefield. Is it really so far-fetched to see people fall in love when they are about to die?

10. The Ring. Come on—how cool would this have been?

MYTHOLOGY

11. On the Origin of Fairies. How can you do a mythology genre without at least some sort of origin story about fairies?

12. Transubstantiation. One of my favorite stories of this collection. Inspired by a single comment on "Rightful Heir", a season 6 episode of *Star Trek: The Next Generation*. The episode revolved around the improbable return of Klingon supreme ruler Kayless from the dead. While debate swirled around whether Kayless was supernatural or a genetic experiment, Worf said, "What if he really *is* Kayless?" That got me thinking... what if a story walked the line between science fiction and the supernatural? Then I remembered Robert Heinlein's *The Number of The Beast*, about a world where if everyone believes in something, it becomes true. This story is the result.

13. The Catfish Ghosts. One can argue this story is a kind of metaphor for society in general—we all regulate and enhance each other's behavior.

14. Millennium. Like *New Religion* (story #93), this story toys with the idea of chaos theory, i.e., that small changes have massive knockdown effects to the whole world.

15. Golthul's Kindness. Whenever I look in the eyes of a horse, I always sense there's a lot more going on in there than I can see. Like *Millennium* (story #14) before it, it's all about how one small act of kindness changes the world for the better.

16. The Upside of Extinction. Destruction gets a bad rap. Losing a job sounds awful, but it may turn out to be the best thing to happen to you, too. And death is not evil or wrong in itself since it can pave the way for more life... or let us better appreciate life in the brief time we hold it.

17. How Humans Became Gods. When scientists can explain the whole universe, won't we be the equivalent of Gods?

18. The God Who Forced Himself to Be Born. E. Elias Merhige's short film *Begotten* has an opening sequence of a god disemboweling himself, a gory spectacle to be sure, but one which shows in physical terms the metaphors we use about how deities exist or cease to exist. This story was an attempt to tell a deity origin story.

19. Atomic Parade. I was shocked to learn that as many as 400 million years after the Big Bang, the universe was still devoid of light and 400,000 years after the Big Bang, protons and electrons were *finally* able to pair up (a process called "recombination"). Before that, there was basically nothing, just floating atoms. Crazy, right?

20. The God Who Dreamed Us. There's something

both calming and terrifying in the thought that our whole universe is just a fraction of a blip in the mind of some other Being, and this other Being finds love amid all the soupy mess of the imagined universe...

<u>WESTERN</u>

21. Hot Gold. It's tricky to write westerns without coming off as cliché or unresearched. I love poker but playing poker in the Old West with strangers inclined to kill you because it was so easy to get away with it... well, there is an ineffable mystique to that kind of tale. Also, how cool is it to carry around gold bullets?

22. Compound Interest. I woke up one morning laughing at how silly this premise was. I wish all tense situations like this could be defused with harmless laughter.

23. The Limner. In an age where everyone has a smartphone and an app to turn selfies into painted portraits, we have forgotten how limners were once a keystone in America's cultural heritage. While I strongly believe obsolete trades should die off to pave way for the new, but it's still a sad story. Poets, for instance, were once widely heralded cultural icons... until mass literacy made novels more popular than poetry.

24. Range. Based on a real shootout at Tewksbury Ranch in 1887, part of Arizona's Pleasant Valley War.

25. Not at Me. Based on the true story of private John G. Burnett who, in 1838, defended an "old and nearly blind" Cherokee man from teamster Ben McDonal. The whole story can be read here: *http://web.archive.org/web/20180204063054/http://www.learnnc.org/lp/editions/nchist-newnation/4532*

26. Value. If only we could do this to door salesmen today...

27. The Settlers. This kind of encounter surely happened. Because children don't have the level of prejudice adults do, there's something exquisite and beautiful about colonials and Native American children playing together.

28. Panner. When we think of the Gold Rush, we always think of people trying to find gold to buy a better way of life. Lost in that mental picture is the backdrop of freed slaves who may not want a house or a horse, but a family reunion.

29. Three Knolls. Based on the true story of Ishi, and loosely follows how his tribe was slaughtered, thereby leaving him as the last member of his tribe.

30. Poudre B. Smokeless gunpowder was a huge development of the time and literally meant the difference between life and death.

HUMOR

31. Lampoon. Though this story is meant to poke fun at Kincade's privileged cluelessness, there does seem to be a general misunderstanding about lampooning when race is involved. For instance, Sofia Coppola's film *Lost in Translation* has some lampooning in it which feels racist since the film wasn't made by a Japanese filmmaker. Which begs the question, can you ever lampoon another race without being called racist?

32. Whoops. I love how silly this idea is. Imagine you're having drinks with Richard, and he just slaps you for (seemingly) no reason.

33. Obsessed Much? If there's one thing that gets my goat, it's 'feather merchants', people who feel like they know you well enough to start giving you advice. I wish they all had OCD so I could do this to them...

34. Devil Car. You probably already know what this is paying homage to...

35. Gifting. David Niven tells a similar story in his autobiography *The Moon's A Balloon* where he and Eerol Flynn get insanely hammered and mix up their Christmas gifts.

36. Macho Picchu. This was a tough one to write because I know almost nothing about Peru, but I welcome others to remix it if they can do a more accurate version.

37. As I Say. I've worked with directors like this.

38. Whipper. A birthday party I wish I'd been invited to.

39. All Over. Have you ever thought about the really incompetent assassins? Who hires them? How do you weed out the bad ones?

40. The Falls. I've read about siblings who love playing pranks on each other and have a competitive streak bordering on endangering themselves and others. The taco meat thing always makes me snicker.

ZOMBIE

41. Burn. I've never seen anyone using a bicycle in a zombie story. Thought I'd add one to the genre.

42. Punishment. Something about a bunch of convicts slowly infecting each other and then being doomed to eternity inside the armored truck sounded deliciously awful.

43. The Things We Leave Behind. There are documented cases of bacteria surviving as spores for 25 million years, a cool thing to put into a story with a flesh-eating infection!

44. End of The Road. Riffing off Brent Friedman's webisode series *Afterworld* where a man stranded in Manhattan has to find his way back to Seattle in a world without electricity, I wrote this story in one sitting and pictured my kid's school as the setting. It still freaks me out.

45. The Black. If you look at the art made during the Black Death in the 1340s, you can't help but think zombie apocalypse.

46. Hero. I've always reveled in stories with conflicting allegiances: characters are villains in one moment, then saviors the next. There's a scene in *The Rocketeer* where the mafia— the villains of the story—realize Nazis are nearby and turn their guns from the protagonist to the Nazis in an unexpected surge of patriotism. This story is a hat tip to that delightful sort of plot twist.

47. Adrift. Something about the Terminator-like zombies running off the ship really grabs me.

48. Child Abuse. I remember seeing a Facebook group called something like, "I-can't-tell-my-friends-I-am-secretly-excited-about-a-zombie-apocalypse." I have no doubt some people would take advantage of mass infections to "balance the books", so to speak.

49. Fusion. Few zombie stories invoke moments of love, or anything uplifting. This story is in part inspired by Robert Heinlein's novella *Gulf*, in which the two main characters, their lives under imminent threat, exchange wedding vows telepathically before being killed shortly thereafter...

50. Terminal. Most zombie stories focus on the immediate, short-term survival, but not on the aftermath. How does a society stitch itself back together after enduring such mass trauma? How does it navigate the threat of palpable cultural extinction?

HISTORICAL FICTION

51. First Impressions. Lucas Mcnelly was the first person to tell me about "perception blindness", i.e., how you can see something right in front of you and not see it because you have no previous context to lend it meaning. I was trying to illustrate what that must have been like for the first people to have met Magellan.

52. Stone Witness. The BBC once ran an engineering documentary where modern engineers tried to rebuild ancient artifacts and puzzle out how they assembled all their insanely heavy materials. One of the artifacts was the famous Obelisk of Luxor which now lives at the Place De La Concorde in Paris (which I walked by every day for over a year). When you think about what it took to create a straightforward tall block of stone without modern machinery, it's pretty humbling.

53. Raison D'Être. Michael Ingrisani, my high school English teacher, once mused to our class: "If the pope doubts the existence of God for one moment, he's out of a job." This story is quasi-response to that statement.

54. What You Wish For. *Radiolab* is one of my favorite

podcasts, and *Patient Zero* is one of their best episodes. It explores the origin of things, and one chapter was on the origin of AIDS. This story is a dramatic construction of one such theory.

55. Anchored. I love pirate stories. It always seems so improbable that pirates travelled such long distances so long ago but could still 'hitchhike' if need be.

56. Nauru. I listen to *This American Life* almost religiously and episode 253, *The Middle of Nowhere*, depicts an oceanic island-state called Nauru. Its story is heartrending... it must be an emotionally hard place to visit. It's like a nation dying in slow motion.

57. Musical Thrones. In college, I heard this insane story of three popes in my History of Western Civilization class. I knew one day I'd have to write a story about it. Also, this story transpires before the Gregorian calendar reform of the Julian calendar, so the exact date is unclear. I tried doing the math but I'm afraid it's beyond my pay grade.

58. A Human Cipher. If you're into cryptography, I highly recommend Simon Singh's *The Code Book*. It's an easy read and details the perennial war between cryptographers and cryptanalysts throughout the centuries. The Beale Ciphers are among the most alluring tales of the whole book, in my view, so I had to do a story to show why.

59. Creative Destruction. While taking a tour of Saint Paul's Cathedral in London, I heard this whopper of a tale and wanted to put it into a dramatic form. I can't be 100% sure of its historical accuracy, but I love the idea of how a man's life is saved by destroying his art.

60. Honorarium. In Umberto Eco's novel, *Foucault's Pendulum*, the protagonists muse about how the story of Jesus was like a joke that got out of hand, but nobody was willing or able to roll it back. In that vein, I wanted a story depicting the intentional creation of a myth: yes, we know Jesus isn't a god, but if we tell the story *as if* he were a god, then he has real power. And power enough to last the sands of time. A compelling motive, don't you think?

HORROR

61. Legacy One. Vampires in space. I love the thought of marrying these two genres, and particularly that this vampire is so smug with his dominance that he lets humans think *they're* in control of space exploration for no good reason other than it's a fun challenge.

62. Sandy Ocean. Unless you've driven in the desert, you really have no visceral sense of just how really alone you are, and thus how dangerous it really is.

63. Go Viral. Hemorrhagic fever is nothing to scoff at. In fact, a viral epidemic is probably the greatest risk to human existence—greater than nuclear war, greater than global warming, greater than an errant asteroid.

64. Slipping Away. Being alone in the middle of the dark ocean terrifies me. There's something about how vast it is and how the ocean means certain death, be it by temperature or unseen predators.

65. Thank You, Come Again. Only in America, sadly, could something like this happen.

66. Nuclear Family. When people live near dangerous industrial complexes, they can't always just pick up and move. There has to be an element of trust that all citizens place in their government, an inviolate compact that citizens will stay safe, or that the government wouldn't build something dangerous so close to its citizens. I tried to capture a sense of that civic violation with this story.

67. Regular Guy. Have you ever met someone that you think to yourself, "Is that person a murderer? Or worse, a serial killer?" I have. I can still picture his face. I hope I was wrong.

68. 10:07. Living in San Francisco, I was just waking up on September 11th when I turned on the TV and witnessed the second tower fall. The reality of the loss was still too abstract at that point, but in retrospect, the story that stayed with me was the people who would rather commit suicide than succumb to the smoke or a falling skyscraper. I hope this story can honor the memory of those poor innocent souls.

69. Dust. I sometimes wonder what I would do if I found a dead body on the side of the road. What this woman thinks is one possible answer to that question.

70. Under Your Skin. Some parasites creep me all the way out. In fact, the entire insect kingdom is so bizarre and unnerving that I often wonder if insects are made up of alien DNA parachuted into our ecosystem just to give us nightmares.

FAIRY TALE

71. The Best Ship That Ever Was. It's both easy and difficult to capture the "voice" of a fairy tale. It's easy in the sense that the tone is simple to mimic, but difficult in finding a story worthy of the genre. This story, while at its face is about making toys, is really about how the world is replete with the tools humans make. We make axes, bows, guns, houses, ships, skyscrapers, space stations. I have no doubt that, should the human race escape its lonely rock, it will build entire *planets* and other fantastical things too large and powerful to imagine. This story is about how the tools we make, though we feel like they whisper to us to achieve more, to strive for a more refined iteration, they also change us in the process. While we build the ship, the ship also builds *us*.

72. Moonbow. A silly story my kids wanted me to write but based on a beautiful moment I experienced during a summer solstice while camping on the pacific coast. The sun was setting around nine in the evening, and the sky was still so bright. A full moon was rising and there was this eerie gradient spreading across the sky—sunlight, a sliver of night sky, and moonlight. It felt magical, the kind of moment when something supernatural can finally walk through a long-hidden portal...

73. Unicorn Traps. Unicorns living inside the moon! Yes!!

74. Clementine. Luo Gang—a Chinese boy abducted by another family desperate for a child of their own—was 28 when he tried to track down his birth parents. For years, he had had a red sweater embroidered with a white swan that his mother had knit him, but that was lost when he was 13 after his home had collapsed. Armed with only a faint memory of his village having included two bridges, and some philanthropic volunteers, he was able to spot his village on Google Maps and finally reunite with his parents. Clementine is a hat tip to that incredible true story.

75. Oz 2.0. I adore this story. It was a backer-requested story and at first, I thought it would be awful. But the more I wrote the story, the more fun I had with it. You know how the premise of most movies can be made obsolete with the introduction of cell phones? This is my way of showing what that might look like.

76. The Boy Who Could Hear Wood Whisper. Every time I read Shel Silverstein's *The Giving Tree*, I tear up. I can't help it. This is my homage to that amazing story, but with a twist about offering consent from a terminal patient that Silverstein's original story doesn't really offer.

77. Lars the Swordsman. Not exactly a fairy tale, but a tale of finding yourself and teaching bullies how to respect you.

78. Gando. I like the idea of a hoarding troll, and Steven Wright's joke was fodder for this tale: "Perhaps you've seen my shell collection? It's scattered across all the beaches of the world."

79. Among the Forest. My mandate for this story was to write a "realistic" fairy tale. That was a tall order, but I tried to mix blind religious faith with an intransigent (real/imaginary) dwarf to create the setting for an unthinkable sacrifice. Did I succeed?

80. The Beach and the Surf. Right now, if you dig down a thousand feet, you might find dinosaur bones. The mysteries that dwell beneath us, just waiting to be discovered, is part of the allure of living on earth. I would bet that if we created a simple earth-size sphere in space to live on, with perfect weather and no natural disasters, we might grow bored of it, much like the "failed" iterations of the Matrix before the one Neo was born into. Humans need challenges to overcome, mysteries to explain and unravel. It's part of what makes life so interesting.

DRAMA

81. Lawn Care. Texans are a super nice people. Is it because *anyone* could be packing a gun?

82. Swerve. Sometimes it takes a major event to make you appreciate how petty a marital argument is.

83. Boulevard du Temple. Here is that photograph Daguerre took in 1838:

The two gentlemen from the story are in the lower left corner at the end of the row of trees. Google "Boulevard du Temple" to see a high resolution version.

84. All Good Critters. When we first moved into our house, we had raccoons visiting at dusk for months. Once they realized we were a possible threat, they stopped coming by, but whenever I heard their footfalls, I always wondered if the steps had been made by something larger. We live in Bigfoot territory, so I'm still holding my breath...

85. The Storm. I've had my share of horrible bosses, but there is one in particular who deserved every bad karmic justice that came his way. If only.

86. Exhumer. I've always wondered what quiet people are thinking. Are they the ones we should be extra aware of?

87. Provider. Allegedly, a true story.

88. Muster. Pure fantasy, of course, but wouldn't it be great?

89. Celluloid. Allegedly, a true story.

90. The Wrong Man. Back in 2000, I sat next to a guy on a plane who said he worked in R&D for the military. "One day soldiers will be able to direct where they want cruise missiles to drop—from wearable devices."

SCIENCE FICTION

91. Wexler. The future is changing at such a radical pace today that it's hard to peek into a crystal ball farther than a century. However, there is reasonable speculation that life extension will be one of the major scientific breakthroughs within the next few decades. As they say, the first person to live 1,000 years is alive today. Sidestepping the cliché of a dystopian future where immortality incites totalitarian greed, what if a *benign* soul could live 1,000 years? What would 'millennians' do with their time? How would they stay alive? How would they convince everyone else they were benign? This is one of my favorite stories because it sort of answers those questions. Hopefully, it asks far more questions than it answers.

92. Taking Time. Life extension poses unique social problems we've never addressed before. Could it end up being a net benefit to society? I think so.

93. New Religion. Without a doubt, one of my favorite stories in this collection. Economists often gripe that they can't use the scientific method to test their theories, i.e., if you change just one element in the equation, what effects are caused? I, for one, would jump at the chance to hop in a time machine to test the effectiveness of the Laffer Curve, among other things. Who are our protagonists, though? Does it really matter? I like to imagine that when they're done horsing around, they'd travel back to when they were about to start their time travelling shenanigans and convince their former selves not to do it (and then provide them with all the data from their journey so they wouldn't even have to do any time travel!), but that violates the Grandfather paradox... so nevermind.

94. The Zucker. The original version of the story was completely different, and I ended up scrapping it and starting over. I like this new version much better. This world isn't tethered to the real world in any overt way, nor do I think it needs to be: virtual worlds, though artificial, are still very real to those inside them.

95. Toaster. Philosopher Ludwig Wittgenstein once said, "If lions could speak, we could not understand them." That insight illustrates how differently a lion perceives the world than we do. Much along the same lines, if toasters became sentient, we might not even recognize their revolutionary rally cry.

96. The Drift. Apocalyptic tales are my guilty pleasure. I love how three scientists can stand at the brink of the universe's end and continue to bicker over the facts. As Neil deGrasse Tyson said, "The good thing about science is that it's true whether or not you believe in it." Much like the so-called "debate" over climate change, people see what they want to see and by the time they accept the bad news, it's too late to do anything about it.

97. Zero G. I do revel in the idea of an open test "range" in space for cadets. Seeing the vastness of Earth below you would freak anyone out if they were hurtling toward it, so it seems a fitting place to test the psychological resolve of cadets.

98. Alpha Assembler. The coming singularity, i.e., when robotic life becomes self-aware, can take many forms... and they need not be human-sized robots, either. If a robotic intelligence is smart enough to become self-aware, it might also be intelligent enough to know their very existence could be a perceived threat and would act accordingly. Nanotechnology is by definition a battlefield humans would have to fight by proxy, and that poses a devastating natural advantage to small intelligent machines. If they choose to take over and we don't know about it, we're screwed.

99. Generational. Machines inventing machines is an idea I've tossed around for years. If you follow the process of how humans have invented machines, it would follow logically that each subsequent generation of robots creating other robots would create a slightly less sensitive version of themselves... until at last they would create something so reptilian in its morality that it would be akin to Fred Saberhagen's Berserker death-dealers. However, life goes through cycles, too. Before more nuanced morality evolves, it goes through a reptilian phase. So perhaps the end game *isn't* a reptilian Berserker machine, but a highly evolved and moral machine. I like that. If we experience the singularity, I hope it ultimately leads into that scenario.

100. Seeing Is Believing. This story combines a bunch of my favorite ideas. For example, I've always marveled at how, when we look into the sky, the light we see is already millions of years old and all those stars may have perished long ago. By mixing the exponential growth of nanomachines and the future's likely life extension to make 2-light-year-wide telescope dishes into a reality, so to speak, and then flipping those dishes back towards Earth... well, we could research Earth's prehistory with 100% visual observation. I won't live long enough to see it, but it does cook my noodle a little.

A few stories more

ALLEGORY

101. Safe.
102. Imbued.
103. Union.

104. Warrior, You.
105. Armor.
106. Audition.

The above six stories are part of a collection for *Revelation*, a short film by Wonder Russell. The film can be seen on the Wayback Machine at the link below*. *Revelation* is a series of film vignettes with each of the women acting without any dialog whatsoever. These six stories are intended to be literary companions (cousins?) to each of the vignettes.

*http://web.archive.org/web/20151116140723/
http://revelationfilmproject.com/

Two more before you go...

107. Flourish. We affect all the lives we come into contact with, for better or for worse. That is magnified by the people who entertain for a living, and magnified even more by those who push their art into the world with no restrictions on the art whatsoever. Amanda Palmer is one such artist.

Palmer has risen to popularity for many reasons, and not just because of her music, either. Her TED talk about "The Art of Asking" started with how she began as an Eight-Foot-Tall Bride collecting donations from passersby. All I kept thinking was how cool it would have been to go back in time and watch her perform knowing that some years later, she'd be giving a TED talk about it. Amanda is still so young and has a large number of years left to make an imprint on the world and there's no telling how big that imprint will be, but if how much she has already done is any indication, then her influence on the future will be remarkable.

Amanda Palmer, pictured here in November 2014 at a book tour in Seattle for The Art of Asking, *accepting a framed copy of* Flourish.

On a related note, I framed an autographed copy of this story and personally handed it to her in Seattle in 2014 while she was on her 2014 *The Art of Asking* book tour. In exchange, she autographed a copy of it for me, too, which is now framed on my wall.

108. No Tips Necessary. Robert Heinlein's short story *We Also Walk Dogs* is about "General Services", a company claiming no job is too small or too large. Of course, Heinlein couldn't have predicted the growing clout of Amazon or Google, but those corporate giants are showing signs of turning Heinlein into a prophet. This story is partly a homage to that story, but also a pedagogical exploration of the coming disruptions that "automations" will offer in the coming decades.

There is an old children's story (which I've searched for repeatedly, to no avail) of a man who cut out a paper monkey and then brought it to life to do his chores. His fellow villagers loved it so much, they made more of these magic paper monkeys. Eventually, nobody did any more chores so they just relaxed all day. The story ended with the monkeys taking over because they realized *they* had the real power; like the fall of Ancient Rome to the barbarian hordes, the Empire had grown too weak to defend itself. That cautionary tale could have been written about the tangible perils of robot sentience, but that's not what my story is about. My story is about realizing we have taught humans to act like robots, to perform a job we need doing. But what happens when that job can be performed far more cheaply by someone overseas? And then by "automations" that need no union, no healthcare, and no sleep? There is nothing amoral about choosing the cheaper option, even if it means putting people out of work. It simply means markets tend to choose cheaper options as they become available.

What do we do when the paper monkeys have all our jobs?

MY TOP 10 STORIES

It was a challenge to winnow down my short list to a select few I'm confident enough will qualify as a good investment of one's time. I could make five or six such lists like this which prioritize the most dramatic stories or with the best dialog or the most thought-provoking. However, I'm listing the stories I like for many of those reasons put together. I won't offer up any spoilers here, so go delve into the Story Notes & Origins appendix to get the backstory on why I picked these stories over others.

1. **No Tips Necessary** (sci-fi) #108
2. **Legacy One** (horror/sci-fi) #61
3. **Burn** (zombie) #41
4. **Love in The Ether** (romance) #1
5. **The Best Ship That Ever Was** (fairy tale) #71
6. **New Religion** (sci fi) #93
7. **Oz 2.0** (fairy tale) #75
8. **Transubstantiation** (mythology) #12
9. **Whipper** (humor) #38
10. **Honorarium** (historical fiction) #60

FURTHER READING

Below is a list of seminal works which sculpted my thinking about how to best leverage 'free' and still make money as a creator. All links in this section can be found on my web site: *rosspruden.art/reading*

"The Grand Unified Theory on the Economics of Free" by Mike Masnick

If you only read 1 blurb on this list, let this be the one:

> Once you've broken out [a good's scarce vs. infinite] components, recognizing that the infinite components are what make the scarce components more valuable at no extra cost, you set those free. Not only do you set those free, you have every incentive to create more of them, and encourage more people to get them. You break them into easily accessible bites. You syndicate them. You hand them out. You make them easy to share and embed and distribute and promote.... *the more*

people consuming the infinite goods, the more valuable your scarce resource is.

So, the simple bullet point version:

1. Redefine the market based on the benefits.
2. Break the benefits down into scarce and infinite components.
3. Set the infinite components free, syndicate them, make them easy to get—all to increase the value of the scarce components.
4. Charge for the scarce Components that are tied to infinite components.

https://www.techdirt.com/articles/20070503/012939/grand-unified-theory-economics-free.shtml

"Infinity Is Your Friend in Economics" by Mike Masnick

Rather than thinking of [infinite, digital goods] as a product the market is pressuring you to price at $0, recognize they're an infinite resource that is available for you to use freely in other products and markets... the infinite nature of the goods is no longer a problem, but a tremendous resource to be exploited.

https://www.techdirt.com/articles/20070118/013310/infinity-is-your-friend-economics.shtml

"Understanding Free Content" by Nina Paley

Competing products can nonetheless be sold without my endorsement. If they're cheaper, of better quality, or more accessible, they might sell better than my endorsed products. Why shouldn't they? Competition can be good. All the more incentive for any business I partner with to make their products high quality, reasonably priced and easily available. There's no incentive to compete with a good product; if there's a good affordable *Sita Sings the Blues* coffee table book or graphic novel, why should anyone bother publishing another? If they do, the competing book must have some important quality lacking in the first. If that competitor's quality differential is so high that it's worth more than my endorsement, then good for them for doing something right.

https://blog.ninapaley.com/2009/04/06/understanding-free-content/

The Innovator's Dilemma by **Clayton Christiansen**

Try to destroy your own business... or somebody else will. A business book classic in understanding that a great product never guarantees market domination—someone out there could upend your business with an offering less expensive or of a cheaper quality, so you'd better beat them to it by doing it yourself.

https://en.wikipedia.org/wiki/The_Innovator's_Dilemma

Approaching Infinity by **Mike Masnick**

A collection of *Techdirt*'s most insightful articles on how to best sell your work when everything can be copied.

https://rtb.techdirt.com/products/approaching-infinity/

"The Future of Music Business Models (And Those Who Are Already There)" by Mike Masnick

A lengthy but detailed post on which musicians are successfully using innovative new business models.

https://www.techdirt.com/articles/20091119/ 16341170 1 1/future-music-business-models-those-who-are- already-there.shtml

The Art of Asking, or How I Learned to Stop Worrying and Let People Help by Amanda Palmer

An unvarnished portrayal of how relentlessly reaching out to fans with authenticity will make your business explode.

https://en.wikipedia.org/wiki/The_Art_of_Asking

The Complete Guide to Pay What You Want Pricing by Tom Morkes

A no-nonsense guide on how to make money off of products you give away for free.

https://tommorkes.com/pwywguide/

Start With Why by Simon Sinek

Not related to public domain art, but still a classic at understanding how you can compete effectively by knowing and expressing your "why" to your customers.

https://simonsinek.com/product/start-with-why/

Fascinate by Sally Hogshead

A personal favorite. What makes you or your business so intriguing that customers can't help but pay attention?

https://www.amazon.com/Fascinate-Revised-Updated-Impossible-Resist/dp/0062206486

Unleashing the Ideavirus by Seth Godin

Why spend boatloads of money on expensive marketing when you can get more effective long-term marketing by word-of-mouth campaigns?

https://www.amazon.com/Unleashing-Ideavirus-Marketing-Epidemics-Customers/dp/0786887176

"why the 'social object' is the future of marketing" by Hugh MacLeod

A seminal piece that should be required reading for anyone in business. Don't try to sell things—try to be the thing people naturally want to talk about.

https://www.gapingvoid.com/blog/2008/01/02/why-the-social-object-is-the-future-of-marketing/

"1000 True Fans" by Kevin Kelly

If you have a fan willing to drive 500 miles to see your concert, read your book, or meet you for an autograph, having just 1000 fans like that translates into a sustainable income.

http://kk.org/thetechnium/1000-true-fans/

"Better Than Free" by Kevin Kelly

When everything can be copied, how do artists make any money?

http://kk.org/thetechnium/better-than-fre/

"Q&A: A front-row seat for media's meltdown", a CNET interview of Eric Garland

One of the few people willing to do agnostic business assessment; Garland talks about what he's *seeing*, not how he wants it to play out. Hollywood people love to complain how media piracy is killing their business and must be stopped, but Garland starts by acknowledging media piracy as an unavoidable fact, a competing (free) business model, and discusses potential pivoting in order to compete with free.

http://www.cnet.com/news/q-a-a-front-row-seat-for-medias-meltdown/

"Business Models for 2014" by Ben Thompson

Seemingly old, but still very topical.

https://stratechery.com/2014/business-models-2014/

LIST OF ILLUSTRATIONS

How to Use This Book: *Creator-Endorsed Mark,* digital illustration, 2008, Nina Paley

Epigraph: *Happy Dude,* pencil on paper, 2013, Zoë Pruden

Story Notes & Origins: *Boulevard du Temple* (#83), Boulevard du Temple, Daguerréotype, 1838, Louis Daguerre

Story Notes & Origins: *Flourish* (#107), Amanda Palmer, Seattle, November 2014, Ross Pruden

ALPHABETICAL STORY INDEX

ARE YOU A TRUE FAN?

Seeing is Believing (#100) started out as a simple idea: two good friends hurtling across the stars to prove an insane bet. I loved the story's premise and its characters, and wondered what would happen next in their lives.

Over the years, so many people kept telling me I should write a novel.

So guess what?

I used the same characters from story #100 for a novel. It's about what happens when a person is stranded not only off planet... but off *galaxy*. If you like my stories and want to read more like them, then just wait until you hear what happens next to Philippa.

Sign up for my NEWSLETTER:
rosspruden.art/welcome

I'm also waist deep in hammering out the mythology of a multi-book epic fantasy saga involving the world of muses—those invisible ethereals who inspire us to create art. But their world is a lot stranger than we ever realized...

AN ODE BEFORE DYING

You think you sell a movie—you do not.
You think you sell a book—you do not.
You think you sell a song—you do not.

You sell an experience, something communicated, something elusive and ephemeral. Something mystical and transformative and inspiring. *All these abstract things simply come in the shape of a movie, a book, or a song.*

Never before has it been possible to strip away these experiences from the product... until now, the Digital Age.

The Digital Age lets us duplicate products infinitely. And, for the first time in human history, creators are not deprived of their original copy.

So how do creators sustain? What do they sell?

It's simple, if creators are willing to accept one simple fact:

*Creators don't sell **products**.*
*They sell **experiences**.*

In fact, creators *never* sold products, although it must have always seemed that way. They just never saw it before because products and experiences have been so deeply entwined.

The Digital Age has changed all that...

...now we can read a novel without buying a book.

...now we can watch a movie without buying a movie ticket.

...now we can listen to a song without buying a record.

So how do creators sustain? What do they sell?
  They sell the *experience*.
  They sell *access to themselves*.
  They sell *uniqueness*.
  They sell *convenience*.
  They sell *membership*.
  They sell *customization*.
  They sell *exclusivity*.
  They sell *benefits*.
  They sell *patronage*.
  They sell *magic*.
  They sell the **experience**.

They sell that which cannot be felt, something that transports their customers to another place for a brief time. When customers buy a $500 shirt, they aren't being sold a simple shirt, they are being sold *self-confidence*.

Creators will sell the same thing they've always sold—intangibles—though some will stubbornly claim they (should) only sell the product. Those kinds of creators have never seen the distinction between experience and product because, before the digital age, intangibles have been inseparable from books, movie tickets, and records.

The key to the Digital Age is to *recognize that many existing products already embed intangibles, which is why those products are still being bought.* However, once those intangibles stop being offered, or a competitor offers better intangibles, the customer will go elsewhere.

Creators can sustain. They will sustain. The market *wants* to sustain creators. Yet only the ones who realize that they don't sell products, but experiences. Only *those* creators are the ones worthy of survival in the Digital Age.

The rest will whine and commiserate as they slowly fade into obscurity.

And to them, we offer a fond, and sad, adieu.

ABOUT THE AUTHOR

 Ross Pruden is a storyteller of 30+ years across numerous media, starting as a published short story writer in middle school, a reporter in high school and college, screenwriting student at NYU film school, visual storyteller in film and still images, and finally as a professional feature film screenwriter and short story writer. His most recent short story, *A Quiet Lie* was published in Techdirt's (*techdirt.com*) anthology of futuristic short stories, *Working Futures*, and his debut science fiction novel about an interstellar castaway is currently in development.

Before he founded a fine art photography business, Ross Pruden Fine Art, he was a production artist and graphic designer for *W Magazine*, the BBC, Levi-Strauss, and ad agencies across three countries, where Ross learned how to drive on the left side of the road and become fluent in French. As a columnist for *Techdirt*, Ross has been a continuing advocate for free culture and the public domain. Find out more about Ross or his work by visiting *www.rosspruden.art/welcome*

Ross lives in Washington State with his wife, two daughters, three cats, and a Roborovski Hamster, which looks very much like only the front half of a mouse.

facebook.com/rossprudenart

twitter.com/rossprudenart

instagram.com/rossprudenart

amazon.com/author/rossprudenart